Praise for
ON BORROWED TIME

"An absolutely irresistible hook . . . No one who picks up this greased-lightning account will rest till it's finished." —*Kirkus Reviews* (starred review)

"Outstanding . . . Anyone who enjoyed Dennis Lehane's *Shutter Island* will love this thriller."
—*Library Journal* (starred review)

"Excellent. All will marvel at the way Rosenfelt builds suspense." —*Publishers Weekly* (starred review)

DOWN TO THE WIRE

"Dynamite . . . Sly humor, breathless pacing, and terrific plot twists keep the pages spinning toward the showdown." —*Publishers Weekly* (starred review)

"Rosenfelt's Andy Carpenter novels are known for their breezy storytelling and humor . . . This one eschews humor to focus on the actions of ordinary people faced with extraordinary trials. It also employs a whiplash plot turn . . . an engaging suspense tale." —*Booklist*

"A terrific plot and a gripping narrative." —*Toronto Sun*

"I am raving about this book . . . a page-turning thriller."
—*[illegible]lly Pleasure*

MORE . . .

DON'T TELL A SOUL

"Stellar . . . Rosenfelt keeps the plot hopping and popping as he reveals a complex frame-up of major proportions with profound political ramifications both terrifying and enlightening."

—*Publishers Weekly* (starred review)

"This fast-paced and brightly written tale spins along . . . *Don't Tell a Soul* is a humdinger."

—*St. Louis Post-Dispatch*

"High-voltage entertainment from an author who plots and writes with verve and wit . . . Rosenfelt ratchets up tension with the precision of a skilled auto mechanic wielding a torque wrench." —*Booklist* (starred)

"Rosenfelt has earned his crime-novelist pedigree."

—*Entertainment Weekly*

"He delivers a fast, inventive stand-alone thriller you'll never put down." —*Kirkus Reviews*

"[Rosenfelt] has pulled together a cynical political thriller that rings true in this age of terrorism, media hype, and Washington scandals . . . it's an enjoyable tale." —*Minneapolis Star Tribune*

"Rosenfelt's first stand-alone novel is a riveting thriller that should boost him to best-seller status . . . Compelling twists and turns, a lightning-fast pace, and breathtaking suspense make this a harrowing ride . . . The book deserves a wide audience."

—*Library Journal* (starred)

Also by
David Rosenfelt

Airtight
On Borrowed Time
Don't Tell a Soul
Down to the Wire

Heart of a Killer

David Rosenfelt

St. Martin's Paperbacks

This is a work of fiction. All of the characters, organizations, and events portrayed in this novel are either products of the author's imagination or are used fictitiously.

HEART OF A KILLER

For information address St. Martin's Press, 175 Fifth Avenue, New York, NY 10010.

Library of Congress Catalog Card Number: 2011036056

ISBN: 978-1-250-01420-7

Printed in the United States of America

St. Martin's Press hardcover edition / February 2012
St. Martin's Paperbacks edition / November 2012

St. Martin's Paperbacks are published by St. Martin's Press, 175 Fifth Avenue, New York, NY 10010.

10 9 8 7 6 5 4 3 2

Prologue

Detective John Novack knew something was wrong even before he stepped in the blood. Though he was a fourteen-year veteran of the force, in this instance his sense of foreboding did not come from an instinct finely honed by experience, nor was it a result of piecing clues together. The voice on the 911 call, as played back to him while he drove to the scene, had said it all.

"I killed Charlie Harrison."

It was a woman's voice, spoken in a dull monotone, without affect or apparent emotion. She had followed that with similar-sounding answers to the 911 operator's questions.

"Yes, I'm sure he's dead."

"We live at one forty-seven Tamarack Avenue."

"He's my husband."

"Yes. I'll wait here."

Novack and his partner, David Anders, rang the bell when they arrived at the run-down garden apartment in Elmwood Park, just twenty minutes from the George Washington Bridge in New Jersey. Since it was ten o'clock in the morning, it was fairly quiet. If this was really a murder, they knew it wouldn't be quiet for long. Police cars, media trucks, and reporters with microphones had a tendency to create commotion and draw crowds.

Two rings did not yield an answer, so the detectives drew their weapons and tried the door. It was unlocked, and they went in, Novack leading the way.

Which was why he was the one to step in the blood.

It had slowly moved from the nearby den to the foyer area near the door; the floor must have been slightly tilted in that direction. It traced a path back to the body of Charlie Harrison, as if the police needed a road map to follow.

Novack did a quick two-step out of the blood, leaving dark-red footprints as he did so. He swore silently to himself, his mind flashing forward to a future trial, when a defense attorney would mock his carelessness at the scene. Anders, the second one in, avoided the same fate, as he gingerly made it around the mess.

Still holding their weapons, they saw Sheryl Harrison, wife of the late Charlie and self-confessed murderess, sitting on a straight-backed chair with her hands folded in her lap, looking toward the detectives. To her left, lying facedown on a blood-soaked couch, was Charlie.

"Is there anyone else in the house?" Novack asked.

"No. My daughter is at school. Someone will have to pick her up and take her to my mother's."

"What is your name?"

"Sheryl. Sheryl Harrison."

"Did you call 911, Sheryl?"

"Yes."

"Did you kill this man?"

"Yes."

Novack was troubled by her answer; it didn't gibe with what he was looking at. But he nodded to Anders, who read Sheryl her rights, then asked if she understood them.

She nodded. "Yes. Will someone pick up Karen? She

goes to P.S. number twenty-eight. She gets out at three-thirty."

"I'll make sure someone takes good care of her and gets her to your mother's. Would you be willing to answer some questions about what happened here?"

"I killed him."

"I have my doubts about that," Novack said, as Anders whirled around in surprise. Of all the things his partner might have said, that was what he would have least expected. "So why don't you tell me the truth?"

"I told you the truth," Sheryl said. "His name was Charlie Harrison, he was my husband, and I killed him."

"Jamie, Mr. Hemmings wants to see you." Alicia Waldman, my assistant, delivered the news. She said it with a stunned reverence, in the way she might say, "God is on line two." Actually, calling Alicia my assistant might imply too high a status level for me; she assisted four other lawyers in the firm as well, all of whom she liked more than me.

I had absolutely no guess why Richard Hemmings would want to see me. I was a twenty-nine-year-old, sixth-year associate in the corporate litigation section of Carlson, Miller, and Timmerman, while he was a senior partner in the bankruptcy section. In non-law-firm parlance, when it came to dumping work on people, he was a "dumper" and I was a "dumpee," but we worked in very different dumping grounds.

We also worked on different floors in our Newark, New Jersey, office building. I was a second-floor guy with a view of the second floor of the building right next door. He was a tenth-story guy, which was as high as it went, with a view on one side of glorious downtown Newark, and a clear sight line to the airport on the other side.

I went right up, and his assistant ushered me directly into his office. He was looking out the window and turned when he heard me. "Jamie," he said, although he had never met me. He must have just known that he had sent for a Jamie, and figured I must be him. He might even have known that my last name was Wagner. Those are the kind of smarts that partners have.

"Mr. Hemmings," I responded, keeping the conversation humming. The culture in the firm was that everyone was on a first-name basis, but when it came to full partners, nobody on my level really trusted that. Better to address them formally, and let them correct you if they wanted.

He didn't, but fortunately came right to the point. "I assume you know that Stan Lysinger is out attending to a personal issue."

I knew that quite well, everybody did, if advanced lung cancer could be casually dismissed as a personal issue. "Yes."

"Everybody is pitching in until he gets back," he said, although we both knew that Stan was not coming back. "I'm taking on his pro-bono responsibilities."

I immediately knew why I was there. Most big firms feel a corporate responsibility, or at least want to look as if they feel a corporate responsibility, to do pro-bono work within the community. They generally like to assign lower- and mid-level people to these jobs, and Stan is, or was, the resident assigner-in-chief.

Most associates dread such assignments, because it takes them out of the mainstream of the firm, and can thus impact their ability to shine and make partner. I had no such concerns, since it had been clear for a while that I was never going to reach those heights. So I viewed a pro-bono assignment with a wait-and-see attitude; it would depend on the specifics of the assignment.

"It's with Legal Aid," he said, as my feelings went from mixed to outright negative. "You're to see an inmate in New Jersey State Prison named Sheryl Harrison."

"They're not going to brief me first?" I asked.

He looked at the file, as if reading it for the first time. "No. They want you to hear it from the client. Seems unusual."

"Does it say what she's in there for?"

He looked again. "Murder. She murdered her husband six years ago; slit his throat. Pleaded guilty. Got fifteen to life."

"Sounds like a nice lady," I said, but it didn't get a smile from Hemmings.

"You'll provide me with written reports on your progress," he said. "Until Stan gets back."

"Yes, I certainly will."

I lived then, and now, on the Upper West Side of Manhattan, which made me semi-unique among my colleagues at the firm. My apartment was on the third floor of a brownstone on Seventy-sixth Street, between Columbus and Amsterdam. It was a walk-up, common among those kinds of buildings in the area, and I tried to think positive by viewing the stairs as a way to stay in shape.

I suspected that my Manhattan residence was not viewed as a positive by my superiors, who no doubt felt that the forty-five-minute commute each way was time better spent in the office, doing work billable to clients.

It wasn't that I was anti–New Jersey; I was pro–New York. If I wanted a pizza at 11:00 P.M., I didn't want to have to preheat an oven. I wanted to go downstairs and get one.

Also, my favorite bars to hang out in were in New York, though I never really gave the Jersey bars a chance. I felt at home in Manhattan, on its streets, in its restaurants, with its women. And if a woman came in one night from Queens, that was fine as well.

The truth is that I would willingly date a woman from any of the five boroughs, with the obvious exception of Staten Island. Even that would be fine, if not for the fact that at some point I'd have to take her home, or meet her parents, or something like that. I've heard that people never come back from there.

I was and am a Manhattan snob, and that's where I'd soon be looking for a job. I was reaching that point at my tenure in the firm where one was either made a partner or encouraged to leave. I was certainly going to receive such encouragement, and I wasn't going to move to any job I couldn't commute to by subway or feet.

I got home from work at about 7:45, which was fairly typical. The phone was ringing as I was walking in the door. It was my friend Ken Bollinger, asking if I wanted to meet him for the first of what would become quite a few drinks.

Ken was and is an investment banker, on track to make ridiculous amounts of money, none of which he was willing to spend. He actually ordered beer based on price.

"Not tonight," I said. "I've got to be at New Jersey State Prison for Women first thing in the morning." It was a line I had never gotten to say before in my life, and I took my time with it.

"Excuse me?"

I explained the situation, after which he said, "There's nothing better than conjugal visit sex."

I knew he was talking about a *Seinfeld* episode in which George dated a female prisoner. He reveled in the idea of conjugal visit sex. Ken and I could talk for days, only using *Seinfeld* references.

"And no pop-ins," I said, since George had also considered it a huge plus that his inmate girlfriend couldn't just show up at his apartment unannounced.

"Can I go with you?" he asked. "Convicts never insist on going to expensive restaurants."

"No chance," I said. "But I'll see if she has a friend. Maybe a nice, frugal arsonist."

The prison was about a forty-five-minute drive from my apartment, though with New York traffic you never know. I didn't want to be late, since I couldn't be sure what the prison punishment for that might be. Solitary? Two weeks in the hole? No sense taking a chance.

Most people I know, and pretty much everyone I work with, are amazed that I keep a car in the city at all. There are trains that could get me to work, but I don't like them. Somehow when I'm in the car I feel like I'm in control, despite the fact that traffic jams can be awful and arbitrary.

I got to the prison a half hour early, which was just as well, because it took almost that long to identify myself, demonstrate that I had an appointment, and go through security. At ten after nine I was finally led into a small visiting room, where Sheryl Harrison was already waiting for me. She was sitting at a table with a folder in front of her.

I almost did a double take. I don't know what I was expecting, but it sure wasn't this. She was young, I would have said about my age, and quite nice looking. There was no hard edge to her, no scraggly hair, or tattooed arms. She was actually pretty, despite the prison garb and obvious lack of makeup, and there was a softness about her that took me off guard. Under different circumstances, this could be someone I'd be willing to follow to Staten Island.

George Costanza may have been on to something.

All in all, she looked like someone that ten years ago I could have taken to the prom, except for the fact that prospective prom dates are rarely handcuffed to metal tables, and almost never have a knife murder as part of their high school experience.

"I'm Jamie Wagner," I said, sitting down. "I'm a lawyer."

She looked me straight in the eye. Eye contact is not my specialty, but she seemed to silently mandate it. "Have they told you why you're here?" she asked.

"No, apparently I'm supposed to hear that from you. But I should tell you straight out that I have no experience in criminal matters."

She nodded. "That's okay; this isn't a criminal matter."

"It isn't?"

"No, and I doubt anyone has experience in what I need." She said it matter-of-factly.

"What might that be?"

"I want to die."

"A lot of women have that initial reaction to me." It was a stupid joke, meant to cover my panic and discomfort. What I really wanted to say was, "Guard! Get me out of here."

She didn't respond either way, not even to reprimand me for the misplaced humor. "I don't have much time," she said.

"Why don't you tell me exactly what's going on?" I asked, though I really didn't want to know.

She opened the folder and took out a picture, which she slid across the table to me. It was of a young girl, pretty but thin, who clearly resembled Sheryl, especially in the eyes. "This is my daughter, Karen. The picture was taken last year, when she was thirteen."

"She looks like you."

"Thank you. She hasn't been well for the last couple of years. Tires easily, poor appetite, not sleeping well. My mother, that's who she lives with, finally took her to the doctor for tests. We got the diagnosis two months ago."

This was not going to be good. "And?"

"She has a congenital heart defect. It's a progressive condition, and it will kill her, unless she gets a transplant."

"I'm sorry, but how does your dying help her?"

"She has a rare blood type, which will make finding a donor almost impossible. So I'm going to give her my heart," she said, definitely, as if the issue was already decided, and only the details were still to be worked out.

"Excuse me?"

She slid another piece of paper across the desk. It was a report from a doctor, with lab results and a written summary. I didn't read it at that point, because she was describing it.

"The prison doctor is a good guy; he took some of my blood and I had it tested on the outside. I have the same blood type, and I'm a perfect match."

"So you want me to get the prison authorities to let you give your heart to your daughter?"

"That's correct," she said.

"You'd be committing suicide in the process."

"You figured that out?"

It was as bizarre a conversation as I'd ever been involved in; this woman was actually asking me to arrange her death. But the situation itself and the surroundings felt even weirder, and that was mostly because of Sheryl Harrison.

People say that certain charismatic people, the Bill Clintons and Ronald Reagans of the world, are the center of whatever room they're in. They control the room by the force of their personality.

Well, Sheryl Harrison controlled this room, and she didn't do it with an entourage of assistants or Secret Service officers around her. She did it alone, wearing an orange jumpsuit, handcuffed to a table. It was surprising to me, and a little disconcerting. I would have thought, just going by our positions in life, that I would have had the upper hand.

I didn't.

Having said that, I was there because of my alleged legal expertise, so I figured I should demonstrate some of it. "Look, this is not a situation I'm faced with every day, but I believe that suicide is illegal, and—"

She interrupted me. "Actually, it's not. Assisting a suicide is illegal."

"And in this case you need assistance."

"Less than you think," she said. "But as you can imagine, it has to be carefully orchestrated. I've done a lot of research on it."

I had no doubt that she had done so; I could already tell that there was nothing impulsive about this decision. "Have you talked to the authorities about it yet?"

"No, I thought it best to have a lawyer do that, at least initially. They will take it more seriously."

I hadn't liked where this was going, and now that it had gotten there, I liked it even less. "Mrs. Harrison . . ."

"Sheryl."

"Sheryl, I'm not sure I'm the right attorney to handle this."

She laughed a short laugh. "You think I picked you?" she said, then softened it with, "You're all I have. This is my daughter, and her life is more worth living than mine."

I looked at the picture again, then at this woman chained to a table, who was probably right in her assessment. But fortunately I don't get to make calls like that. "What does Karen think of all this?" I asked. "She would certainly have to consent."

"She doesn't know yet. I don't want to tell her until it's arranged. And at her age, consent isn't necessary."

"And your mother?"

"She knows. She's opposed to it." For the first time, I thought I detected a bit of frustration, or an impatience. "But none of that need concern you. That's for me to deal with."

I felt as if I was being dismissed and I wasn't crazy about the feeling. "I'm going to need time to think about this, and research it."

She nodded. "That's fine. Just do me one favor, please."

"What's that?" I asked.

"Hurry."

"So she's a nut job?" The questioner was Julie Ammerman, the closest I had to a real friend in the entire firm. There are a limited number of partnerships at the end of the eight- or nine-year rainbow, so a natural competition exists among the associates vying to receive them.

Somehow Julie and I had always mostly gotten past that, and since it became obvious I was no real threat for one of the coveted spots, we'd gotten even closer. We'd slept together twice, which qualified as a semi-long relationship for me, but the last time was six months prior, and we'd since settled into a platonic friendship.

Julie had gone to a much lesser law school than me; actually, everybody by definition had gone to a lesser law school than me. But she certainly never resented it, and worked tirelessly and successfully to prove those Ivy admissions offices wrong.

We were in the firm's cafeteria, moving through the line with our trays. The food was extraordinarily good and inexpensive; it was the one aspect of big-time lawyering that I was likely to miss.

"That's what I thought while I was talking to her, but . . . yeah, she might be nuts."

"Maybe you should report her," she said.

"To who? About what?"

"Well, if she's suicidal, shouldn't you tell someone? I mean, if she hangs herself in her cell and they come to you, what are you going to say? 'Oh, right, she mentioned cutting her heart out, but it slipped my mind'?"

"She's not going to hang herself in her cell. She wants to do the whole thing under medical supervision. And I can't tell anyone about it; it's covered under attorney-client privilege. Did you cut class the year they taught that in law school?"

"Sorry, Mr. Harvard." The fact that I went to Harvard Law somehow has always qualified me for ridicule among my colleagues, all of whom would have sacrificed their future firstborns to have gone there. "And if it's all privileged, how come you're telling me?"

"Because we work for the same firm; I consider you my cocounsel."

"I suggest you reconsider that. Are you going to take her case?"

"No way. If I lose, which I would, I'm a loser. If I win, which I won't, my client dies. Not exactly a fun way to pass the time."

"And her daughter is really going to die?"

"That's what she said; I have to assume she wouldn't lie about it."

We were quiet for a while; I was thinking about Sheryl's situation and I imagined Julie was doing the same.

Finally, she said, "I'm trying to imagine my mother giving up her heart for me." She laughed. "If she did, I'd never hear the end of it."

I wasn't quite into the humor of this; I could still picture Sheryl in that prison, trying to control her desperation, relying on me.

But Julie was on a roll. "Every day I don't get married, she tells me I'm tearing her heart out."

We finished lunch and headed back to our respective offices for another torture-filled afternoon. At 6:15, I got an instant message from her asking me if I was almost done for the day. I wrote back that I was planning to be out in fifteen minutes.

You want to grab a drink? Julie asked.

More than one, I responded.

We went to Hurlihey's, on Columbus. It's where I went when I was with someone, and therefore not interested in meeting anyone new. They have great burgers, crisp on the outside and rare on the inside, and a bunch of TVs always tuned to sports.

I started ordering dark and stormies, a combination of Gosling's Rum and ginger beer that a friend in Boston had introduced me to the previous summer. Julie was drinking bloody marys, and like always was sucking them down to what must have been a hollow leg. No matter how much she drank it never seemed to affect her.

"You seem preoccupied," she said. "Talk to Mama."

"I'm fine. Just tired."

"Bullshit. You're thinking about your nut-job client in prison."

"Actually, I was thinking about the shooting in Tucson. The one where the congresswoman got shot, and a bunch of other people died. You remember?"

She nodded. "Of course I remember. What about it?"

"There was a judge there with his wife. He was one of the people who were killed."

"And?"

"The killer had pointed the gun at the judge's wife and fired, but the judge jumped in front of her and took the bullet."

Julie could be somewhat impatient when a story wasn't

being told fast enough for her taste. "Land the plane on this, Jamie."

"So he was considered a hero for saving her life. Their friends went on the *Today* show, columns were written, it was a beautiful story. He gave up his life for the person he loved."

Julie nodded slowly. "Which is what she wants to do."

"Right. And he did it in the spur of the moment, with barely enough time to think about it. She's had nothing but time to think, and to make a reasoned, careful decision."

"Maybe she's not such a nut job after all," Julie said.

I was always considered an underachiever.

There were a number of reasons for that, the most obvious being that I pretty consistently underachieved. This I managed despite finishing near the top of my class in high school, then doing the same at the University of Pennsylvania, and graduating from Harvard Law.

The thing about underachieving is it is all based on expectations, and the ones for me were way up there. A lot of that was my own fault. I'm really smart, with an IQ off the charts, and perfect scores, or damn close, on every college board and achievement test I ever took.

So that raised the bar quite a bit, but it was starting from a ridiculously high level. My father is Dr. Thomas Wagner, the head of Respiratory Medicine at Columbia Presbyterian. You know how everybody always says that their doctor is "the best"? Well, if they're talking about respiratory medicine, and they're not talking about Thomas Wagner, then they have no idea what they're talking about.

Mom is Theresa Lynne Wagner, and she is extraordinarily formidable in her own right. A graduate of the

London School of Economics, an MBA from Harvard, she went on to become CFO for a Fortune 500 company.

She left that position, voluntarily, at the age of forty-seven, in order to become involved in every charitable foundation in the history of Earth. She is also on the board of directors of six different companies, and writes an occasional op-ed in *The Wall Street Journal*.

They're just a pair of typical parents, except for maybe the part about driving the kids to soccer games. And except for their unnerving ability to make every night feel like parent-teacher night, with them playing both roles.

I saw a shrink the summer after my sophomore year in college. My parents suggested it, concerned that my academics was not up to their expected standards. Parents all over America were dealing with kids dropping out of school and/or strung out on drugs, and my parents were panicking that I had a 3.7 at Penn.

I didn't pick the shrink from my father's approved list, which for me qualified as a fairly rebellious act. The one I did pick didn't help me very much, but I did come away with the understanding that I couldn't stand my parents. I realized it during a session when I heard myself blurt out, "I can't stand my parents."

So on the Sunday before the Monday that I was to return to the prison to see Sheryl Harrison, I used her as an excuse to be late arriving at my parents' house in Greenwich, Connecticut. It was a fund-raising cocktail party, which by 4:00 P.M. would be filled with worthy people raising money for a worthy cause. When I did finally arrive, I would be the only person there who didn't write a check.

But I had a job to do, and a client to maybe represent, so I opened Sheryl Harrison's case folder to learn what she was about and how she came to find herself in prison.

The first thing I looked at was a color photograph of Charles Harrison lying facedown on the couch. Blood had spread from his neck, at least twelve inches out to both sides. It was as if the photographer had said, "Charlie, lie down over there, with your head on that bloody Rorschach test."

It was among the most disgusting things I had ever seen, though it quickly took a spot near the back of the list when I saw some of the other photographs. Those had Charlie turned facing up, revealing the wound that caused his demise. It was literally ear to ear, and it made me glad that Sheryl Harrison was handcuffed to the table when we met.

The file wasn't terribly thick, though the truth is I wouldn't know a thick murder file from a thin one. But in this case it wasn't exactly a whodunit; Sheryl said she "dunit" immediately, and the police, led by Detective John Novack, seemed to have competently crossed all the "t"s and dotted the "i"s. There was some written evidence that Novack initially doubted her confession, but no indication that ever went anywhere.

There was some background information on the victim, and it's safe to say that Charlie's life was not an exemplary one. He had been arrested four times and convicted twice of nonviolent crimes, though his nonviolence only seemed to extend to his felonies.

Police had been called to the home four times in the previous six months for domestic violence incidents, including twice when Charlie claimed he had hit her because she came at him with a knife.

Charlie had managed to avoid prison for the felony convictions, and was never arrested for domestic violence. In fact, Sheryl was arrested one of the times that Charlie claimed she went after him with a knife, something that in retrospect must have seemed more credible once Charlie had his throat slit. Sheryl also had a history of drug use, though that had been a number of years earlier.

The couple's only child was Karen, eight years old at

the time of the murder. Fortunately, she was at school when her mother took a blade to her father's throat.

Maybe my parents weren't as bad as I thought.

By the time I finished the file, I knew there was no way I would feel comfortable representing Sheryl Harrison. What she did, no matter how big a slimeball Charlie was, was reprehensible. Even though the loss of life that she was now hoping for would have been a good thing if it saved her daughter, Sheryl was just not someone I wanted to spend time with. Let somebody else do it.

I arrived at my parents' house at 5:00 P.M., an hour after I had been told to be there. If they were annoyed, they didn't show it, though annoyance was not something they ever displayed in public.

They made a big show of introducing me to everyone. I knew I had met at least half of those people before at similar functions, but no one admitted to it, and I certainly didn't. The same thing would happen next time if, God forbid, there was a next time.

It wasn't until at least an hour later that my father called me aside and reminded me that the invitation had said four o'clock.

I nodded. "I know, but I'm on a big case, and I got caught up in the work."

He looked pleased. "That I'm glad to hear. What kind of case is it?"

"Murder," I said, and happily waited for the double take, which came on schedule. I waited just a beat before dropping the bomb. "Pro bono."

His faint, ironic smile told me that he felt he should have expected something just like this. "Sounds like quite a career move. Murder . . . you're starting at the top. No sense fooling around with armed robbery, or embezzlement."

"But there's still a chance for some upward mobility," I said. "I mean, it's not like she's a mass murderer."

"She?"

"Yes. She cut her husband's throat with a steak knife."

Just then my mother walked over, probably curious and a little concerned about what the conference was about. "Our son is representing a murderer," Dad said.

She recoiled for a moment, and then said, "Jamie." Mother could make the word "Jamie" mean "Jamie, you're an asshole and a complete disappointment," merely by adjusting her inflection.

"Jamie, this is simply not a good idea," Dad said.

"Yet it feels right," I said.

My mother frowned, something she was incredibly accomplished at. She had at least fifteen different frowns in her repertoire, which covered every possible displeasure she wanted to exhibit. "It's like I've always said, he has his uncle's genes."

She was referring to Dad's brother Reggie, a criminal attorney for almost thirty-five years, during which time he had made virtually no money at all. Reggie occasionally showed up at family functions, but he was not exactly welcomed with open arms, and was obviously even less happy to be there.

The conversation quickly came to an end, and my parents went back to circulating among their guests. It left me with a slight feeling of triumph, but then a stronger one of horror.

I had decided not to represent Sheryl Harrison, but if I followed through on that instinct, my parents would think they won, that I had obeyed them.

I had just gotten myself a client.

For Sheryl, Sunday was either the best or worst day of the week. The sole determining factor was whether Karen came to visit; it was literally the only thing in the world that Sheryl looked forward to or had any interest in. Which meant that this particular day was going to be a "best" day, the first one in more than a month.

For a long time Karen was there almost every Sunday, but the percentage started to decline as her health worsened. What also declined was the level of honesty between them; what were formerly open, candid conversations had become guarded and secretive.

On Karen's part, it represented a desire to protect her mother. She knew that she was her mother's entire world, and that Sheryl would do anything for her. She also knew how helpless Sheryl felt because of her imprisonment; there was literally nothing she could do for Karen in any area of her life, other than provide love and understanding. But for what was ailing Karen, love and understanding simply wasn't going to do the trick.

So Karen avoided talking about her health, which was to say that left nothing in her life she really could talk honestly about. Because her health was gradually taking over everything, impacting all that she did, or didn't do. And as she grew weaker, the "didn't do"s were dominating.

On this day, the conversation began pretty much the same as always, with Sheryl asking, "How are you feeling, honey?" She couldn't help inquiring even though she already knew the answer.

Her mother, Terry Aimonetti, had cared for her granddaughter Karen since Sheryl's arrest, and had done the best she could in an awful situation. She considered it her obligation to keep Sheryl fully informed of Karen's condition, even though Karen had sworn her to secrecy. It was one of a number of issues in which Terry was caught in the middle between daughter and granddaughter.

Terry waited outside, as she did on all these visits. She wanted the two of them to be able to talk alone; she thought they could connect better that way.

Karen was fourteen years old, but she seemed stuck on twelve, or maybe thirteen. Her disease had made her more frail, or at least she seemed that way to Sheryl, and the physical changes made her seem younger than she was.

"Pretty good," Karen said, although Sheryl would have known better even if Terry had not kept her current. Karen looked exhausted, pale, and washed out, and Sheryl had to catch herself so as not to react to Karen's appearance when she first walked in.

What Sheryl didn't realize was that Karen was there this morning, and had started coming on mornings more than previously, because by the afternoon her strength had been pretty much sapped.

"You getting enough rest?" Sheryl asked.

Karen frowned. "All I do is rest."

"It's good for you. How is Tommy?" Tommy was the latest of Karen's boyfriends, though "boyfriend" was not a word Karen would ever have used. In Karen's mind, she and Tommy just "hung out." Sheryl wasn't sure what that meant in the modern parlance, and wasn't sure she wanted to know.

"Okay, I guess."

"Trouble between you two?"

"No, we just . . . whatever. I'm staying home a lot . . . studying." Karen seemed frustrated, which was completely understandable to Sheryl. She of all people knew what it was like to be prevented from doing what she wanted, when she wanted, though obviously it was for a different reason than the one her daughter faced.

Sheryl put her hand on her daughter's. "Karen, it's going to be all right, I swear. Before you know it, you'll be feeling better and have more energy than you've ever had before." This was one of the areas in which Sheryl was not forthcoming; she would not tell Karen her transplant plans until they were about to become a reality. Karen would be upset and never willingly go along, which was why Sheryl had no intention of giving her a choice.

They talked for a while, but it was a guarded, strained conversation, since neither could broach the only subject that was on their minds, that was dominating their lives.

Five minutes before the hour was up, Karen asked, "How do things look for the parole hearing?"

Sheryl's parole hearing was coming up, a biannual event that Sheryl had spent absolutely no time thinking about. "Same as last time," Sheryl said. "It's just a formality, Karen. No one is granted parole this early."

It wasn't the first time Karen had heard that, but each time was like a slap in the face. She had always invested most of her hope in that process. In her view, people were gathering to decide whether her mother should stay in prison. Surely they could decide "no" just as easily as "yes."

"Can I talk to them this time?" she asked.

"I don't think so, honey. It's not done." Sheryl would

never want to put Karen through that, especially since she was telling the truth. The hearing was a formality; there was no chance that at this stage of her term she would be let out, no matter who testified.

"But he was my father. If I tell them that I forgive you, maybe they will."

"I'll talk to my lawyer," she said, which was partially true. She would be talking to her lawyer, but not about Karen testifying before the parole board.

She would be talking to her lawyer about being allowed to die.

Jamie Wagner's visit to the prison was a major opportunity for Lila Baldwin. A guard at New Jersey State, Lila had been keeping a close eye on Sheryl Harrison for the past six years, watching for anything unusual, anything that she could report. In all that time, there had been nothing really even worth mentioning; Sheryl had been a quiet, model prisoner.

It wasn't the prison authorities that were particularly interested in Sheryl; in fact, Lila wasn't sure who she was reporting to. She had a phone number that she was to call. When the process first began, soon after Sheryl's incarceration, Lila had reported a few insignificant matters, simply to show that she was on top of things and could be relied on. Soon she stopped bothering to do that.

The truth was that Lila never really thought it would last this long; she had never been that lucky. She remembered the first anonymous package she had received, filled with ten blank one-thousand-dollar money orders. A phone call followed, equally anonymous, instructing her on what she should do, with the promise of more money to come.

The person had done their homework about her, Lila

knew. Not every guard would have been susceptible to the proposal, even though technically she was doing nothing illegal. For her the call had been an easy one; she would take her money and follow those kinds of orders as long as they wanted.

And the money orders continued to come, one thousand dollars the first of every month. No return address on the envelope, and no indication who her employer was. She didn't really care, maybe didn't even want to know, so long as the money kept coming.

So when Lila learned about Jamie, it represented an opportunity to cement her employment, to show that she still had value. She dialed the number, the first time she had done so in almost four years. And this time, just as the few times back then, it was answered on the first ring.

"Yes?" It sounded like the same male voice as in the previous calls. The man's name was Ray Hennessey, but Lila did not know that, and had never felt like she should ask.

"This is Lila Baldwin, I . . ."

"Yes?"

"I'm calling about Sheryl Harrison; I've been watching her for you, and . . ."

"I know who you are and about whom you are calling. Say what you are going to say." There was a trace of impatience in the voice, which worried Lila. She wanted to stay on this person's good side.

"Okay . . . sure. The thing is, Sheryl met with a lawyer on Friday."

"What was the subject of the meeting?" Hennessey asked.

"I'm not sure. I'm trying to find out, but she's being really quiet about it. I've had some people ask her, but she refuses to say."

"Might it be her parole hearing?"

"No, she told someone she's not preparing for that at all. That if things go well there won't be a hearing."

"What else do you know?" The voice sounded more interested than before, which Lila took as a good sign.

"The lawyer's name is Jamie Wagner. He works at a firm called Carlson, Miller, and Timmerman. They're in Newark. I'm trying to find out more about him."

"Report in when you do," Hennessey said.

"Of course." Lila momentarily was struck with a desire to ask if all of this information, which was clearly of interest to her employer, warranted a bonus. She thought better of it; if it developed further, that could happen down the line.

"What area of the prison is Sheryl in these days?" the voice asked.

"She's in with the general population."

"Good."

Click.

The word "good," just before the man hung up, unnerved Lila more than a little. He had seemed relieved to learn she was in the general population, and Lila was certain that wasn't because he wanted Sheryl to be able to socialize.

No, it sounded like he was pleased because if it became necessary, Sheryl could be gotten to. In the context of prison life, that was a very ominous concept. Lila worried about what might happen to Sheryl, and whether she should intervene in any way.

If she did say something, her receiving the money all those years would be uncovered, her career would be over, and she might well switch places and become one of the guarded, rather than the guard.

For Lila, the decision was an easy one: Sheryl Harrison was on her own.

But the truth was that Lila misjudged Hennessey's reaction. His use of the word "good" was simply expressing his pleasure that he would have more information to tell his own boss. Hennessey did not care where Sheryl was in the prison population, nor did he care what happened to her or why she was talking to a lawyer.

Hennessey's job was strikingly similar to Lila's in one major respect. He was supposed to acquire information, and report it up the ladder. Where they differed was that for Lila, that was the end of it. For Hennessey, there was always likely to be more.

In this case, it could be anything. Maybe he would have to kill Sheryl, or maybe even the lawyer. That would depend on more information, which he would acquire. Gathering information was one of his specialties.

Hennessey's next actions would be decided later, and not by him. He would simply do what he was told, what he was paid to do, and he didn't care much either way what it was.

On my second visit to the prison, I felt much more comfortable. I knew the security procedures, so that went more smoothly. I recognized some of the guards, and they seemed to remember me as well. In only two trips, I was feeling just as much at home as I did at Carlson, Miller, and Timmerman.

My new friendship with my guard buddies apparently was not going to get me any special favors, since it took almost an hour before Sheryl Harrison was produced to meet with me. We met in the same room as the last time, and she was handcuffed to the same table.

Once again I was taken aback by how good she looked, and how incongruous her appearance seemed to the reality of her situation.

"Hello, Sheryl."

"What did you come up with?" She didn't seem in much of a sociable mood; I'd had corporate clients who were significantly less businesslike.

"Well, I've been familiarizing myself with your case," I said.

"Which case?" She didn't so much say it as snap it.

"The murder case. The Charlie Harrison murder."

She was clearly annoyed. "What the hell does that have to do with anything?"

"It's the reason you're here."

"Listen," she said, pausing to try and compose herself. "I know why I'm here. Everybody knows why I'm here, and now you do as well. But focus on what I'm saying, okay? The reason I'm here has nothing at all to do with the reason you are here."

She was either impatient or disgusted with me, or both, and it was starting to get on my nerves. "I understand," I said, "but—"

She interrupted me, which was just as well, since I had no idea how I was going to finish the sentence. "You are here to save my daughter's life."

I nodded. "And I will try to do that. I've decided to represent you, if you still want me to."

"I have no alternative," she said, clearly not pleased by her lack of options.

"My eyes are filling with tears," I said, displaying my normal tendency to substitute sarcasm for angry speech. "You could get another lawyer."

"How?"

"I don't know . . . however you got me. You can just go through the same process; trust me, I won't fight it."

"You know how long that took?" she asked. "Three weeks, and look what I wound up with. You know how long three weeks is in this situation?"

I'm not sure why I didn't walk out of the room; that was certainly my inclination. But for some reason I didn't. "Sheryl, you are clearly not happy to have me as your lawyer. And I've got to tell you, I didn't rub the lawyer genie's ass and wish for you either. But it seems like I'm all you've got, and I'm willing to do my best. I'm a pretty good lawyer."

"Where did you go to law school?" she asked.

"Harvard."

She tried to stifle a moan, but failed. "Oh, shit."

"You don't approve of Harvard?"

"Jamie, none of this is going to be pretty, or clean. You understand?"

I nodded, annoyed that I was pleased she had used my first name. "I figured that much."

"So your Harvard clubs, and your secret handshakes, won't help us. Still with me?"

"I'm trying, but I can't seem to focus."

"Why not?"

"I'm trying to remember the secret handshake. Which worries me, because if I can't remember it, no one else will tell it to me. It's a secret."

She laughed, an incongruous laugh considering the circumstances, but a great laugh considering any circumstances. It was a laugh that you expect to hear in a bar, after a bunch of beers and a bunch of stories. Not in a prison while figuring out how to die. And it was a laugh that matched her eyes, which were much warmer than when we had first met.

It was the kind of laugh that invited others to laugh along, and I did.

"You going to work your ass off on this?" she asked, her tone changed. Weirdly, my joke about the secret handshake had for the first time implausibly earned me some respect.

I could have given her a knee-jerk "yes," but I didn't, because her question jarred me a little, and made me think. The concept of working my ass off, not because I had to but because I wanted to, was not one I was very familiar with. The last time I had voluntarily worked my ass off was never.

"I'm going to do the best I can, Sheryl."

She paused, maybe because someone doing the best

they could for her was not exactly an everyday occurrence. Then, "Let's get it done, Harvard."

As motivational speeches go, in that moment "Let's get it done, Harvard" ranked up there with "Win it for the Gipper."

Uncle Reggie's office was the size of a broom closet. Actually, I think it had been a broom closet before Reggie converted it into a place where the accused could find salvation, coffee, and a way out of their legal troubles.

Reggie was a legend in New Jersey legal and criminal circles, which in itself was quite revealing. He believed that everyone deserved a competent, vigorous defense, and their ability to get such a defense should not be predicated on their ability to pay. That also happens to be what the justice system purports to believe, which is why it was sort of a surprise that Reggie always stood out so much.

On a per-square-inch basis, there was more paper in Reggie's office than anywhere on Earth. It was possible to pace the office, or sit down, without ever actually touching floor or chair. The paper was strewn everywhere, and Reggie always claimed that if a single piece were cleaned up or moved, he wouldn't be able to find anything.

"Well, if it isn't life's great disappointment," he said when he saw me, softening the verbal blow with a warm hug.

"Thanks, Reggie. I can always count on you for a pick-me-up."

"How's my pain-in-the-ass brother?" he asked.

"I would describe him as unchanged," I said.

"That's not always such a bad thing." He thought for a moment, then, "Make a note of this . . . that's what I want on my headstone. 'Here lies Reggie Wagner. He was unchanged.' "

"You've got me making notes about your headstone?"

"Why not? You're the executor of my will. You're also the sole beneficiary."

"Are you serious?"

"Don't be too flattered," he said. "You didn't beat out any other serious contenders, and I have no money. In fact, you're probably going to have to spring for the headstone."

I laughed out loud; Reggie was one of the few people on the planet who could make me do that. "Then stone might be the wrong thing to call it. 'Headwood' might be more accurate. Balsa wood."

"So what brings you here? Planning the next family circle?"

"I was in the New Jersey State Prison for Women this morning," I said.

"Who bailed you out?"

"This is serious. I have a client in there."

He nodded. "Let's hear it."

I told him the whole story, and he listened attentively, not interrupting once. When I finished, I asked, "What do you think?"

"Sheryl Harrison. That's the woman who slit her husband's throat?"

I hadn't mentioned how she killed him, only that she had. "Yes, you remember it?"

"I pretty much remember every significant criminal

case in this county for the last thirty years. It's a curse. But this one was near the top of the list."

"Why?"

"Because it didn't make sense to me. I never really bought that she did it."

"She confessed."

He nodded. "I know, which doesn't say much for my theory. And don't forget, I think everyone is innocent."

He stood up. "Let's go."

"Where?"

"I've got to be in court in twenty minutes. We can finish talking on the way."

We started making our way from Regg's Main Street office in Paterson to the courthouse, about a fifteen-minute walk. It should take ten, but each store seems obligated to have stands set up out in the street with their merchandise, as if the junk, when seen in the light of day, will prove too enticing to pass up. It makes walking on the streets very difficult. Since at many points the walking area was only one-person wide, it wasn't that well suited for talking either. Especially since Charlie walked at about forty-five miles an hour.

"So what do you think of her chances?" I yelled up ahead, while trying to simultaneously catch my breath.

"She doesn't have any chances."

"What does that mean?"

He stopped for a moment, to let me close the gap. "They won't go for it. They won't come close to going for it."

I had come to the same conclusion, but his certainty still annoyed me. "Why not?"

"You're asking them to kill her. There is no death penalty in New Jersey."

"They don't have to do the actual killing, and this isn't a penalty; this is the granting of a wish."

He nodded as if that cleared it up. "Ohhh, why didn't

you say that before? That changes everything; prisoners get three wishes that are always granted. This could be her first and last one."

"So they would let her daughter die?"

"Her daughter is not their problem; she is. Take your best shot, Jamie, and let me know how I can help. I think she's right, and I approve of what you're doing. But you and she have no chance."

We reached the courthouse, and he shook my hand and told me he had to get inside for jury selection on his next trial.

"Are you going to win this one?" I asked.

He laughed. "You must be kidding. I've got less chance than Sheryl Harrison."

He started to walk across the street, then stopped and came back. "Who was the detective assigned to the case at the time?"

"John Novack," I said.

"He's the best. Let me know if you want to talk to him."

"Why would I want to do that?"

He shrugged. "Because pretty soon you'll be grasping at straws, and maybe he'll be able to help."

The way to get through life is to reduce the number of potential "no"s. Most people in most jobs are trained to say "no"; it's much easier and much safer. A "yes" involves a lot of risk, and it's very public and easy to trace back. A "no" has a good chance of remaining anonymous, and anonymity is a valued perk in our workforce.

A "no" stops something cold, often leaving little or no chance to appeal. So if you want an answer on something, you go as high up as you can, bypassing as many potential "no-sayers" as possible.

This is the reason why I didn't go to the director of inmate affairs at the prison, or even the warden. They would be very likely to say "no," and no doubt powerless to say "yes." The best I could hope for, and that would be a long shot, was that they would pass it up to their superiors for a ruling. The more prudent move for me would be to go straight to those superiors, if I was able to.

So that's what I tried to do, and I tried to do it quickly. Just four hours after promising Sheryl that I would work my ass off, I called Sidney Williams, the commissioner of the New Jersey State Department of Corrections.

Williams's position is a political one, appointed by the governor. I wasn't sure which way that would cut, but I basically saw it as a negative. Sheryl was counting on someone to do the right thing. When people concerned with doing the best thing politically actually do the right thing, it's generally a coincidence.

I told Mr. Williams's assistant that I needed to talk to him on an urgent matter, concerning a prisoner in his system. When the woman didn't seem impressed, I told her that it "is a matter of life and death," and that "time is a crucial factor."

I had a feeling that she wasn't cowed, because she started reciting the procedures I would have to take, starting with the officials within the prison itself. When it became clear that I wasn't going to get through the impenetrable bureaucratic wall, I asked who was the next person below Williams on the chain of command.

She told me that the first assistant commissioner was a woman named Constance Barkley, so I hung up and called Ms. Barkley next. She had a male assistant, I guess they go boy-girl, boy-girl, and I told him my name was Jamie Wagner, and that I needed to see Ms. Barkley on an urgent matter.

It was pretty much the same story that I told the previous person, except for purposes of this conversation I wasn't Jamie Wagner, a prisoner's attorney. My new persona was Jamie Wagner, reporter for the Bergen *Record*, who was giving the Department of Corrections a chance to be quoted in a page-one story that was going to run the next day. A story that was focused totally and unflatteringly on that very department.

An hour and a half later I was in Ms. Barkley's office. She appeared to be in her late fifties, petite with a kind face. You wouldn't pick her out of a lineup as a person second in command of a stateful of felons.

"You're not a reporter," she said, after we shook hands. "You're a lawyer."

"What gave it away? My sweaty palms?"

She laughed, which made me figure she wasn't too annoyed by the deception. "No, the Bergen *Record* did that. When we checked they had no idea who you were. So we searched the system, and found you had recently registered as a lawyer for one Sheryl Harrison."

"Why did you agree to see me?" I asked.

That brought a shrug. "Why not? I was curious, and what's the worst that could happen?"

"That's my philosophy of life," I said. "Actually, the story I gave you was partially true. What I wanted to talk to you about does have the potential to be a very big story. I'm hoping you can help me avoid that, and do the right thing in the process."

"I assume it's about Ms. Harrison. What is it that she wants?" she asked.

"She wants to save her daughter's life."

"Sounds reasonable. Where does the Department of Corrections come in?"

So I laid it straight out for her, chapter and verse, and she listened without saying anything, except a single "I see," when I got to the part about Sheryl being the only match for a heart that Karen was likely to find.

When she finally responded, it was slowly and carefully. "I'll move your request quickly through the system. You were wise in coming straight here; had you gone through the local prison authorities it would have been bogged down for weeks."

"Great. Do you have a point of view on the request itself?"

"I want you to understand that what I'm about to say does not represent the point of view of the commissioner, or the state of New Jersey."

I nodded. "Understood."

"I think it's a wonderful thing she's doing; I'd like to think I would do the same. But you don't have a chance in hell. Not one."

That was becoming a familiar refrain. "Why not?"

"Because we don't kill people in New Jersey; we don't have the death penalty. She should have committed her murder in Texas."

"This is not a penalty; this is her wish. Hopefully, in her mind, her dying wish."

"I understand, but it makes no difference. There is no jurisdiction I know of, not even Texas, where the death penalty is voluntary. And even if it were to be approved by the commissioner, even by the governor, the doctor performing the surgery would be breaking the law. Assisted suicide is illegal, and make no mistake, that is what we're talking about here."

"We are not asking a doctor to perform the surgery while she is alive, simply that transplant preparations be made should she die."

That didn't sway her, so I thanked her for her time, asked that she expedite the process, and left. She had said exactly what I knew to be the truth. She put it more bluntly than I expected, but not as bluntly as I would have to put it to Sheryl Harrison.

She was not going to get what she wanted. She was going to live, and unless a donor could be found quickly, her daughter was not. Nothing could change that, not even a lawyer who knew what he was doing.

If she could find one.

I didn't feel like going home, so I called Ken Bollinger on his cell, and was not surprised he was at one of the bars we'd go to, on Amsterdam in the upper seventies.

"Well, my man, you got here just in time. I was going to have to give my credit card for the tab; now you can have that honor."

"Ken, I think you have enough money that you can spend some on beer and not run out."

"You miss the point, Jamie. When it comes to money, the fun is in having it. If you spend it, then you have less, which means less fun."

I shrugged and took out my credit card and gave it to the waiter.

After a few minutes of me doing very little talking, Ken said, "What's the matter, pal? You're even more boring than usual tonight."

"It's about that case I told you about. I'm not sure I see a way through it, and I might be in over my head. It's bothering me a lot."

"Take some advice, Jamie," he said. "Don't bring your work home with you. And definitely don't bring it to the bar."

I nodded. "Wise counsel."

"One more thing," he said. "Don't go growing up on me. I'm not ready for that."

At that moment, Alex Cahill wished his father could be there. There was nothing shocking about that; Alex had been wishing that since his father died, thirty-three years ago, when Alex was five. His other main wish, for all but the first few of those years, was that he could remember his father.

Randy Cahill, by all accounts, had been a powerful man. He was a landscaper, and if you called him a gardener you were in for a hell of a lot of trouble. When someone bought a house, they called in Randy, and he designed the outside, down to the last shrub. Randy felt it was easily as creative as interior design, but somehow didn't get the same respect.

And Randy did the work himself. He had helpers, but they were there to take direction. Randy literally got down in the dirt and created, and his wife, Nancy, used to say that she spent half their honeymoon futilely trying to get the dirt out from under her new husband's fingernails.

And then one day, while planting bougainvilleas, Randy died. No warning; he just tilted over and fell facedown. It took about ten minutes for his coworkers to even notice, but the paramedics said it wouldn't have mattered. He was probably dead before he hit the ground.

Alex saw newspaper clippings that Nancy had saved, what passed in their small-town paper as an obituary. They mostly focused on the fact that Randy had been a great high school athlete, and they mentioned that he left a young son behind.

Nancy told Alex that his father's heart just stopped, that the rhythm with which it beat was somehow interrupted. No one had known he had that problem, though back then there was little they could have done about it.

When Alex was sixteen, he lost his mother. Nothing sudden about that; she contracted throat cancer from smoking and withered away. Alex decided that of the two ways to go, Randy had it right, albeit way too early.

Alex never married, never wanted to have kids, and he figured it was because he didn't want to leave anyone behind, like he was left behind. He moved from his southern Californian birthplace to north Jersey, and carved out a successful career for himself as a software designer and consultant.

But the reason Alex especially wished Randy could have seen him on that particular day was because Randy had saved his life, if inadvertently. Alex had gone to a heart specialist when he was twenty-one, armed with information about the ailment that killed his father. Tests showed that Alex had the same problem, though it hadn't yet completely developed.

Alex was told to come back every six months to be rechecked, and he did so religiously. For seventeen years, they sent him home without recommending any special treatment, until six months before that day. Then the doctor dropped the verbal bomb that the condition had worsened, and for the first time posed a threat.

A pacemaker was recommended, which would maintain the rhythm of the heart. Had that kind of awareness and technology existed for Randy, Alex could have watched him grow old.

But Alex intended to grow old, and he very willingly had the procedure that implanted the pacemaker. It was much less of a big deal than he imagined, and once it was inside of him he really didn't notice it at all.

Following his doctor's instructions religiously, Alex began a diet and training regimen designed to support his already supported heart. He was down to 170 pounds on his six-foot-one frame, and had done cardio work at the gym every day.

Alex's doctor was by this point telling him that there were no restrictions on him at all, that he could be as active as he wanted, within reason.

So on this day Alex was doing exactly that; he was being as active as he wanted. He was going to run five miles in the park near his home. The distance was not particularly daunting, since he had frequently done more than that on the treadmill.

But it was outdoors, so it was somehow special, and it would have been nice for his father to be there, to root him on as Alex had always heard fathers were wont to do. But of course he wasn't there, never would be, and Alex said a silent thank-you for the knowledge that Randy had provided, which had saved his son's life.

Karen Davies, a nineteen-year-old student at Seton Hall with a secret dream to run the New York Marathon, was the one who found Alex, lying facedown in the dirt like his father all those years before. She called paramedics, who arrived quickly but could do nothing.

An autopsy was performed, and it was determined that the pacemaker had inexplicably failed. Not only did it not prevent Alex from suffering Randy's fate, but its malfunction had caused it. It had speeded his heart up to levels that caused it to literally burst from the pressure.

It was left to a woman who claimed to be Alex's widow, even though he was never married, to file a lawsuit, seeking four million dollars in damages.

A claim that was paid and collected.

I can't remember the last time the local TV morning news had anything that interested me. I only watch it to get the weather report, which enables me to complain to anyone who will listen that the weather forecasters don't have a clue what they're talking about.

I wasn't even going to turn it on that day, because I was rushing to get out of the city early, in order to beat the traffic into Jersey. Almost no one, besides me, lives in New York City and works in New Jersey, yet there's always heavy traffic in both directions. It's baffling.

But I turned it on, jumped in the shower, and didn't pay any attention to it while I was getting dressed. I walked into the kitchen, and got back to the bedroom just in time to hear the news guy say, "Harrison's lawyer is James Wagner, but he has not commented on the report."

My initial, desperate refuge was in the mention of the lawyer's name as "James," rather than "Jamie," but since James is my real name, that is how I am listed with the bar association. In any event, I knew down deep that another James Wagner having a client named Harrison, in a situation that was newsworthy, was too much of a coincidence to really hope for.

I went right to my computer and turned it on. I have Yahoo! as my home page, and the first thing I noticed was the name Sheryl Harrison. It was at the top of the "trending now" list, which probably meant her name was at that moment the most searched name on the web.

My hope was that Sheryl somehow gave an interview from prison, but I knew that wasn't going to turn out to be the case.

The story was everywhere; I had my choice of where I wanted to read it. I chose *The New York Times*; there would be time to check out the more sensationalized versions later. And sure enough, it was a straightforward recounting of the facts, at least in its initial paragraphs. It then eased into a legal analysis of the law as it relates to assisted suicide, both in New Jersey and nationally.

It was completely clear that either Constance Barkley went to the press after I left, or she went to her superiors, who then decided to go public. It made sense for them, especially since I had stupidly threatened to do so myself. This way they got to frame the story in their terms; the first time the public saw the facts they would be getting the government version.

Also mentioned in the story, as it had been on television, was the fact that I was not available for comment. Then I realized why. I turn off the ringer on my phone during the night and let the machine pick up. Late-night phone calls have always scared me; nobody calls after midnight with good news. So I avoid them.

There were eighteen messages on the machine, since that was all that it could hold. I didn't know how many people couldn't get through, and I had no desire to find out.

Seventeen of the calls were from media outlets, imploring me to call them back. Quite a few of them implied that they were on my side, and that I could use them as a platform to spread our word.

The one call not from a media person was a woman's voice that I recognized as Sheryl's. Even if I hadn't recognized it, the message would have made the identity of the caller crystal clear.

All she said was, "Harvard, you are an asshole. A major asshole. Thanks for telling my daughter and the entire world that she is going to die."

Had Sheryl Harrison employed a cadre of advisers for twenty years, giving them as their only task coming up with words to cause me pain, they couldn't have done as well as she did with that message. I hadn't even considered the effect on Karen, how stunned, frightened, and devastated she would be.

I hadn't thought through the impact my actions might have; I just blundered ahead with the first idea that popped into my head. And now it was too late; nothing I could do from that point on could make up for what Karen Harrison had to be going through.

I decided not to call any of the reporters back, for two reasons. First of all, I hadn't decided what to tell them, and I had already said enough to regret for a decade. More important, Sheryl deserved to be the first one I talked to. That way she could fire me, and it would no longer matter what the hell I said to anyone.

They were waiting in front of the building; I would call it a small army of media people, except for the fact that it wasn't small, and it wasn't just people. There were also trucks, and cameras, and microphones.

The garage where I parked was about two hundred feet from the front door of my apartment, and it took me twenty minutes to navigate it. I decided to make one statement, so as not to look as if we had nothing to say on our side.

"I'm not going to comment publicly at this moment. This is a very serious matter; a young girl's life is at stake. Just because the Corrections Department decided she is not entitled to privacy and compassion does not mean we should stoop to that level."

I didn't mind taking a shot at the Corrections authorities. It was by then completely obvious that they were never going to relent; if we were going to prevail it would be in the courts. And it was just as obvious that this would be as much a public relations war as anything else, with the PR ball now obviously in our court.

The other reason I attacked them was because I was pissed, and I wasn't going to just sit back and take what they dished out. The desire to fight, and to win, was a feeling I hadn't experienced since maybe never.

It was a feeling I liked, except for the nauseous part.

Ray Hennessey got the call the way he always got the call. His phone rang with a number that began with the area code 406. Hennessey had once checked and learned it was a Missoula, Montana, number. He had even called it once, from a pay phone, but the recording said it was out of service.

He knew the drill; once the phone rang from that number, he was to turn on his laptop computer forty-five minutes later. He did so, and five minutes after that the familiar voice came through the speakers. It was a normal voice, a little tinny from the speakers, and it spoke with a fairly dull monotone. This would be the primary way that they would communicate, though Hennessey did have a number to call, albeit through a circuitous route, that could put him in touch with the contact.

Hennessey had never met the person speaking to him, though they had talked at least fifty times. More significantly, that person had paid Hennessey more than five million dollars in the past seven years, with the promise of more to come.

Much more.

Hennessey had given up an earlier desire to know more

about the caller, and where he was calling from. This time, as always, there was no background noise at all, as if the caller were in a sealed, silent room.

He had no way of knowing that there were two men besides the caller in the room. Their names were Daniel Churchill and Peter Lampley, and they had quite a bit in common. Both were in their late twenties, and were workaholics. At that moment, as always, they sat at their desks, staring at their elaborate, state-of-the-art computer systems. Neither had girlfriends, other interests, or anything resembling a life away from their work; there would be plenty of time for that later.

The other thing that Churchill and Lampley had in common was that they were both dead by the time they were ten years old.

The man who conducted this and all conversations with Hennessey was Nolan Murray. He was considerably older than his handpicked colleagues, but he referred to them as his "partners." He was in actually their leader, and their boss.

Murray and Churchill knew each other first, and developed what had become their incredibly profitable "business" together. It took a while to find a third person who could meet their strict requirements to join their club, but Churchill finally found him in Lampley. Once they added Hennessey for the "hands-on" work, their workforce was complete.

And once Murray worked his way into the Limerick nuclear plant, they knew that their business was going to expand rather dramatically.

"Hello, Mr. Hennessey. I received your report on Sheryl Harrison," Murray said. He spoke through a voice synthesizer, so the sound that Hennessey would hear bore little resemblance to his real voice.

"Obviously things have since changed," Hennessey said, referring to the media outburst that had just occurred.

"Obviously. The situation has gone from slightly worrisome to decidedly unsatisfactory."

"I'm working on finding out more information," Hennessey said. "Not just what's in the papers." He said this without conviction, since he really had little prospect of finding out anything useful to the caller that wasn't already public.

"Information is not what I'm looking for now. We're coming up on a sensitive time, and this is an intolerable interference."

Hennessey had no idea what he meant by a "sensitive time," because he really hadn't a clue as to what Murray's goals were. "Okay. What are you looking for?"

"Ms. Harrison wants to die."

"Yes."

"Grant her wish."

A media contingent was waiting for me outside the prison. They looked exactly like the group in front of my apartment; there seemed to be no limit to the number of people assigned to this story.

Once I got past them and went inside, the people in the reception area and the guards seemed somewhat more responsive than they had the previous times. I assumed it was because they now knew the world was interested and watching, and scrutiny might be visited upon them.

I was brought into the same room Sheryl and I had met in twice before, and once again she was waiting for me. It was a conversation I was not looking forward to. I realized that I was seeking her approval, and I was about to get anything but that.

"I'm sorry, Sheryl. I screwed up big time. I don't know what else to say."

"Tell me what happened," she said. "Don't leave out anything."

So I told her about calling the Corrections Department, pretending to be a reporter, and meeting with Constance Barkley. I also told her that I had threatened the matter would become public, which I believe provoked them to take the initiative. "It was stupid," I said. "And I never thought about Karen. Not once."

"At the end of the day it's not going to matter," she said, once again demonstrating the gift of surprise.

"What?"

"We had to go to them eventually anyway, and at least you got heard by the person at the top. This way we didn't waste time with the losers at the prison. And this was the type of thing that the media was going to grab on to whenever word got out."

"But we could have framed it with our point of view." Weirdly, she didn't seem angry, or even upset. To her it was another mountain to climb; I suspected she had climbed a few in her life.

"We still can," she said.

"And Karen?"

"I'm very unhappy about that, but she was going to find out anyway. I wanted to be the one to tell her, but my mother will handle it."

"Are you trying to make me feel better?" I asked.

She gave me the eye contact thing again, in full force. "Harvard, believe me when I tell you this. I totally do not give a shit if you feel better."

"I believe you."

She nodded. "Good. Now let's figure out what we're going to do next."

"Before we do that, there's something else we need to talk about," I said.

She seemed wary, as if another bomb was going to be dropped on her. "You raising your fee?"

"Sheryl, remember the trouble you said you had getting a lawyer? When I suggested you could change lawyers you said you couldn't go through that process again."

"I remember."

"Well, at this point lawyers would be throwing themselves at you. This has a high media profile now; you just say the word and you could hold bar association meetings in here."

"Is that right?" she asked, as if she hadn't thought of that before.

"That's absolutely right."

"Harvard lawyers?" she asked.

"Hopefully not."

She thought for a while, more than a minute, apparently giving it serious consideration. Finally, "No. I'll stick with you."

"Why?"

"Because you feel guilty about what happened, and because you're pissed off. You're invested in this."

I was happy with her decision; no, more than happy. I felt vindicated, and maybe even energized. I'm not sure why I wanted to keep a hopeless case that wouldn't earn me a dime, but I did.

We talked for almost an hour, planning our strategy, such as it was. We came to the conclusion that our approach had to be two-pronged, both public relations and legal. It was not exactly inspired genius, since the PR battle had already begun, and I was a lawyer.

"I'm going to file a lawsuit," I said.

"On what grounds?"

"I don't know yet, but I'll come up with something. We need to pressure them, come at them from all angles."

I doubt that Sheryl was reassured, but at least by now she trusted I would give it my full effort. What I hadn't told her was that I was going to be adding a third prong. I didn't know whether I could get anywhere with it yet, so I was waiting to broach the subject with her. But I made a mental note to call my uncle Reggie, to get that wheel in motion.

As I was leaving, a guy dressed in a suit and tie, which

meant he was neither a guard nor a prisoner, approached me. "Mr. Wagner, have you got a minute?"

"For what?"

"Warden Dolan would like to see you."

I let him lead me to the warden's office, which was surprisingly spacious and well appointed, and seemed incongruous for the prison environment. Dolan was in her mid-forties, with looks that gave new meaning to the word "nondescript." If I met with her ten times, I still wouldn't recognize her on the street.

"Mr. Wagner," she said, dispensing with any pleasantries, "I have some information for you relating to your client."

"What might that be?"

"She has been placed on suicide watch."

"What exactly does that mean?"

"She is being removed from the general population, into a cell and area of the prison that is constantly monitored by cameras and guards. Anything that could be considered remotely dangerous will be taken from her."

"Why are you doing this?"

"It's quite common, really. We do it whenever we judge that an inmate might be a candidate for suicide. Today's media reports clearly indicate that she is a textbook case. Not only does she intend to commit suicide; she wants the state to facilitate it."

"She would only do it under medical supervision," I said.

"Perhaps. But perhaps in her desperation when her plans are thwarted she would take her own life, hoping that the medical staff would arrange for the transplant." She showed a small, smug smile. "That is no longer possible."

"So you are intent on keeping her alive, so that her daughter can die."

"Mr. Wagner, I would have preferred that you had followed the chain of command with your initial request."

"You mean I should have come to you?"

"That is correct."

"Why would I want to start at the bottom?"

I left, having taken a petulant shot at someone in a position to make my client's life more difficult. It was not my finest moment, but it was unfortunately getting to be a typical one.

I write great briefs; even the partners at the firm wouldn't dispute that. They cut straight to the salient points, which judges like, and are concise, which judges like even more. It's not a talent that gets you the big prize of partnership at a law firm; it's sort of like winning Miss Congeniality. But in any event, I'm sort of known for it, even among my colleagues.

So I set out to write a brief in support of the lawsuit I was filing on Sheryl's behalf. It's disheartening to write something like that, knowing down deep that if I were a judge I would rule against it myself. The law was simply not on our side.

Which, of course, did not stop me from claiming that the law was exactly, precisely on our side. The specific law I relied on was *Griswold vs. Connecticut,* a landmark 1965 Supreme Court case. It invalidated a Connecticut law against the use of contraceptives, with seven justices taking the position that it violated the constitutional right to privacy, in this case the marital variety. This despite the fact that not even the like-minded seven justices could point to an actual mention of privacy in the Constitution. Instead they pointed to other areas of the document, especially the fourteenth amendment, as justification.

The Griswold decision has had very far-ranging, significant implications beyond whether Connecticut men could use condoms. It has since been cited again and again by the court, most notably in *Roe vs. Wade*. In that decision, as well as numerous others, the court accepted a woman's dominance over her own body, saying that all such decisions were private and between her and her doctor, without the government having any right to interfere.

So I cited Griswold repeatedly throughout my brief. Our position was that Sheryl Harrison had total control of her own body, including ending its life in order to save that of her daughter. It was, essentially, a "private" matter, and none of the government's business.

I recognized that one of the counterarguments would be that once Sheryl was convicted and sent to prison, she gave up control of her body, so completely that the government had the right to imprison it. I thought that argument was easily refuted; for instance, surely her being an inmate didn't give the authorities the right to experiment on her, or sterilize her. Her essential bodily privacy was maintained, even in prison.

My counter to the law against assisted suicide was considerably less effective. I argued that the intent in this case was not suicide; the intent was simply to save a life by providing a transplant. The fact that she would die in the process was a secondary effect; in fact, if an artificial heart could keep her alive after the operation, she would certainly consent to that.

When I finished, I was struck with a realization that made me understand how far in over my head I was. I had never so much as argued a case in any court before, which in itself is not unusual for a person on my level within the firm. The senior partners handle the courtroom roles, and we associates provide them the backup they need, and demand.

But now here I was filing suit in the New Jersey Supreme Court, asking that they hear this on an expedited basis because of the urgent time considerations. It was comparable to the clubhouse custodian at Yankee Stadium suddenly being called on to replace Derek Jeter at shortstop.

I didn't even have any idea how to do it, so I called my uncle Reggie, who walked me through the fairly easy mechanics. I would literally drive to the courthouse, walk in the front door, and hand it to the clerk.

"But don't go alone," he said.

"You want to go with me?"

"What do I look like, a valet? Why the hell would I go with you?"

"You just said I shouldn't go alone," I pointed out.

"Right. You should go with every reporter and cameraman you can find. And bring the daughter; have her faint a couple of times on the courthouse steps."

I couldn't help but smile. "You don't think that's a little too subtle?"

"Jamie, here's your only shot. You've got to get every person in America on your side. They need to think that if their elected officials turn you down, they are murdering a teenage girl."

Reggie's comment jarred me, but not for the reason he would have thought. It made me realize that this really was about that teenage girl, slowly dying, probably scared out of her mind. She and her mother were what I should be focusing on.

Of course, I also knew that Reggie was right, and that it was in Karen's best interest to have the media on her side. I didn't know how one attracts "every reporter and cameraman," so Reggie said he would take care of it with one phone call. "Just wait a half hour and head for the courthouse."

I hung up, and as soon as I did the phone rang. Assuming it was one of the media people, I picked it up, so that I could announce my intentions.

"Jamie, this is Gerard Timmerman."

He didn't need to mention that he was the Gerard Timmerman of the firm of Carlson, Miller, and Timmerman, the firm that gave me a paycheck twice a month. Everybody referred to him as Gerry, but apparently when talking to someone of my level, it was Gerard.

"Yes, sir."

"I see that this pro-bono assignment has taken a somewhat unexpected turn."

"Yes, sir," I said, for the second time, since the first time seemed to have gone fairly well.

"Come in and let's talk about it."

"Okay . . . will do. When?"

"Let's say in one hour," he said.

"I'm afraid I can't do that, sir. I'll be at the courthouse in one hour. I can be there tomorrow morning . . . if that works for you."

He was quiet for a few minutes, probably deciding the words he was going to use to fire me. Then, "Nine-thirty."

I started to say that was fine, and that I'd see him at nine-thirty, when I realized he was no longer on the phone.

By the time I drove to the courthouse, which was in Newark, you would think that the president of the United States or Lindsay Lohan was arriving. I had been so busy that I don't think I fully understood the media firestorm Sheryl's plight had created. Demonstrations were well under way on both sides of the issue, but I would say the definite tilt was toward our side.

I worked my way through the crowd into the courthouse, where the security guards seemed to be waiting for me. They guided me to the clerk's office, and the actual filing took just a few minutes.

The case of *Harrison vs. New Jersey Department of Corrections* was a reality.

That was the good news. The bad news was we had almost no chance of prevailing, and if we did, it almost definitely would not be quick enough. Which meant that we were going to have to be very aggressive on the public relations side of the equation.

I had exactly as much experience dealing with the media as I had with the New Jersey Supreme Court, but I figured that was as good a time as any to learn on the job. I walked out of the court and stopped at the top of the steps, which seemed like a logical place to hold an impromptu news conference.

The assembled reporters threw about five million questions at me, none of which I even tried to answer. Instead I just waited until the din quieted down a little, then raised my arms and said I wanted to make a statement.

"About six weeks ago the president of the United States held a ceremony at the White House, at which he posthumously awarded Captain Timothy Myerson the highest honor he could bestow, the Congressional Medal of Honor. Captain Myerson had fallen on an unexploded munition, so that the seven other men in his command would not themselves be killed."

The reporters looked confused by what I was saying, as if they had wandered into the wrong movie and couldn't find an usher.

"Captain Myerson did exactly what Sheryl Harrison wants to do, to give up her own life to save another. But she is not honored at a White House ceremony; instead she is prevented from performing this act of heroism by bureaucrats in the New Jersey State government.

"As a grateful American, I am thankful that heroes like

Captain Myerson do not have to check with bureaucrats and politicians before they perform their acts of tremendous generosity and courage. With the lawsuit we are filing today, we will try to give Sheryl Harrison that same freedom."

With that I declined to take any questions, which didn't deter them, and they continued to yell them out as I walked away. It took me a while to physically extricate myself from the media mob, but when I was finally and safely in my car, I could reflect on how well it had gone.

Maybe I wasted my time in law school.

About two years ago, Ryan Palmer got the scare of his life.

The fifty-one-year-old periodontist had gone in for his yearly physical, and expected to receive the same clean bill of health he had gotten the last five years.

Instead he got the "C" word.

The good news, according to his doctor, was that it was thyroid cancer, detected early and very, very curable. The bad news, thought Ryan, was that when it comes to cancer there is no such thing as good news.

Having thought that, it came as a relief to him that the oncologist that he saw told him he would not need chemotherapy. The thyroid would be removed surgically, and its loss of function would easily be compensated for by taking pills, which he could do for the rest of what should be a very long life.

Starting three weeks after the surgery, Ryan would get three radiation treatments, spaced a week apart. He was lucky in that his local hospital had just gotten a state-of-the-art radiation machine. It was renowned for its ability to target massive dosages of radiation with incredible precision, eliminating the possibility of damage to any surrounding, totally healthy organs.

Upon receiving the diagnosis, and prior to the surgery, Ryan did the responsible thing and got his affairs in order, as best he could. His wife, Alice, and twelve-year-old twins, Jeremy and Andrew, would be reasonably well taken care of. Ryan had invested well, and also had a $750,000 life insurance policy, with Alice as the beneficiary.

But by the day of the surgery, no one was thinking negative thoughts, not even Ryan. And that optimism proved warranted, as he came through the procedure with flying colors. The surgeon expressed confidence that the entire malignancy was removed, and the biopsy tended to confirm that. The radiation would make extra sure.

Ryan spent three days in the hospital, and was then released. He would rest up for the three weeks, have the radiation, and thus put all of it behind him. He lobbied the radiologist, Dr. Stephen Robbins, to start the treatments early, but Dr. Robbins refused. The original plan was the safest way to proceed.

Alice took Ryan in for his first treatment, just as she had done for the surgery. Dr. Robbins explained that he would be put under a light general anesthesia, and the treatment itself would only take about twenty minutes. Once he awoke and was completely coherent, Alice could take him home.

Because he was sleeping, Ryan didn't get a chance to see the large piece of machinery that would dispense the radiation. It was just as well; it could be rather intimidating. And it would certainly have been hard to believe that even with the most advanced computers ever made controlling it, it could be so precise.

Everything went as planned, and Ryan was home five hours after arriving at the hospital. Dr. Robbins had told him to expect to be tired for a couple of days, but Ryan didn't feel that way at all. He wished that he could go back the next two days for treatments two and three, but he knew better than to waste his time trying to convince Dr. Robbins to speed up the schedule.

One week later, Alice took Ryan to the hospital for the second treatment. This time, once he was taken back to the room to be prepped, she left to run some errands, planning to be back well before the time she was supposed to.

Ryan was put under anesthesia, and brought into the radiology room. He was positioned under the machine, in the same manner as the first time. The technician directed the computers to correctly position it, and then monitored them as the radiation was delivered. Dr. Robbins, though he really had no role to play at this point, watched over the technician's shoulder.

The computer display indicated that the radiation was being effectively delivered to the target area, and it took almost four minutes for them to come to the horrific realization that it was not.

In fact, the radiation was being directed more than six inches from the correct spot, to an area near the bottom of Ryan's brain. It wouldn't be until much later that day, long after Ryan's body was taken away for an autopsy, that they also learned that the radiation had been delivered at more than seven times the directed strength. It had charcoal-broiled his brain.

Within weeks, the grief-stricken Alice had hired a lawyer, and the hospital, as well as Dr. Robbins and the company that manufactured the machine, had all quietly consented to a very large settlement. Ryan's family would be wealthy, but it was small consolation to them for his loss.

The life insurance company paid off the $750,000 to Alice, as well as the $1.5 million policy to Daniel Shaw, whom Ryan had never met nor heard of.

If one wants to hire a murderer, prisons are a great place to start. Especially maximum security prisons; when mining for murderers that's pretty much the mother lode.

The key is to find someone with expertise and experience; MIT has the engineers, Vegas the gamblers, Manhattan the great pizza makers. But if a headhunter is looking to hire a literal "headhunter," a maximum security prison is the place.

If you throw a dart in a maximum security prison, you'll most likely hit a murderer, though that would probably not be the wisest thing to do. Ray Hennessey didn't have to throw a dart; all he had to do was put out the word that $100,000 was up for grabs.

The fact that the killers in prison by definition had previously gotten caught meant nothing to Hennessey. Whether his hired killer was apprehended after killing Sheryl Harrison was of no concern to him, and likely wouldn't be to the killer either.

New Jersey's lack of a death penalty was the reason for that. Many of the convicted murderers were already put away for the rest of their natural lives. So since they couldn't be put to death, or sent away for any longer than they already were, why would another conviction be of concern?

Money always talked, even behind the prison walls. Not only could it buy perks on the inside, many of these people had families on the outside, and being able to provide them with substantial cash was very appealing.

So once Hennessey put the word out that he was looking for someone on the inside to kill Sheryl Harrison, he had a wide array of possibilities to choose from. Since it was a women's prison, they were all women, which was not something that Hennessey was used to.

The person he chose came highly recommended both for her ruthlessness and for her discretion. Even though Hennessey's identity remained a secret from her, if she were caught she would still reveal nothing about the facts behind her hiring.

But none of that mattered. He had arranged for Sheryl Harrison to be murdered. It was to take place in the prison laundry, where she worked, but on the appointed day she didn't show up for her shift. The killer made inquiries, and learned that she had been moved to suicide watch.

That meant that she would be isolated from the other prisoners and carefully guarded twenty-four hours a day, with constant camera surveillance. Under those circumstances, she simply could not be gotten to, not even by someone willing to reveal their identity for the chance to make the kill.

The word was passed to Hennessey by his hired killer, who could not accomplish the job because of the suicide watch.

Sheryl Harrison, the inmate who wanted to die, could not be killed.

Terry Aimonetti was cooking, which had lately become a delicate balancing act.

Terry was one of those instinctively great cooks. No matter what was lying around in the refrigerator, she could make a uniquely wonderful meal out of it. She was an artist, and she generally loved practicing her art.

But she had been trying to balance two conflicting needs, and it was a struggle. Karen's appetite had waned; the weaker she became the less interest she had in eating. Since she had always loved Terry's cooking, it fell to Karen's grandmother to make special dishes that would overcome her lack of appetite and get her to eat.

But also as Karen became more ill, her doctors kept making her diet progressively more strict. No spices, no seasonings, nothing that Terry ordinarily used to work her magic. With so few weapons at her disposal, making something that Karen would be anxious to eat became a near impossible task, but that didn't stop Terry from tackling it head on.

Terry had been cooking for almost an hour, making a whole wheat pasta with a sauce that Terry's own mother would have scorned as belonging in an old age home. But it was as good as it was going to get, and Terry had called out to Karen to sit down at the table.

She called three times, but Karen didn't answer. This was not terribly unusual, as Karen had been sleeping during the day a great deal, and had a teenager's immunity to sleep disturbances.

"Karen?" Terry kept calling, with increasing loudness as she walked to her room. She was by then starting to worry, moving more quickly as she approached.

Karen's door was open, but she was not there. The door to the bathroom off her room was closed, and Terry moved toward it. She thought she could hear water running, so she called out, "Karen? Karen, sweetheart, are you okay?"

There was no response, so Terry called again, louder and more insistent. Still no answer, so Terry opened the door. "Karen, I'm sorry, I . . ."

Karen was on the floor, facedown, blood coming from the top of her head. Terry screamed and went to her, fearing the worst. She slowly turned her so that she could see her face, and she saw the blood coming from a cut, which was actually just above her eye.

But she was breathing, and starting to open her eyes groggily. She said something, so low and muffled that Terry couldn't make it out.

"It's okay, baby . . . you're going to be okay," Terry said, then took a folded towel and placed it gently between Karen's head and the cold floor. She pressed another towel lightly to the cut, but it had mostly stopped bleeding by then.

Terry ran into the bedroom, grabbed the phone, and called 911, asking that an ambulance be sent. Within ten minutes the emergency medical people were in the house and putting Karen onto a stretcher, for the trip to the hospital.

Terry drove with her in the back of the ambulance. Karen was awake and coherent, but she was scared, and Terry tried to console her. "You must have slipped on the wet floor," Terry said, but they both knew better.

Karen was taken to the emergency room, but admitted to the hospital as a patient. It was not because of the cut, but because of her condition. Her heart was weakening at an alarming rate, and it was felt that she would be better off in the hospital, where she could be monitored and cared for.

Stress was something that her doctors wanted her to have none of, so it was decided, at least for the time being, that the furor surrounding her mother would be kept from her. This was not as easy as it sounded; it meant that she could only watch television when supervised, and could not take phone calls from her friends.

Terry was having a difficult time. The horror of watching her granddaughter go through this, coupled with the nightmare going on with Sheryl, was enough stress for ten people, and it was weighing heavily on Terry.

But life had never been easy for her, and it had made her a remarkably strong woman. She was going to get through this, no matter which direction it went, and she was going to be there for her family.

And the part that made this particularly unbearable, and so terribly, terribly unfair, was the secret that she had promised never to reveal.

Uncle Reggie called me at seven o'clock in the morning. I was sleeping, having been up until 1:00 A.M. the previous night doing media interviews over the phone. When they say that cable news is a 24/7 operation, they mean it literally.

"He'll see you at eight-thirty behind the tennis courts at Eastside Park in Paterson," was the opening Reggie used instead of "hello." "And he said if you bring any reporters, he'll cut your tongue out."

"Paterson? I'm in New York."

"Then you'd better get your ass moving; he's doing this as a favor to me."

I jumped in the shower, dressed, and was in my car in fifteen minutes. I had a vague idea how to get to Paterson, but no idea where Eastside Park was, so I figured I'd ask when I got in the area.

I made very good time and was approaching Paterson on Route 4 at about eight o'clock. I stopped at a gas station and asked the attendant where Eastside Park was, and he didn't have a clue. He told me his boss would be back in a minute, and that he would likely know.

The mention of "boss" jarringly reminded me that I had a meeting at nine-thirty scheduled with Gerard Timmerman, an appointment I would not be able to keep.

Once the gas station boss gave me directions to the park, I called Timmerman's office, and got his administrative assistant, an imposing woman named Mildred. She was the only person under sixty that I had ever met with that name, but I wasn't about to tell her that.

"I'm sorry, but something important has come up, and I'm going to have to reschedule my meeting with Mr. Timmerman this morning."

She didn't answer at first, no doubt finding it difficult to process. Then, "You're rescheduling?"

"Yes, I'm afraid so. What time works for him?"

"You're sure about this?" she asked, clearly incredulous. Her tone was screaming at me that this was an ill-advised career move.

"Listen, I know this is unusual, but I'll explain when I see him. And I'm in something of a hurry. I'm late for a meeting."

"You set up a different meeting?"

I was getting in deeper, but there was nothing I could do. Finally, she told me that Timmerman had an opening on his schedule for eleven-thirty, and she would pencil me in for then. If Timmerman found that unacceptable when she spoke to him, she'd call me.

I got to the tennis courts five minutes early, and exactly five minutes after that former detective, now lieutenant, John Novack pulled up. He got out of the car and walked toward me, glancing around, probably to make sure he didn't see reporters, which would force him to cut out my tongue.

"Speak," he said.

"Thanks for coming."

"Speak words that matter."

"Okay. I'm representing Sheryl Harrison; you've probably seen the media coverage about what's going on."

He didn't say anything, so I pushed forward. "You were the arresting officer in the murder case, and the first one on the scene. Sheryl confessed to you."

"You planning on telling me something I don't know?" he asked.

"Actually, I'm not. I'm more interested in learning what you do know, or more accurately, what you think."

"About what?" His tone was still belligerent, and it was getting on my nerves. Unfortunately, I couldn't afford to alienate him.

"Look, Reggie told me you don't like defense lawyers, but that's not what I am. I just sort of wandered into this, and I'm doing the best I can. I'm trying to save a girl's life."

"And lose your client's in the process."

"I'm not happy about that, but it's her decision, or at least that's what I'm hoping to make it."

He seemed to think about this for a moment, and then seemed to soften a little. A very little. "What does this have to do with me?"

"I don't give us much chance to win in the courts, and even if we do, Karen won't make it that long. Public opinion is on our side, and we can milk it as we go along, but it's not so one-sided that the state is going to back down."

"So?'

"So Sheryl has a parole hearing in three weeks. It's just a formality at this point, but I want to make it more than that. I want her to get the parole and go out in the world. Then there will be nothing to stop her from saving her daughter's life."

"She won't get paroled," Novack said.

I nodded. "Not on the current evidence."

"You have something new?"

I shook my head. "No. That's where I'm hoping you come in."

He laughed. "Let me go check my car; I think I've got some new evidence in the trunk."

"Reggie doesn't think she did it," I said.

Novack didn't say that Reggie was an idiot, or that Reggie didn't know what he was talking about, or that I should stop wasting his time with this bullshit. What he said was, "Yeah."

"More importantly, I looked at the discovery, including the murder book."

"So?" he asked, though he knew where I was going.

"I saw your reports; you had doubts that Sheryl was guilty. I think that's why you agreed to meet me this morning."

He seemed to run through his mind where to go with this, and then he asked, "You know that thing you attorneys have, where you take an oath to keep things in confidence, and you pretend you have integrity?"

I smiled. "I'm vaguely familiar with it."

"Well, you better keep what I tell you in confidence, because if you don't, you won't get disbarred. You'll get dis-balled."

I smiled an uncomfortable smile. "You have my word."

"Good. It's true that I was never sure she did it; none of the pieces fit."

"What do you mean?"

"Well, for one, the victim was lying facedown, which means she had to lift his head from behind, reach around, and slice him."

"She couldn't have done it from the side?"

He shook his head. "Not in the direction it was done. I

could explain that, but take my word for it. Also, the autopsy showed there were indentations on his back from the killer's knees. But for her to have done it the way the evidence showed wouldn't make sense anyway."

"Why is that?"

"Couple of things. One, she risked waking him up by doing it that way, which would not have gone well for her. Two, if she was an enraged, battered wife, she would be far more likely to plunge the knife into his back a bunch of times. The way this was done was surgical; not a crime of passion at all. More like an execution."

"Anything else?"

He nodded. "There was no blood on her. She would have had to be very, very careful to avoid the blood; it was everywhere. And why go to all that trouble if she was going to call 911 and confess?"

"Maybe she's squeamish."

"Squeamish people don't slit throats. They put poison in coffee. And the victim had a gun in his pocket, a thirty-eight. It was unregistered."

"So?"

"So he was a used-car salesman. Why did he need to carry an unregistered handgun? Plus he had a fake ID in his wallet, a professional job."

I wanted to sound like I knew what I was talking about, like I had some insight. But I was impressed at the way this was pouring out of Novack, with little prompting. Either he had amazing powers of recall, or he had been thinking about this over the years. "So?"

"This guy wasn't getting carded in bars; why would he have a fake ID?"

"Did you do anything about this at the time?"

His stare was the reason the phrase "If looks could kill" was invented. "You may find this hard to understand, but police have a tendency to use their time and resources to solve crimes that haven't already been solved. It's not a whodunit when somebody has already said, 'I done it.' "

"Why would she confess if she didn't do it?" I asked.

"I don't know. I'll ask her the next time we have a client conference."

I decided to ignore the insult and get to the real reason why I was there. "I need your help."

He just stared at me, waiting.

"I don't have any money, and Sheryl sure as hell doesn't. So I can't hire any investigators."

Still just stared, waiting.

"So I was wondering if you could conduct at least some of the investigation you didn't conduct back then," I said, and then softened it with, "Not that you should have, I mean, back then."

"I'll get back to you," he said, and then walked back to his car. I had no idea what his intentions were, or what he was going to get back to me with.

So I went to meet with my boss, which would probably be a lot like meeting with my parents.

Probably worse.

Jamie Wagner's question had gotten under Novack's skin. He had asked why Novack didn't do anything about his suspicions at the time of Charlie Harrison's murder. The answer had been the right one; once Sheryl Harrison confessed, there were other cases that more urgently needed his attention.

But it was bullshit, and Novack knew it. The case had bothered Novack ever since, and he had the autonomy to have pursued it if he thought it was worthwhile. But he never did, and even though he made the excuse to Wagner, he knew better.

Of course, time was always a factor, and there was never enough of it, but at this point he was going to make the time. He would try to find out what really went on in that room that day, and whether Sheryl Harrison killed Charlie or not.

He was tired of beating himself up over this case; he had plenty of other cases to beat himself up over.

Sheryl's mission to save her daughter's life and give up her own was not the motivating factor for Novack. He wasn't sure where he came down on the issue, and didn't spend much time thinking about it. Deep philosophical thinking was not really Novack's thing, especially when the issue at hand was strictly other people's business.

But if he were pressed, he'd probably be on the side of saving the daughter's life. He and his ex-wife Cindy didn't have any children, but if they had, Novack would do everything he could for that kid, including giving up his own life, if that became necessary. So he admired and respected Sheryl's guts, whether or not she slit Charlie's throat.

Novack had discussed it the night before with Cindy. She was pretty much the only person in the world that he ever had an outside-of-work conversation with that didn't include the words "Knicks," "Mets," "Giants," or "Jets."

He and Cindy were married for seven years, which could best be described as turbulent. Novack was simply impossible to be married to; he was moody and difficult, and his level of impossibility exactly mirrored what was happening at work.

There were many good moments, and she loved him, but he was just too unpredictable, and she didn't want to walk on eggshells all the time. So finally, she couldn't take it anymore, and she threw him out. She immediately filed for divorce, which he did not contest, and began the process of overhauling her life.

She finished her masters in speech therapy and got a good job in an already thriving private practice. She started dating, nothing too serious, which was just as well, since there was a problem.

Its name was Novack.

For all practical purposes, Novack didn't recognize the divorce. He took an apartment of his own, but considered the post-marriage situation simply a phase. He kept showing up at Cindy's house, helping her whenever he could, and just hanging out until she told him to leave.

It definitely inhibited her dating, since Novack was six foot two, a hundred and ninety pounds, was trained in martial arts, and carried a gun. Prospective suitors found that to be a somewhat unappealing combination.

And the truth was that Cindy didn't mind. This was a different Novack, attentive, respectful, and even, her mind boggled at the thought, sensitive. Plus, since they didn't live together, she could throw him out whenever he started to get on her nerves, though that happened on surprisingly few occasions.

Sex between them, though always satisfying to both, became even better. And money, a cause of some friction in the past, was not an issue, since they kept separate finances. Cindy actually made more than he did, which was a secret she would carry to her grave and beyond.

They were planning a vacation, for one week starting that Monday. Nothing fancy, they were heading to Long Beach Island, New Jersey. Surprisingly, Cindy was looking forward to it without any trepidation, even though it was the first vacation they would take together since the divorce. She figured that if any problems came up, they were advanced enough to handle it.

Cindy knew how much the Sheryl Harrison case had troubled him and stuck with him over the years, so she was not surprised when he brought it up the previous night. When Reggie told him that Jamie Wagner wanted to meet with him, Novack basically knew where that was going to go, and he discussed it with her.

She had encouraged him to do whatever he had to in order to clear his mind of it once and for all. She also felt for Sheryl, and strongly supported her goal of saving her daughter.

Cindy was not surprised when Novack showed up at her office after his meeting with Jamie Wagner. He started to make small talk, which was decidedly not his specialty, and since a client was waiting for her, she attempted to cut through it.

"What's up?" she asked. "How was your meeting with Wagner?"

"Fine . . . no big deal."

"Great," she said, trying to hide her amusement. "I was afraid it might interfere with our vacation."

"Don't be ridiculous," he said.

"Because I know you wouldn't want anything to interfere with our vacation."

He gave her a kiss on the cheek and said, "Every day with you is a vacation."

"You're a piece of work, you know, Novack?"

"I'm aware of that, yes."

"You came here to tell me we're not going away next week, and you don't know how to bring it up."

"Cind, it's a perfect chance to get to the bottom of this. And that poor girl, lying in that hospital . . ."

"You're playing the 'poor girl' card on me?"

He smiled. "I can only play the cards I'm dealt."

"You know, all the other women, their ex-husbands take them on great trips after they get divorced. I had to get stuck with you? You won't even take me to New Jersey?"

"I'll make it up to you. Next year I won't take you to Paris."

She laughed. "Deal. Now get out of here."

Gerard Timmerman kept me waiting in his anteroom for ten minutes. It was probably some type of revenge for my postponing our meeting, or maybe he was on the phone with HR determining if they needed to give me any severance, or just throw me out without paying me a dime.

Ordinarily I wouldn't mind; Timmerman could keep me waiting until August and I'd be fine with it. It would have meant less time at my desk poring through contracts, and I was getting paid whether I actually did any work or not. But I was anxious to get to the prison and talk to Sheryl, so I was hoping the great man would hurry up and see me.

When I was finally summoned, I saw that I was meeting with not one, but two exalted leaders. In addition to Timmerman, Harold Carlson was there as well, which meant two-thirds of the founding fathers were present, plus me.

There was a famous double-play combination in baseball about a million years ago, that my uncle Reggie used to tell me about. They were way before his time, but he is a baseball history geek, and he said these guys were legendary. The combination was referred to as "Tinker, to Evers, to Chance," since those were their last names. Looking at these two guys, I had to stifle a laugh, as for some reason it hit me that I felt like I was alone with Tinker and Evers, and I had no Chance.

I decided to open the meeting with an apology about missing the meeting earlier, but Timmerman shrugged it off as if it were of no importance. "As I mentioned on the phone," he said, "Harold and I are concerned at the direction your assignment has taken."

The truth was that in our brief conversation, he hadn't mentioned that he was concerned, nor had he mentioned "Harold." But I decided correcting him wouldn't be a good plan, so I just gave a half nod and waited.

"We also don't think it's the kind of case our firm is well equipped to handle. It's well outside our areas of specialization, as well as yours."

Was he trying to take the case away from me? "What are you saying?" I asked, but I soon realized that my questions or feelings were of no consequence to the conversation. In fact, it wasn't a conversation at all. He was going to say what he was going to say; I could jump on his desk and tap-dance and it wouldn't matter.

"It's a very difficult matter . . . very difficult," he said, shaking his head sadly at the difficulty of it all. He looked over at Harold, who sat impassively, not joining in the head shaking. "So we are prepared to take an unprecedented step."

He paused; this might have been my chance to jump in, but I didn't.

"We will hire an experienced criminal attorney to represent Ms. Harrison, at our expense. Our involvement will be behind the scenes, of course. We are not looking for publicity."

"It's not really a criminal case," I said.

He smiled. “I assure you the attorney we hire will be equal to the task.”

“So you’re asking me to withdraw from representing Sheryl? Ms. Harrison?”

“I’m not sure I would categorize it as ‘asking,’ ” he said. “You are currently representing her on assignment from this office. We are reassigning you to something more in line with your skill set. It is better for her, and much better for your future with the firm.”

“I don’t have a future with the firm.”

He seemed surprised by my directness, but recovered and shook his head. “Not true. I’ve been reviewing your record; it’s a strong one.”

“So I have a chance at partner?”

“You will certainly receive every consideration,” he lied.

I was furious, and wanted to tell him what he could do with his consideration, but he and Harold and the surroundings were somewhat intimidating.

But then I thought of Sheryl, sitting in that shit hole relying on me in a way no one had ever relied on me before, and I realized that these assholes were not in her league. I had only spent a couple of hours with her, and I worked for these people for six years, yet I cared more about her than Gerard and Harold and their whole goddamn firm.

“I’ll talk to Sheryl about your offer,” I said. “It is ultimately her decision.”

Timmerman’s voice immediately got about twenty degrees colder. “Your withdrawal from the case is not her decision; she will be adequately represented and cannot compel you to continue. To be completely candid, it is also not your decision. It is the decision of this firm.”

I put my hands on his desk, partially to steady myself. I was annoyed that this asshole had the power to literally make my legs shake. “Mr. Timmerman, Mr. Carlson, here’s how this is going to work. I am going to tell Sheryl your offer. If she takes it, that's fine. If she wants to keep me, then I will remain her lawyer."

"You don't—" he started, but I interrupted him.

"You can keep paying my salary while I do so, or you can fire me. That's the only part that is in your control. But if you fire me, I'll see to it that you'll be chin deep in all that publicity you don't want."

"I'm not sure that's the attitude you want to take," he said. "And I'm not sure we're the people you want to threaten."

I nodded. "I'm not either. But what I am sure of is that Sheryl Harrison is going to be calling the shots. She's dealing with enough bullshit, without adding yours to the pile. So let me know what you want to do, fire me or not. Either way I'm fine with it."

As exit lines go, I wasn't going to come up with anything much better than that, so I walked out. I think Timmerman was saying something as I closed the door, but I'm not sure.

Novack had waited six years to investigate the case; he wasn't waiting another day. He told his partner, David Anders, what he was doing, and Anders had said, "What a surprise."

"Which means what?" Novack asked.

"Which means this has been bugging you for six years. When this story about Harrison broke, there was no way you weren't going to dive into it."

"You think it's a mistake?"

"I think it's a mistake, and I think it's a waste of time. I told you that then, and I'm telling you now. She said she did it. She was alone in the room with the victim. End of story."

"Then I'm doing it," Novack said. "Proving you wrong will only add to the satisfaction."

Anders laughed, and since their caseload was not that busy at the moment, and since he was Novack's friend as well as partner, he agreed to cover for Novack, so that he might begin his "vacation" project four days early.

The first thing Novack did was retrieve the murder book from the archives. It was easily found, because much of it had just been copied for Wagner when he was appointed as

Sheryl Harrison's new attorney. And it was easy to go through, because there was almost nothing of real consequence in it.

Novack immediately knew how difficult this was going to be. It was much tougher than diving into a cold case, because invariably those cases would have gone cold after every investigative avenue was exhausted. The file would be filled with information that could be reexamined and rechecked.

In the murder of Charlie Harrison, almost no investigation had taken place, because the obvious killer was in custody within minutes of the murder.

Whereas the victim's life is usually taken apart in an effort to find out who might have wanted him dead, Charlie Harrison's life had undergone no such scrutiny. The only aspect that had been documented in any detail at all was his relationship with Sheryl, which had been a rocky one. And that information hadn't been gathered for the purpose of finding the killer; it was more to guarantee that Sheryl would pay for her crime.

So that was where Novack would start; he would learn who Charlie Harrison was, and maybe that would reveal why he died. His first stop was Arcadia Chevrolet on Route 4 in Paramus, where Charlie worked for seven years as a used-car salesman.

There was always the chance that few if any people would even remember him, six years could have seen a lot of turnover in the dealership's employees. Novack arrived and flashed his badge, asking to see the person in charge.

Within five minutes he was in Danny Duncan's office. The sign outside his office door said "manager," and the small sign on his desk confirmed it. Duncan quite obviously wanted to make sure that everybody knew he was the top banana at Arcadia Chevrolet.

Duncan looked to be in his forties. The percentage of

his hair that he had maintained over the years was in the twenties, and it was obvious to Novack that careful combing was designed to maximize what he had and conceal what he didn't. It didn't work, thought Novack, but then again it never did.

Duncan had a bunch of commendations on his wall, proclaiming him the top salesman of various months, going back as far as 2002. That told Novack that he had worked his way up to manager, and that he had been a colleague of Charlie's when his throat was intact.

"He was a great guy," Duncan said, "just a great guy. And a real practical joker, you know? You never knew what he was going to do next."

"Did he have any enemies?" Novack asked.

"Charlie? No way."

"Do me a favor, think before you answer, okay? It's been six years, so you probably haven't thought about this stuff in a while. Take your time, and tell me everything you know about him. The good and the bad."

"Okay . . . sure."

"Did he have any enemies?"

Duncan delayed answering, as instructed, trying to figure out when he could respond without being accused of jumping the gun. Finally, he said, "I guess his wife, you know?"

"Did you ever meet her?"

"Nah, Charlie never brought her around. Didn't talk about her much either."

"Were there any customers that were angry at Charlie, maybe they thought he ripped them off?"

"We have a satisfaction guarantee in place here."

"I'm sure you do, but maybe some customer still wasn't completely satisfied? Do you keep records of things like that?"

"Well, we keep a file with complaints, but that's going back a ways. I could look for it."

"Good, do that. When you heard that Charlie had been murdered, did you hear at the same time that his wife had been arrested?"

Duncan thought back on the moment and said, "No, I don't think I did."

Novack nodded. "In that moment, did you have an instinct as to who might have done it?"

Again Duncan took his time, and finally shook his head. "No, I don't think so. I just remember how weird it was that Charlie was gone, and like that, in that way, you know? It gave me the creeps; I mean, we had just been out celebrating the night before."

"What were you celebrating?"

"It was Charlie's going away party. A bunch of us went to the Crow's Nest on Route Seventeen."

"Had be been fired?"

"Charlie? No way," Duncan said. "He quit."

"Why?"

"Because he was coming into all that money."

It was a totally weird sensation; I couldn't get used to it. Whenever I turned on the radio or television, I was the person they were talking about. Sheryl was the center of attention, but they never failed to mention me, and I was almost always pleased that they did. Until now, I never really thought of myself as having an ego, and here I was finding out how much I liked having it stroked.

The one thing my ego and I didn't like was that some of the analysts were turning their attention to whether I had the experience and savvy necessary for the job. It was obviously a legitimate question, but I couldn't help wondering if Timmerman was feeding the flames. I decided that it was too soon for that, since I had just turned the guy down. But I certainly wouldn't put it past him for the future.

It seemed like more polls were taken to gauge the public's point of view on the Harrison case than the average presidential election. In sum they said that about 55 percent of Americans sided with Sheryl in her fight to save Karen's life; 38 percent were against her, and 7 percent had no opinion.

The people opposed basically broke down in three

camps. The fervent pro-lifers, mostly devoutly religious people, simply could not countenance the state taking someone's life in such a manner. All life, they reasoned, was precious and had to be protected.

A second segment worried about the "slippery slope" that might be greased by granting Sheryl's wish. They sympathized with her plight, but worried where it might lead, who else might petition the government for the right to die. These people vaguely worried about governmental death panels, which might go even further and make decisions about whether some people no longer were worth keeping alive.

The third group, the smallest of the three, was opposed simply because it was against the law. Neither the Corrections Department, nor the governor himself, had the right to disregard a long-standing statute. If they wanted to let Sheryl die, let the Congress pass a law giving them and her that right.

The irony of it all was made crystal clear by another survey, which asked people whether someone who slit someone's throat while their victim was sleeping should receive the death penalty. A large majority said yes, meaning many people thought it was okay for the state to kill Sheryl, but just not on her terms.

I headed to the prison to see Sheryl, and found that I was looking forward to it. I liked her, she was straightforward and didn't bullshit, traits which were not exactly commonplace in my world. I also had to admit that I saw her as a benefactor in a strange way; I was enjoying being in the action, and she was the reason I was there.

I was searched even more carefully than usual before being allowed in to see her; it was invasive and irritating. They must have thought I was smuggling in a scalpel, some anesthesia, and a team of surgeons.

Sheryl was getting less access to the outside world now

that she was on suicide watch and thus in solitary, so she asked me to update her on everything that was happening. I told her about the lawsuit I filed, and she pumped me for details with surprisingly perceptive legal questions. She had clearly been studying.

She seemed fine with my answers, but less so with my public relations efforts. "You've got to step it up," she said. "Public pressure is the only way this is going to happen."

I told her that I had plans to do another round of cable TV interviews the next day, and that seemed to mollify her somewhat, but not all the way. "You should be doing a 'full Ginsburg,' " she said, and I laughed out loud.

She was referring to William Ginsburg, an attorney for Monica Lewinsky, who once hired went on every Sunday morning TV news show in one day. It redefined television ubiquity, and the feat was dubbed a "full Ginsburg."

She laughed herself at my reaction. She had an easy, appealing laugh, and she was able to work it into the most serious conversations, without apparent incongruity. But she was focused, and that focus was on a process that, if successful, would end her ability to laugh, or cry, or breathe.

We started talking about Karen, and Sheryl said that as far as she knew, Karen was still unaware of the furor. "This is the longest she's been in the hospital," she said. "Each time gets longer." It was an obvious sign that her condition was growing ever more serious.

When she had exhausted her questions, I told her about my meeting with Timmerman and his offer to pay for her representation, as long as it wasn't by me.

She barely gave it a moment's thought. "No, I want you."

"There are better lawyers out there."

"But none that I can manipulate so easily," she said, and laughed, even though she probably wasn't joking. "And that Medal of Honor thing you used on the media was cool . . . I liked that."

"I was pretty pleased with that myself," I said, smiling, before I dropped the bomb. "Why did you confess to killing your husband?"

She flinched slightly, or maybe not, and said, "Because I killed him."

"I'm not so sure," I said. "And the cop that arrested you isn't so sure, either."

"Well, you're both wrong, so drop it, okay? Keep your eye on the ball, Harvard."

"I'm doing just that," I said. "Public opinion is on your side, which means the politicians making this decision would like to be on your side as well. But they most likely see themselves as trapped, because their lawyers are telling them that you don't have a legal leg to stand on."

"So?"

"So they just might want to have a way to do this that doesn't break the law, or at least gets you off their plate. Getting you off their plate means getting you out of prison."

"So you think I'm innocent, and that you're going to prove it in time to save Karen? What the hell are you smoking, Harvard?"

"I do think you damn well might be innocent, but I don't have to prove it. All I have to do is give the parole board enough evidence, enough of an excuse, to let you out."

"That's not the way things work, Jamie. And even if they did, they don't work fast enough."

"Sheryl . . ."

"Harvard, I killed the son of a bitch."

While it might seem unusual for a lawyer, at that moment I was glad that I thought my client was lying.

Novack spent the better part of the morning digging into Charlie Harrison's financial life. It had taken a substantial, albeit strange, turn about six months before his death. Prior to that time, his only source of income appeared to be his work at the Chevy dealership, which earned him a decent, if unspectacular, living. Each December there was an extra amount in the middle of the month. It was of varying size, and Novack suspected it was a bonus, dependent on sales for the year.

But nine months before he died, he received a wire transfer in the amount of $50,000. He subsequently received four more payments, also of $50,000, at odd times in the remaining months. They were also wire transfers, and the last one was three weeks before he got his throat slit.

Novack was able to accomplish a lot of this work on the police computer, something he would have been far less able to rely on six years earlier. But there was a limit to what could be found, or at least what he was capable of finding. Fortunately, he had other resources at his disposal.

Novack called Sandy Barone, an FBI agent in the Newark office. They had met when their paths crossed on a murder case Novack was working on. The suspect was also one of the targets of a large-scale fraud investigation the Feds were knee-deep in, and Barone had approached Novack about it.

Her specialty was in financially related crimes, and as is the FBI's policy, she tried to get Novack to, if not back off, be deferential to the Bureau. At first Novack thought she was joking, since his case was a murder, and he learned in Police Work 101 that killing was worse than stealing.

Barone's position was that she was not trying to hurt Novack's case, but that the fraud investigation involved many people, huge amounts of money, and had international implications. She was of the opinion that the Bureau should have some leeway, and that Novack's case would not be imperiled, merely delayed a short time.

They clashed, not exactly a news event since Novack clashed with everyone, but ultimately they worked it out. Novack even developed a respect for Barone, one reason being that she was one of the rare federal agents who didn't threaten to go over his head. All of this brought the total number of FBI agents that he respected to one.

From Barone's perspective, once she got past the fact that Novack was the most annoying person on the face of the Earth, she recognized that he had at least two worthwhile qualities that were in short supply in the population: He was a dedicated, talented cop, and if he told you something, you could absolutely take it to the bank. Of course, very rarely did you like what Novack told you.

"It's your favorite cop," Novack said when he got her on the phone.

"That's a short list to be on top of," she said. "How are you? More importantly, how's Cindy?" Barone and Cindy had met and immediately hit it off.

"She's fine; still hopelessly in love with me."

"The woman is a saint," Barone said.

"Are we through chitchatting? I need some information on a company."

"What a surprise; the man needs a favor."

"You know, I could have called a hundred other people," Novack said.

"You want me to transfer the call?"

"No, you'll do," Novack said. "The company is called Cintron Industries. All I know about them is that six years ago they were wiring money to someone I'm investigating."

"When do you need it?" she asked.

"How about at the end of this sentence?"

She laughed and told him to hold on, then came back about five minutes later. "Sorry I took so long," she said. "But it's harder to find information on a company when there is no such company."

"It's a dummy?" Novack asked, not surprised.

"No, you're a dummy. It doesn't exist. I'll do some more checking, but my guess is it never did."

"Maybe it's foreign?" he asked.

"Who do you think I work for, Mayberry PD? Our database includes every company on the planet, no matter what country they're located in."

"So how could a company that doesn't exist wire money?"

"I can't help you with that," she said. "Maybe you should call a cop."

When Novack got off the phone he was quite confused, but he was nowhere nearly as confused as he was aggravated and pissed off at himself. In one day he had uncovered a truckload of suspicious information, information he should have learned six years ago if he had taken the time.

The money Charlie Harrison had received was substantial, but not nearly life changing. He would not have quit his job had he not been expecting a huge upcoming payoff, or at least the prospect of continued payments on the level he had been getting them. Fifty grand every month or so definitely would reduce the incentive to keep saying, "What will it take to put you in this 2006 Chevy Malibu today?"

The money was real, even if it seemed to come from nowhere. Maybe it was money that provoked Sheryl Harrison enough to kill her husband, but Novack instinctively didn't think so. Although he did consider it quite possible that the money was the reason Charlie died.

Charlie did something for that money, and the payment schedule made it likely that he kept doing it. Finding out what he did, six years earlier, was not going to be easy, and the truth was that Novack really didn't know where to begin.

Then he remembered one of the curious things about this very curious case. In Charlie Harrison's wallet when he died was that fake ID. Novack had no idea whether or not it had anything to do with the case, but chasing it down had one major advantage to it.

It gave him something to do.

Nolan Murray was a football fan. For a time he thought of himself as a football player, and even tried to be a walk-on for Rutgers, the year before he dropped out. A few scrimmages against the first team defense convinced him his future was not on the gridiron.

Nolan had the mind for the game; he had the mind for pretty much any game ever invented. He just didn't have the physical skills, and he was smart enough to know it.

The first thing he had learned from his high school coach, the first thing every quarterback had to know, was that he had to see the whole field. He had to know where every player was, on both teams, and where they were likely to go. In short, he had to be completely aware.

Nolan Murray was completely aware, not on the football field anymore, but in his work. He was able to see everything, and that was important, because to stretch the football analogy a bit, he was about to compete in the criminal equivalent of the Super Bowl.

For instance, Nolan knew that Novack had reopened the case; he knew it within moments of Novack turning on his computer. He knew that he was investigating Charlie

Harrison's life, and that he had discovered the wire transfers.

With the resources of the government at Novack's disposal, Nolan also was aware that he would discover, if he hadn't already, that Cintron Industries didn't exist. Unless Novack was incompetent, and Nolan knew that he wasn't, the cop would understand that the payments Harrison received were on some level tied into his death.

But Novack would never get to the bottom of this. He wouldn't have been able to if he had the six years, and now he had barely three weeks. After that it wouldn't matter what he learned; the mission would have already been accomplished, and Nolan would have disappeared with an almost unimaginable amount of money.

Nolan was the type to make a decision and move on, rather than replay it over and over again in his mind. But the way he got to this place was a combination of brains and luck that would change the world.

Two years ago, almost to the day, he was out with his girlfriend in a bar. Actually, "girlfriend" might not be the word many people would use, since the relationship for Nolan was totally about sex. He had no desire to be open or emotionally available or intimate or any of the things a real relationship generally called for.

It happened that the "girlfriend" met another friend in the bar that night, who in turn had just met a guy who was clearly smitten with her. He lived outside of Philadelphia, and was in town visiting friends for the weekend. They all got to talking, and when the man, Stan Wollner, mentioned where he worked, the idea hit Nolan square between the eyes.

From there it was surprisingly easy. He hacked into the young woman's Facebook account, and in subsequent days began to pretend to be her as "she" flirted with Wollner. She raised the prospect of them spending a weekend together, but kept it just out of reach for a while. Then "she" requested that he send a message to her at a time when Nolan knew he would be at work. What sweetened the pot was a clear inference that sex was becoming a definite possibility.

Wollner could have ignored it, or he could have left work and contacted her from somewhere outside. Had he done that, Nolan would have given up and gone back to focusing on his already very, very profitable business. Wollner was not supposed to go on the Internet from work, but as Nolan suspected, he couldn't resist the temptation and did so.

With a few keystrokes, Nolan was therefore able to break in to the computer system of Wollner's employer, and everything else Nolan was doing immediately paled into relative insignificance. Because Nolan Murray was now inside the cyber walls of the Limerick nuclear power plant, and no one would be aware of it until he was ready to tell them.

The planning from there had gone far more smoothly than Nolan could have predicted. Each step of the way he was prepared to abort if necessary, but that never came close to being necessary. Security was incredibly lax, well beyond Nolan's expectations, and he had not expected great competence.

Even after the Japanese tsunami, and the focus on safety measures that the damaged nuclear plant prompted around the world, Nolan was surprised by the poor preparation at Limerick. It was as if they were daring him to proceed; if that was the case, he was quite willing to accept the challenge.

That's not to say that everything was going as well as it could have. This stupid thing with Harrison's daughter, while impossible to have predicted, had shined a light on the case that was extraordinarily unwelcome. It also confirmed to him that he had made a mistake in judgment those six years ago.

Sheryl Harrison should have died alongside Charlie. She was allowed to live because her confession would have given the police no reason to look into Charlie's background and especially his finances, which was why Novack didn't discover the wire transfers back then.

But ultimately it was a mistake, but it wouldn't matter; by the time anyone might be able to figure out what was going on, it would simply be an academic exercise to do so.

And by then Nolan would be long dead, living happily ever after.

I couldn't remember the last time I was this nervous. Maybe high school baseball, if I was up in a key situation against a pitcher I was afraid I couldn't handle, which would describe just about every pitcher I ever faced. Certainly there were times I was nervous around my parents, at least back in the day when I still had the notion that I could please them.

I don't think I had ever been nervous in my work life. In fact, I can safely say that nothing ever happened at work that I considered important a week after the fact. I did what I was assigned, and then I went home, came back the next day, and did it again.

The point was that it had been a while since something seemed crucial enough for me to be anxious about it. And nothing had ever, ever made me as nervous as I was when I found out that the New Jersey Supreme Court was about to issue a ruling on my motion.

I heard about the impending ruling on television. My developing ego was a little miffed that the court had not itself made efforts to alert me, but the truth was I had no idea if any lawyer would have gotten that courtesy. It more likely was just not the way things were done.

But the decision was coming down at two o'clock. It could go in any of many directions; this was a complicated case and a simple "yes" or "no" was not necessarily called for, though "no" was a distinct possibility.

I had been asking for an injunction of sorts, but not in the traditional sense. An injunction, if granted, ordinarily puts a stop to something. For instance, if a building were to be knocked down and people were opposed to that, they could seek an injunction stopping the demolition, so that the matter could then be considered by the court.

I wasn't asking for anything to be stopped, other than the edict by the Department of Corrections that Sheryl's wish to die not be granted. The problem was that even if the court stopped that edict, they were not in a position, at least not yet, to reverse it. They weren't about to say at this point that her wish must be granted; I hadn't even had the nerve to ask for that.

What I wanted was for them to tell the lower court that they must hear the lawsuit immediately, and what I didn't want was for them to tell me to go shove it. We needed this to go on, to give us some forward momentum, so that we could keep the public relations pressure on.

A "no" from the New Jersey court, which meant a refusal to order that the lawsuit be heard on a very expedited basis, would leave us with the Federal Court of Appeals as our next option. But that would be a ridiculous long shot, and everyone would know it. The legal air would have come out of our balloon.

At least on this day there would not be any dramatic moment in the court; they were going to post the ruling on their website. So my choices were to watch TV and wait for them to announce it, or sit in my apartment and keep hitting refresh on the website. I chose the latter, but planned to turn off my phone at the appointed hour, so I wouldn't be told by a media person calling for a reaction.

At a quarter of two, before it was posted and before I turned my phone off, it rang. I answered it against my better judgment, since I had no desire to give the media a preruling reaction.

"Hello?"

"It's Novack. Ask your client where Charlie would have kept his personal papers."

"Why?" I asked.

"Because I want to know."

"Are you working on the case?" I asked.

"No, six years after everybody dies, I try and find their personal papers. It's a hobby of mine."

Novack was not the most agreeable guy in the world, but I was thrilled he was doing at least some investigating. "Anything else?" I asked.

"Yeah. Find out if he had a safe-deposit box."

"Okay."

Click.

He hung up before I could say, "Welcome aboard." It was probably just as well.

I shut my phone off and waited, and by two-thirty there was still nothing up on the court website. I was tempted to turn on the TV, in case they already had the ruling, but I resisted. It was almost like a superstition, like I had to see it on the website for us to have a chance, as if I ever waited for a ruling on a website before. Or waited on a ruling anywhere before.

At 2:38 the refresh button finally had the desired effect, and the court's ruling appeared. It was only two pages long, which my pessimism took to be a negative, but I plunged ahead and read it.

We won, at least that round. The court found a compelling public interest in the case being heard immediately, and ordered the lower court to do just that. They took two paragraphs to make the point that they were not rendering an opinion on the merits of the case itself; they were simply affirming our right to be heard, and heard quickly.

Actually, the court distinguished between our lawsuit and the underlying issue. Since a lawsuit could naturally involve damages to the state if it lost, they were entitled to sufficient time to prepare. The court could not fairly reverse that, though they encouraged the lower court to move rapidly.

It was in the matter of judging whether the Corrections Department made the right decision in the first place that the court insisted on an almost immediate resolution, and that was the area we would have to focus on. The lawsuit could be handled later, and the sad truth was that the potential damages would hinge on whether Karen, and Sheryl, lived or died.

I turned on the phone and started answering the calls, which came in rapid succession. I basically said the same thing to each reporter: "We are happy the court ruled the way it did, and Sheryl Harrison looks forward to her day in court. The system works, and it will continue to do so. The net result, we hope and expect, will be that an innocent young girl's life will be saved."

Then I went outside and tried to pretend I was still a normal, noncelebrity human being by going outside and walking to the supermarket. The media was waiting for me, and walked along with me every step of the way, with me waxing eloquent about the court's ruling.

It was a simple, three-block walk, but it felt like a victory lap.

Karen learned the news from her grandmother. As much as she dreaded the conversation, Terry decided that she couldn't wait any longer. Karen, though still hospitalized, was feeling stronger and was certainly more alert. That meant she wanted to watch television, and wanted the remote control in her hand.

It also meant that she wanted to talk on the phone, and text with her friends. It was the way of the fourteen-year-old, and therefore it was well beyond Terry's ability to control the flow of information.

So Terry told her that they needed to have a very serious conversation, and she laid it out, straight and direct, the way they always talked. The only shading of the truth was Terry's saying that Karen's mother wanted to do this "if necessary."

"How do I get her to change her mind?" was the first thing Karen asked.

"The best way is for you to get better." Karen was not fully aware that she was dying, or that the chances of finding another heart were as remote as they really were. "It's a backup plan," Terry said. "But the way the media is, they build up the story, you know? Just stay strong and healthy, and all this will go away."

After a while, Karen started to sob. They were soft, quiet sobs, which reflected not an anger but an unspeakable sadness. Terry held her as she cried, and they cried together. It wasn't the first time, and Terry hoped it wouldn't be the last.

When there was no crying left, Karen said, "Grandma, I can't let that happen."

"Then stay strong."

"It's my heart that doesn't work, not hers. I can't let her die. I can't kill her."

"You would not be doing anything to her, Karen. It would be her choice, and her joy."

"Would you do it? For her?" Karen asked.

"Would I give my daughter my heart? Is that what you're asking?"

"Yes."

She smiled. "In a heartbeat."

"I'm serious," Karen said.

Terry nodded. "So am I. I would do it for her, and I would do it for you. And my mother would have done it for me. That's the way we're wired, sweetheart. You'll know what I mean when you have a child, and a grandchild."

"But how could I live, knowing she did that?"

"The same way I live, knowing that my daughter is in prison for something she did not do."

Terry regretted the words as soon as they came out of her mouth. She had never said them before; it was a solemn oath to Sheryl, that she now had broken.

"What do you mean? She didn't kill him?"

"No, in my heart I can't let myself believe that she did."

It was a deception; Terry knew that, but it was the only way she knew to cover her mistake. And it worked; Karen didn't press her on it anymore.

"We live one day at a time, sweetheart. And before you know it, it's tomorrow. And if that isn't any better, the good news is that there's another day coming right after that."

She hugged her granddaughter closer. "We just need to keep those days coming."

The fake ID in Charlie Harrison's wallet was in the name of William Beverly. It was a Pennsylvania license, with an address in King of Prussia.

Novack assumed that it was a fake name and address, as most fabricated IDs are. But with a very short time on the computer, and one phone call, Novack learned otherwise, and he was able to gather a good deal of information on the real William Beverly.

Beverly was thirty-five years old at the time of Charlie's murder, which made him two years younger than Charlie. He worked for a major clothing manufacturer as a salesman, which put him on the road almost constantly.

It didn't take much more digging to learn that Beverly had lived in King of Prussia all his life. He went to Penn State for two years, but dropped out to earn money soon after his parents died in a car accident. That left just William and his brother, James, who was two years older than William.

At first nothing seemed unusual or particularly relevant to the Harrison case, except of course for the fact that Beverly's driver's license was in the dead guy's wallet.

But then something else caught Novack's eye, and his cop's instinct alarm instantly went off. James Beverly was dead, the result of mistakenly taking two incompatible drugs. And according to the public records, he died two weeks before Charlie Harrison.

There was obviously more to be gained by digging further on the computer, but Novack was a street guy, and he felt that this was the time to be on the street. In this case the street was Carbondale Road in King of Prussia, specifically number 241, William Beverly's address, as indicated on the ID in Charlie Harrison's wallet.

Novack made the normally two-hour drive in an hour and forty, and with the help of his GPS found the house easily enough. It was on a hill near the top of a private road. There were three houses on the hill, and their mailboxes were at the bottom of the road.

There were two cars in the driveway of number 241, and that, plus music coming from inside the house, made it obvious that someone was home. It was rap or hip-hop or something; Novack wasn't sure which, but it didn't matter, since he hated them both.

Novack rang the bell, and the door was opened by a teenage boy, probably fifteen years old.

"I'm looking for William Beverly," Novack said, talking loudly to be heard above the annoying music.

"Who? Beverly? Never heard of her."

"William Beverly. Is anybody else home?"

"Just my mother. But she's busy."

Novack took out his badge and held it up. "Get her."

The young man did just that, and within thirty seconds had fetched his mother, a beleaguered-looking woman who turned off the music as soon as she entered the room, earning Novack's undying gratitude.

He identified himself as a policeman, and said that he was looking for William Beverly.

"I'm sorry, I don't think I know the name," she said. "Who is he?"

"He used to live here," Novack said. "As recently as six years ago."

"No, sir. I've lived here for fourteen."

Additional questions from Novack got him nothing more than that, so he went to the other two houses on the hill. The family living in the nearest house had only lived there three months; they were renting. But they had never heard of William Beverly.

The family in the other house had lived there close to forever; the woman Novack spoke with was in her fifties and she grew up there. She said quite definitively that no family named Beverly had ever lived on that street, or in that neighborhood.

Next stop for Novack was Finley Fashions, the dress manufacturer for whom Beverly worked. Their office was in downtown King of Prussia, and it was a small one. Their actual manufacturing was done in Vietnam, and their materials came from Thailand. With their salesmen spending most of their time on the road, there was no reason to have a lot of employees in their local office.

Novack's questions at Finley brought the same response as in Beverly's home neighborhood. The manager, a woman named Hilda Stenowitz, clearly thought Novack's arrival was incredibly exciting, and she tried her hardest to be helpful.

Even though she had been in that office for fourteen years and would certainly know Beverly if he had worked there, she dutifully went to the files to check. The process took about ten minutes, and Novack was impatient, since by now he knew what the result would be.

"Never had an employee by that name," she said.

Novack nodded, thanked her, and left. His next stop was city hall, where the physical documents in the records department confirmed that no one named William or James Beverly ever lived in King of Prussia, or for that matter, anywhere in Montgomery County.

Novack had the drive home to try and make sense out of all this. The fact that Harrison's fake ID was of a fake person with a fake address wouldn't ordinarily be much of a surprise.

What was apparently inexplicable was the fact that cyber records had shown Beverly to be very real. Novack's online search before his trip confirmed Beverly's address, listed his employer, and gave him a fairly full history.

He would dig into it more, as well as everything related to James, William's brother. Maybe he'd discover that there was a rational explanation for all of this, and that everything was as the online information made it seem.

Or maybe William Beverly, real or not, was the reason that Charlie Harrison had his throat slit.

Captain Larry Whitaker's mind was wandering. Daydreaming in this fashion while working is generally frowned upon in the pilot community, though it's understood that they all do it. Especially when flying runs like Southern Air Flight 3278, Atlanta–Charlotte, as Whitaker was doing for the fifth time that week.

At fifty-two years old, Whitaker found his daydreams during that particular flight involved looking ahead three years, to retirement age, when his pension would kick in. His two kids were long out of the house, doing well on their own, and he and his wife, Ginny, wanted to travel.

Atlanta to Charlotte was not in their travel plans.

The weather was perfect on that particular day, and once Whitaker settled the Regional jet in at 31,000 feet, the plane could pretty much fly itself. In fact, since it had made this particular run more than Whitaker, he wouldn't be surprised if the onboard computers could reach Charlotte, land on their own, thank the fifty-five passengers, and unload the luggage.

That day was coming, but Whitaker was thankful he wouldn't be around to see it.

Flight 3278 was about fifty-five minutes from Charlotte, close to entering the domain of Charlotte air traffic control. The controller who would be bringing it in to its uneventful landing would be Denise Weber, herself just finishing fourteen years on the job.

It was approaching 2:00 P.M., a comparatively slow time of the day, and Denise was having a cup of coffee to keep her alert. She did this because everybody else did, not because she had ever been able to discern any such effect from caffeine. The truth was, she could drink a gallon of it at night and go right to sleep.

A moment later, Denise got more of a jolt than the coffee could have ever provided. Her phone rang, flashing red at the same time. It was the emergency line, and in all her time on the job it had only rung twice before.

She picked it up on the first ring. "Weber."

"I think there's something wrong with one of your airplanes." It was a little girl's voice; Denise thought she couldn't be more than five years old. She had absolutely no way of knowing that a grown man, Nolan Murray, was actually doing the speaking, with his voice going through a synthesizer to change it to the sound of a little girl.

"Who is this?" Denise asked.

"Tammy."

"Tammy, how did you get this number?"

"I don't know, I just have it."

"Well, you're not supposed to call it. You could get in trouble." Denise's voice had gone from reflecting her worry to one of amusement. This would be even funnier, if it didn't mean she would have to write a lengthy report about it.

"But there's something wrong with your plane." The little girl's voice was insistent.

"What plane?

"Flight three two seven eight."

"How do you—" she started, but was interrupted by a message coming in from one of the airplanes.

"This is Southern three two seven eight," said Larry Whitaker. "We have an onboard problem; request technical assistance."

Denise tried to process this information. How could this little girl know that? Where was she calling from? "What's the issue, three two seven eight?"

"Onboard computer is preventing our descent. We're actually gaining altitude."

Denise pressed a button, which would alert her supervisor to a looming emergency. "Roger, Southern, will get you assistance."

She then turned her attention to the little girl on the phone. "Tammy, how did you know there is something wrong on that plane?"

"Because I am controlling their computers, silly. I'm making it go up, up, instead of down."

"How can you do that?" Denise asked. It was getting more bewildering by the moment.

"Easy." Nolan was getting a lot of enjoyment out of this, but that was not why he was doing it. He felt that the people he was talking to would find it somehow more disconcerting, more terrifying, to have a conversation of this deadly importance with a voice that sounded like a little girl.

Whitaker then came in through Denise's headset, more urgency in his voice, reporting that they were at thirty-five thousand feet and rising. "Request immediate assistance."

"Tammy, what are you doing?"

"I'm making the plane go up until you give me a million dollars."

The words sent a cold chill through Denise; however this caller sounded, there was nothing childish or funny about what was going on. At that moment the supervisor, Ray

Pierce, arrived. From the moment Denise had buzzed into him, he had been monitoring what was going on, though had no more explanation for it than Denise did.

Pierce became the person talking to Whitaker, and they patched in Southern Airlines' top technical person. "Thirty-nine thousand," Whitaker reported. He was clearly very upset, since it had only taken a couple of minutes to gain seven thousand feet, and the plane could likely not survive about fifty-five thousand.

Denise continued to talk to "Tammy." "Tammy, you have to stop this. We'll give you a million dollars, but you have to let the plane land." She realized how ridiculous she sounded, but the facts were dictating her response.

"But I want the money first." The voice was that of a petulant child.

"I don't have a million dollars, but I'll get it for you. I promise."

"I don't believe you," Tammy said. "Show me."

"How can I do that?"

"Put it on television. Nickelodeon."

The passengers on the Southern flight were starting to notice the problem. At a time when the plane should have been starting its descent, it was clearly climbing. The captain hadn't yet said anything, but the flight attendant announced that air traffic control was adjusting their altitude because of traffic in the Charlotte area, and that there was nothing to worry about.

The strain in her voice said otherwise.

Whitaker, meanwhile, was trying to control his own panic. He had no control of his aircraft at all; he might as well have been sitting back in coach. The computers were in command, and they were either out of control, frozen, or being run from an external source.

And the altitude was forty-six thousand feet.

"Tammy, please, let me talk to someone else," Denise

pleaded. Security had arrived and they were telling her what to say, though no one had been through anything like this before. "The person that is doing this."

"I'm the only one here," the little girl's voice said, "and you didn't give me my money."

"It takes time, okay?" She was still talking in that gentle, singsongy way that adults talk to small children, which was incongruous and bizarre in this situation. "Stop hurting the plane, and you'll get your money. I promise."

"I don't believe you," Tammy said. "I'm not talking anymore."

The oxygen masks came down a few seconds later, sending the passengers into a near panic. They had noticed some trouble breathing moments before, and hungrily grabbed the masks, as the flight attendant came on again and offered both instructions and confident words.

No one believed her.

"Fifty-two thousand feet," said Whitaker. He kept trying to take control of the aircraft, but it was completely unresponsive.

Both Whitaker and the people on the ground knew what was going to happen very soon. The plane would not break apart, nor would the pressure differential inside the aircraft become so pronounced as to harm the people on board. And the oxygen masks would continue to function and let them breathe.

Before any of that could happen, the air outside would become too thin to support the aircraft, and it would stall and begin a plunge toward the ground. In normal circumstances, the pilot could then attempt to restart it and come out of the dive, and often would be successful in doing so.

This case was different, though. There was no way to know if the aircraft shutting down would have the effect of restoring control to the pilot; that could only be determined in the moment. And that moment would be terrifying.

It was clear that Tammy had not hung up, but was not responding to Denise's pleas. The call was traced to Dubuque, Iowa, and the FBI was responding, but none of that was going to matter to those people in the air.

Whitaker could only watch as the plane reached 55,700 feet, sputtered, and died. He braced himself and geared for what would come next; the plane would dive and he would have to bring it back to life. But he would only have a chance if it had reverted to his control.

The plane began its plunge, and with the screams of the passengers behind him, he grabbed on to the controls and got to work.

There was a full four-minute interval between the time he realized that the computer was still in total control and the moment the plane smashed into the earth.

All Tammy said before hanging up was, "Next time you better listen to me."

Sheryl was less enthusiastic than I expected. I had come there that morning to give her the good news, hoping she would hear it from me first. At this point I could pretty much come and go as I pleased; the fact that the case was prominent in the media meant that the prison authorities would try to appear accommodating.

But Sheryl reacted if not coolly, then matter of factly, to my report, and that was probably because I never seemed to give her credit for being as smart as she really was.

"You did well," she said.

"I thought you'd be euphoric."

"Is the lower court going to rule in our favor? Are they going to order that I can give Karen my heart?"

"It's very, very unlikely," I said.

"Then why exactly should I be overjoyed? We either win it all or we lose, Harvard."

She was right, of course, but I didn't want to fully give her that. "Because, and you should pardon the expression, right now this keeps us alive. And as long as we are alive in the courts, there's a chance for public pressure to build."

"And then what?" she asked.

"And then maybe they'll cave. If we haven't come up with anything else in the meantime."

"Like what?"

I ignored the question, at least for the moment. "Where did Charlie keep his personal papers?"

"Why?"

I hit it straight on. "Because I'm working with the cop that arrested you. He doesn't think you murdered Charlie, and I don't either."

She was clearly annoyed. "We've been through this."

I nodded. "And now we're going through it again. Look, there's a two percent chance we'll uncover something to get you paroled. But that's double the chance we have of winning in court, so I'm going to pursue it."

"No, you're not."

"Sheryl, my job is to protect you, which in this case means getting you what you want. This is the best way for me to do it, to go down both avenues. If that doesn't work for you, then you need to get yourself a different lawyer."

I'd never been that forceful with her, and she seemed taken aback by it. She took time to gather her thoughts, and I realized that, just like with every woman I've ever met, I had absolutely no idea what she was going to say.

Finally she said, "He had a desk in the room he used as an office. There were drawers that locked, and he kept important stuff in there."

"Where would it be now?"

She laughed. "Good question. After I was arrested and he was dead, the house was empty. Within two days, I was told that someone had broken in and ransacked the place. The bastards must have read about what happened in the papers, and they swooped in. It's like when they read the obits, so they'll know who to rob during the funeral."

I didn't know why Novack had asked the question about Charlie's papers in the first place, but I was immediately suspicious about the robbery. It seemed very possible, even likely, that it was not a theft of opportunity by predators who knew from the newspaper that the house would be unoccupied. They could have been after whatever Novack was after; unfortunately they got there six years ahead of him.

"What about a safe-deposit box? Did he have one of those?"

She thought about it for a while, and then nodded. "I think we had one together, though I never used it. I remember when we took it out."

"Do you have the key?" I asked.

She shrugged. "I don't think I ever did."

"What bank?"

"Probably Citizens Trust on Broadway. That's the branch I always used."

"Thanks, Sheryl," I said, and then had an idea. "Would you talk to the cop if I brought him in here? His name is Novack."

"Believe me, I remember him."

"Would you talk to him? I'd be in the room as well."

"I'd rather not," she said.

"I'd rather you would," I said.

"You're turning into a pain in the ass, Harvard."

"Not true. I've always been a pain in the ass. You're just learning it now. Where have you been?"

She smiled. "In here."

"So maybe we can change that. I'll talk to you soon."

I started to leave, but then stopped at the door before the guard saw me. I turned back to her, and came fully back into the room. "Sheryl, I'm sorry to be difficult about this, but I just can't see you slitting someone's throat."

She shrugged but didn't say anything.

"How did you do it?" I asked.

"With a knife."

"No, I mean, well . . . was he lying on his back or his stomach?"

"Do I really need to relive this?" she asked.

"This is the only time I'll ask you about it; I promise," I said.

"He was on his stomach."

"And where were you? Did you just walk up to him and raise his head?"

"Yes. He was sleeping."

"So you were standing next to him?" I asked.

"Yes."

I knew from Novack's description, and from the discovery documents, that the killer made knee imprints in Charlie's back. "You're lying, Sheryl. You don't even know how the hell it happened."

She yelled "Guard!" and when he came in, she added, "We're finished with our meeting. Get my lawyer the hell out of here."

I didn't wait for the guard; I left on my own. I had done what I needed to do; I had shaken her up. I was pleased by that.

Ten more times and we'd be even.

“We’re going to have to work together on this.”

Novack just laughed when I said it, as if the idea was too absurd to warrant an actual verbal response. But I knew that I was going to have to get my way on this, ever since I left the prison that morning.

We were sitting and eating pancakes in Paula’s Pancake House, on Route 4 in Elmwood Park. It was three o’clock in the afternoon, and we were at one of only two occupied tables in the place. The other patron, sitting on the other end of the room, was an elderly man in his seventies, drinking a cup of coffee so slowly it seemed it might last into his eighties.

I would assume that pancake consumption decreases as the day goes along, and at Paula’s that day it had apparently ground to a halt. The ones I was eating seemed as if they were cooked around 9:00 A.M.; at that point they were somewhere between pancakes and hockey pucks. Novack was suffering through his as well.

The lack of other customers was a good thing, since it meant we didn’t have to whisper. Arguing in hushed tones always seems awkward.

I had called him here, so I was the one with the agenda, and I was going to push it. "I'm serious," I said. "It's the only way that works for me, and for you as well."

"How do you figure?"

"You're going to need access to Sheryl; she's the only one that can answer questions about Charlie. She won't talk to you without me there; she trusts me and knows I'm on her side. She doesn't see you as her best buddy; you put her where she is."

"She put herself there," Novack said.

"True. But I'm crucial to you and her getting along. And there's a more important factor."

"Keep talking."

"The only way to do this in time, at least from her point of view, is to use whatever we can come up with in her parole hearing. I've got to prepare for that hearing, so I must know what's going on as soon as you do. You not including me is a deal breaker."

I was pushing it, but I had nothing to lose. If I didn't have immediate access to everything he came up with, he did me no good.

He laughed. "Why would I care if you break the deal? You think I have nothing else to do?"

"I think this thing has been bugging you for six years, and you want to get to the bottom of it. So I think you've got plenty to do, but this is at the top of your list, and you want to cross it off."

He thought about it for a few seconds, and then said, "When can I talk to her?"

"When you tell me why you want to."

He took me through his trying to find William Beverly by going to what was supposed to be his home in King of Prussia, and his listed place of employment. He had done some further checking, and still could not find anyone who had been in physical contact with Beverly, or had any recollection of him. Yet his life was chronicled in cyberspace in fairly significant detail; there was far more evidence of him than just an ID in Charlie Harrison's wallet.

"Weird," I said.

"Wow . . . that could be just the insight we need," he said. Then, "And it gets weirder. I've been checking into Beverly's brother, James. He died two weeks before Charlie Harrison."

"Murdered?" I asked.

Novack shrugged. "Depends on your definition. He was admitted into a hospital in Camden for blood clots. They put him on some medication, and within ten minutes he was dead."

"Did the drugs cause the death?" I asked.

"Doesn't seem like it," he said.

"So what did he die of?"

"Nothing. As far as I can tell he didn't die at all, because he was never in that hospital. At least nobody there remembers him, and they swear that's the kind of event that they would never forget. But he's in their computer; he's in a bunch of computers, just like his brother William. But nobody remembers either of them. Nobody."

"Any theories?" I asked.

"Not yet. How about you, counselor?"

"James Beverly supposedly died at about the time Charlie quit his job, and he quit his job because he believed he was coming into a bunch of money. It seems logical to infer that the two things are connected."

"Unless they're not," he said.

"Look, I've never done this kind of stuff, and I'm certainly not going to tell you your business. But the timing here is such that we're not going to be able to cross the 't's you usually cross, or dot the 'i's you usually dot. We're going to have to trust our gut instincts."

He seemed amused. "You have a gut instinct?"

"A few more of these pancakes and I'll have a gut. The instinct will follow."

Novack asked me what I had found out about Charlie Harrison's personal papers, and I related what Sheryl had told me. He already had learned about the robbery, and was as suspicious about it as I was.

"What about the safe-deposit box?"

"They had one together," I said. "But Sheryl never used it; she doesn't even think she had a key. I could use my power of attorney to get into it."

He nodded his satisfaction with that. "Good. Let's do that tomorrow."

We talked some more, and Novack said that if he could gather more information, he could go off vacation mode and officially open the case, which would bring the resources of the department to bear on it. Then we discussed the public relations side of things.

"Your publicity campaign took a hit," he said.

He was referring to the fact that we were no longer page-one news. An airline had crashed near Charlotte, North Carolina, killing fifty-nine people. The authorities were claiming to have no idea what caused the crash, but conspiracy theorists were already calling it an act of terrorism, and no one was denying it with any vehemence.

People are always interested in plane crashes, and when there is even a hint that it might not have been an accident, it crowds everything else out of the news until that possibility is credibly discounted.

"You think it was terrorism?" I asked.

He shrugged. "Beats the shit out of me. We'll know soon enough what the government thinks."

"You think they'll tell the truth?"

"It's not what they say, lawyer, it's what they do. And what's really important is who does it."

"What do you mean?"

"If the FBI takes the lead, it means they think it was terrorism. And then your story goes to page forty."

He was right, of course. Sheryl's was a fascinating human interest story, but humans are far more interested in something that could threaten them personally, and since most people get on airplanes at least once in a while, the plane in Charlotte was a huge news event.

We made plans for Novack to talk to Sheryl at the prison the next morning, and were out of Paula's by three-thirty. We both had a lot to do, and if I sat there and waited until I could digest the pancakes, it would be way too late.

The NTSB was already taking an uncustomary backseat on Flight 3278. Whenever there was an aviation accident, or near accident, the National Transportation Safety Board completely and immediately took over the investigation. They were famously and sometimes annoyingly painstaking and thorough.

The drill was replayed over and over. After a serious incident with multiple fatalities, with the public clamoring for an explanation, an NTSB official would hold a press conference and make it crystal clear that the answer was a very long ways off, and that no speculation would be forthcoming.

But this case was different. While it was unclear exactly how the ability to control the aircraft was taken away from Captain Whitaker, nobody in a position to know was under the illusion that it was an accident. The plane was intentionally taken down, which meant the FBI would be the preeminent agency.

Within twenty minutes of Flight 3278 hitting the ground, Special Agent Mike Janssen was in the air, heading for Charlotte. Working out of the Chicago office, Janssen had a number of attributes to make him the logical choice to head up the investigation, besides being tough, smart, and relentless.

Janssen had successfully investigated the crash two years earlier of a Brazilian jet near São Paulo. The FBI traditionally offers its superior resources to allies in particularly difficult cases, especially in situations like that one, where two Americans were among the dead.

Terrorism was suspected in the Brazilian crash, and Janssen had brought the investigation to a successful conclusion, determining that lax security measures had allowed a passenger to bring an explosive on board. The deranged individual, not representing any terrorist organization or cause, but merely wanting to commit a spectacular suicide, had detonated the device and brought the plane down.

Another key quality that Janssen possessed was an antipathy for the press, coupled with an ability to effectively control it. Actually, he pretty much had a disdain for all people, including those he worked for. Every time there were politically motivated executive changes at the Bureau, he likened it to the daily event at Buckingham Palace, but referring to the personnel shuffles as the "changing of the assholes."

Janssen had handled quite a few high-profile cases in his career, and his unwillingness to share things with the media enabled him to be successful in maintaining a wall of secrecy when the situation required it.

And this situation certainly required it.

Janssen had the ability, or the curse depending on one's perspective, to singularly focus on an issue, to the exclusion of everything else. It was why his colleagues nicknamed him "Laser," and why he did not have to call his wife and tell her he was heading for Charlotte. Janssen wasn't married; he had tried it once and his wife simply could not deal with his devotion to his job.

It was not that he worked twenty-four hours a day on a case, though he came close. It was more that the case of the moment was all he thought about, ever. Which left very little time to think of his wife, or friends, or anything else.

By the time he reached the scene, he had digested all available information, such as there was. The phone call from "Tammy" was traced to a home in Dubuque, Iowa, in which Kyle and Stacy Danforth lived with their five-year-old daughter, Tammy. Federal agents descended on the house, at which point they were told by the petrified Stacy that little Tammy was at preschool.

A trip to the preschool confirmed that Tammy Danforth had been finger-painting at the time the plane went down. It was an embarrassing moment for the agents and Bureau, though less so since it had not been made public.

Though it could not be proved at that point, there was no doubt in Janssen's mind that the voice of Tammy was filtered through a voice synthesizer. It was determined to be the voice quality of a child less than five years old, and no person of that age would be capable of conducting such a conversation, even when prompted.

The reason that the perpetrator would have felt it necessary to use that voice was, like everything else at that point, completely unclear. Perhaps it was felt that it would seem even more bewildering and terrifying, and strike more panic into people that heard it. Or perhaps it was simply an amusement for the killer, or a sign of some personality defect or derangement that would become more clear later, and might even lead to the killer's downfall.

Certainly, the voice synthesizer could have been programmed to sound like any kind of voice, and it would have masked the real voice just as completely.

The more important questions, of course, were how the plane was taken down and why. The NTSB investigators were working on the first part of that, and it was obvious to them from the transcript of the incident itself, especially Captain Whitaker's description of what he was facing on board, that it was a computer issue.

The onboard computers had taken over from Whitaker, and simply did not let him regain control. It's as if he had put it on automatic pilot, and that automatic pilot subsequently refused to relinquish command. Of course, in this case the automatic pilot had decided to become a mass murderer. It would be up to the scientists to discover how Tammy had managed the hacking feat, and they were counting on the recovered black boxes to help them.

The "why" was even more bewildering. Tammy had demanded money, which was the only thing about the case that could be considered standard procedure. But the truth was that she had set up the incident so that there could never have been enough time for money to be paid, even in the unlikely event that an immediate decision was made to do so.

To Janssen it was as if the perpetrator conducted the whole operation as a way to demonstrate his or her power. Since money was the expressed purpose, it seemed logical that money was the ultimate goal. But if a planeload of people was not considered enough of a prize to be selling, something bigger was coming down the road.

Which was why each of the many times Janssen listened to the recording, a chill ran through him at Tammy's last line of warning:

"Next time you better listen to me."

Novack should not have had the pancakes. Not just because it felt like he had eaten two manhole covers, but more because Cindy was making an anniversary dinner for them that night. She was making chicken parmigiana, his absolute all-time favorite, and he was going to be called upon to eat a prodigious amount.

They celebrated the date of their divorce, rather than that of their marriage, since it was because of the divorce that they seemed able to live happily ever after. Novack always spent the entire anniversary night at her house, unless he started driving Cindy crazy, in which case she had the right to throw him out, as per the rules they had long been following.

Of course, the amendment to that anniversary rule was that before she could throw him out, they would make love. That was a rule they were both inclined to enforce.

Another rule that was in place on anniversary nights was that Novack not talk business. Cindy just wanted a break from hearing about graphic crime scenes, or families decimated by drugs. The problem was that on some nights, she could tell that Novack couldn't take his mind off those things, even if he obediently prevented the thoughts from working their way into the conversations.

This was one of those nights.

"You thinking about Sheryl Harrison?" she asked.

"During our anniversary dinner? Are you nuts? No chance. Sheryl who?"

"You're full of shit, Novack."

He shrugged. "What else is new?"

"Tell me what's going on," she said. "This is one that I'm interested in."

"Why?"

"I want her to be able to save her daughter's life. And it's a weight I want lifted off your shoulders."

"My shoulders are fine. It's a case, Cind. That's all."

"Did I mention that you were full of shit?" she asked. "When cases bother you, you get sarcastic and annoying. I can tell how much they bother you by how sarcastic and annoying you get, and by how long you get that way. I have a ten-point scale I rank it on."

He smiled despite himself. "And when I arrested Sheryl Harrison?"

"Ten point five," she said. "Off the charts."

So he told her the story, and she came to the same conclusion as Jamie Wagner, that it had to be about money. "Money that Charlie didn't get because he was killed."

"Or maybe he got it and they took it from him," he said.

"I doubt it," she said. "You probably would have found some record of it somewhere. And you said his boss told you the party was the night before, and he referred to it as money Charlie was going to get. Right?"

"Right."

"From what you've told me, it sounds like Charlie was the type that if he had money, he'd flaunt it."

Novack nodded. "I think that's true. I also think the

money was tied into Beverly's brother's death. That's if his brother really died. And if he and his brother really existed."

"Maybe he was suing whoever was responsible for the death," she said. "That would explain his believing he was going to get big money, but not having it yet."

"Then why was he killed, unless Sheryl really did it? He would only be valuable to anyone after he got the money, and lawsuits take a lot of time, even when the insurance company settles. Killing Charlie eliminated his value."

"He must have had some value already," she pointed out. "Someone kept wiring him fifty thousand dollars, even if it was from a company that didn't exist. Just like those people didn't exist."

"You're pretty smart," Novack said. "And not bad looking. Why did I divorce you?"

"As I recall, I dumped you, and said I wanted nothing more to do with you."

"Right," Novack said, nodding. "I knew there was a reason. But you hit on the key point. However Harrison was using Beverly's identity to make money, it's very likely he was doing it all along, maybe with different people. Because someone was sending him that cash long before Beverly's brother supposedly died."

"So you need to find out who was sending him the money, and why." She smiled. "No big deal."

"Do I have to do it tonight?"

She looked at her watch. "Yes, and you better hurry. I've got a date, and he should be here any minute."

"I'll wait for him," Novack said. "I'm glad I brought my gun."

Cindy smiled. "Let's go upstairs. I'll give you your anniversary present."

"Well, the big-time lawyer returns to his small-time roots."

Ken Bollinger had seen me at the bar, and had gotten up from his table to come over. "It's about time you reentered the real world."

I smiled. "It's only a brief visit. I'm picking up a couple of burgers to take back to the fake world with me."

"Well, change your plans, big guy. Don't stare too hard, but take a look over at my table."

I looked over and saw that Ken had been sitting with two young women, of the attractive variety.

"See the one on the left?" he asked, talking in a low voice, though there was no possibility they could overhear us. "Her name is Maggie. She and her friend came over to me because they heard we're best friends. You believe that? They're impressed that I know you. I've spent the last five years being ashamed of it, and they're impressed."

"Why were they impressed?"

"Are you kidding? You're on TV more than Oprah Winfrey. You're a celebrity, and celebrities get women. As do friends of celebrities."

I smiled. "I can't believe these words are coming out of my mouth, but I'm working tonight."

"Well, put them back in your mouth, asshole. Because with you joining the party, my chances improve geometrically, in case you didn't study geometrics at Harvard."

"It's called geometry."

"That's good . . . big words like that will impress them even more. Come on," he said. "I'll introduce you."

"Ken, I've got to be in court in two days. And tomorrow I'll be at the prison, meeting with Sheryl, so . . ."

He interrupted. "You're meeting with Sheryl? You've got a chance to take Maggie back to your apartment tonight, but you can't, because you're going to the prison to meet with Sheryl tomorrow? You got a thing going with Sheryl?"

He had quickly crossed the line from amusing to irritating. It was a line he rarely crossed, which might have been a reflection of the fact that I was drawing it in a different place than I used to.

"Yeah, I've got a thing," I said. "I'm trying to save her daughter's life. So tell Maggie I'm sorry, but not tonight. I'm getting my burgers, and then I'm going to work."

The words came out a little harsher than I would have liked, but not so much that I wanted to say anything to soften them. It wasn't Ken's fault. The truth was that the events of the past days had already changed me, but Ken hadn't gotten the memo, because I hadn't sent one out.

Burgers and beer in hand, I went back to my apartment to receive good and bad news. The bad news was a call from my mother, telling me that she and my father wanted to have dinner with me over the weekend.

"We've been reading about you in the papers," she said, a dig at the fact that I hadn't been calling and bringing them up to date on my life. "It all sounds very exciting."

The good news was the mail, which brought a copy of my direct-deposit pay, which had gone from the firm to my bank on schedule. Apparently, I hadn't been fired, even though the pay stub made me remember that I had not officially told anyone there of Sheryl's decision to keep me as her attorney.

So far, in my dealings with the press, I hadn't mentioned Carlson, Miller, and Timmerman, thereby saving them from what they perceived as embarrassment. Which meant that maybe my not being fired wasn't such good news; I probably could have gotten a terrific termination package from them, in return for my going quietly and not bringing them into the publicity fray.

As I was thinking about this, I realized I had already made a momentous decision, without having consulted with myself about it. I do that a lot; my thoughts go in a logical progression, and they take me to a place where I feel like I have already been, without realizing it. It almost feels as if I haven't decided something at all, but rather that I've been let in on it.

The revelation this time was simple and obvious; I was going to quit the firm at the conclusion of this case, win or lose.

There was plenty I could do. I could write a book; I could even read a book. I'd never done the former, and it had been a really long time since I had done the latter.

Having decided my future, or at least what my future would not be, I set out to work on the present. That meant finishing the brief and readying myself for the hearing less than thirty-six hours away, in which I would try and convince a judge that Sheryl should be allowed to die.

I would also have liked to be preparing for another, possibly more important hearing, that of the parole board. But I had nothing to tell them yet; that would have to wait for Novack to come up with something. And no matter what it was, it would ram smack into Sheryl's confession.

I stopped at around eleven, and turned on CNN to see if

our case was anywhere to be found. We did get a brief mention, focusing on the upcoming hearing. But for the most part the news was all about the plane crash in Charlotte.

The authorities were remaining tight-lipped as to the cause, and public pressure was building. Families of the victims were being trotted out to complain about the lack of information they were receiving. They were being told what everyone else was being told; the investigation was in its early stages, nobody wanted to jump the gun, blah, blah, blah.

Unidentified sources were reporting that the FBI had taken over as the primary investigating agency, with the NTSB in an unaccustomed second position. Novack had said that was the thing to watch, and it was obviously significant if true. If the cause was simply something like failed equipment or pilot error, the FBI would not have to play a major role.

Apparently also revealing was the report that FBI Special Agent Mike Janssen was assigned to head the investigation. I had never previously heard of him, probably because he didn't hang out in bars on the Upper West Side of Manhattan, or get involved in much arcane corporate litigation.

But those in the know referred to him as an expert in domestic counterterrorism, which meant that there was a strong possibility that was what they were dealing with.

I watched for a half hour, then put in another hour of legal preparation. I would compensate for my inexperience with hard work, and I took some emotional refuge in the understanding that no one had experience in a case of this kind.

Very few lawyers try to arrange their client's death. That led me to another belated understanding that I had not been in touch with, but which seemed to represent the ultimate conflict of interest.

I was fighting for Sheryl Harrison's death, but I sure as hell did not want her to die.

Ray Hennessey was following Novack. He wasn't sure why; he had simply been assigned to do so by Nolan Murray. His instructions had been to report back on everything Novack did, everywhere he went, and everybody he talked to.

So he had followed him to King of Prussia, and noted his various stops there. He had dutifully told that to Murray in detail, but Murray had listened impassively, not revealing to Hennessey if the information was of any significance to him.

Which it certainly was.

This particular morning brought something that even Hennessey found interesting. Novack went to a branch of Citizens Trust Bank, where he met Jamie Wagner, who Hennessey knew was Sheryl Harrison's lawyer.

While Hennessey was being extra careful tailing Novack, since the cop could be expected to be savvy in that area, he took a chance and went into the bank after them. When he got inside, he saw them talking to a manager, presenting the woman with some papers. She then led them into the safe-deposit room.

The two men were inside that room for almost fifteen minutes, and when they came out Novack was carrying a manila envelope that he hadn't had when they entered.

Hennessey quickly left, got in his car, and waited. When Novack and Wagner came out of the bank, they each got back in their own car, but both drove out to the prison where Sheryl Harrison was an inmate.

The two men were in there for almost two hours, during which time Hennessey contacted Nolan Murray. He repeated exactly what he had witnessed that day, leaving out nothing. When he finished, Murray had very few questions about the events that Hennessey had related.

Instead, he asked, "What kind of car does Novack drive?"

"A Ford Taurus."

"What year?"

"I'm not sure, but it's not more than a year or two old."

"Confirm that. If you're wrong about it, I want to know it immediately."

Hennessey knew better than to ask why Murray wanted the information. "Anything else?"

"Where does he live?"

"In a high-rise in Edgewater."

"So he parks his car in an indoor garage at night?"

"Yes. But he's spent the last two nights at his ex-wife's house. She lives in Fair Lawn. My guess is he'll be back there tonight."

"Where does he park when he's there?"

"On the street."

"Can you enter the car without setting off an alarm?" Murray asked.

"Of course."

"Good. Call me tonight if he is at his ex-wife's house, and you believe he has settled in for the night, and I'll give you further instructions."

Once he was off the phone, Murray had to decide which of his two colleagues would be most capable of handling the assignment. He realized with some satisfaction that either could do it with relative ease, but he decided on Daniel Churchill.

He had more of a comfort level with Churchill, and though he knew he could also rely on Peter Lampley, Churchill was usually his first choice. He called Churchill in and explained it to him, then was not surprised when Churchill asked a couple of obvious questions, and then said it would be no problem.

Novack was proving to be more annoying each day, and though there was still little danger that he could ultimately pose a threat, there was no sense sitting idly by and waiting for that possibility to develop. And then there was the matter of the safe-deposit box, which Murray had not realized existed. There was no way to know what was recovered from that box, but the fact was that both Novack and the lawyer were now familiar with it. And they wouldn't have taken it with them if it did not have any significance.

Even with Novack about to be effectively removed from the picture, Murray was feeling that it was time to move things along. He had wanted to give the authorities time to let their worry grow to panic as to where and when he might strike again, and he had done that.

The time seemed right to move forward.

"I hear you think I'm innocent." That was the first thing that Sheryl said to Novack, when he and I were brought into the room. She said it as if it were amusing to her, but I was getting to know her better and better, and I don't think she was amused at all.

I think she was scared.

Novack shook his head. "I had thought it was possible, but now I have my doubts."

"Really?" she asked. "Why is that?"

"Because you obviously would be willing to die to save your daughter. Yet if you're innocent, it means you're sitting on information that could do just that. Doesn't make sense."

Sheryl didn't say anything, but it was clear that Novack was hitting home in a way that I couldn't. Finally, she asked, "Why are you here?"

"He has a few questions for you, Sheryl," I said. "As we discussed."

"Does anyone else know you're here?" she asked Novack. It seemed like a strange question, and Novack obviously thought the same.

"Who are you worried about?" he asked.

"Nobody. Ask your questions, and then you and Harvard can get the hell out of here."

Novack turned to me. "You went to Harvard?"

"Yes."

"No wonder," he said, and then turned back to Sheryl. "Have you ever heard of William Beverly?"

Sheryl thought for a moment. "No. Not that I can recall."

"Daniel Shaw?"

"No."

"Craig Simmons."

"No. Who are these people?"

"Your husband had identification, with his picture, for each of these people. The Beverly one was in his wallet when he was killed. He was pretending to be Beverly, and I suspect the other people as well. Do you have any idea why that would be?"

"None whatsoever. But Charlie and I were not exactly close near the end, you know?" The sarcasm in her tone was heavy, but not necessary; both Novack and I knew from his investigation that their marriage was a violent disaster. "He could have been doing anything, and I wouldn't have known it."

I spoke up. "So you had no idea what he was doing?"

"That's what I just said, didn't I, Harvard? I didn't know and I didn't care."

"Then why did you kill him?"

The question seemed to jolt her, and I realized it was possible she never had to answer it before. "It doesn't matter now," she said.

"How were things for you and Charlie financially?" Novack asked.

"What do you think? You saw where we were living. You think I had my pick of places to raise Karen, but I chose that dump?"

"Somebody wired Charlie two hundred thousand dollars in the six months before he died," I said.

She did a double take. Then, "Who?"

"We were hoping you could tell us that."

"I have no idea. He never mentioned anything like that to me. Where is that money now?"

"That was my next question," Novack said. "It was taken out of the account."

"Not by me," she said. "I would have fixed up my cell much nicer."

"What are you afraid of, Sheryl?"

"I'm not afraid of anything except my daughter dying."

Novack shook his head. "There's more to it than that," he said, and then turned to me. "You going to be long?"

"A few minutes."

"I'll wait for you outside."

As soon as he left, Sheryl asked, "So what's up, counselor?" She was trying to act nonchalant and in control, and had been in that mode since Novack and I arrived.

"I'm in court tomorrow. I submitted my brief this morning."

"Good. Please come tell me what happens."

I nod. "Of course. But there won't be a decision tomorrow."

"There never is."

I stood up to leave, when Sheryl asked, "Can I trust him?"

"Who? Novack?"

"Yes. How do I know if I can trust him?"

"Sheryl, you don't even know if you can trust me."

"Answer the question, please."

"I don't know; I just met him myself. But he's using up his vacation to try and help you. Or at least to find out the truth. I don't know what he'd have to gain by lying."

"Okay," she said.

"Okay what?"

"Okay, good luck in court tomorrow."

I nodded my thanks, and walked to the door. Her voice stopped me and I turned.

"Harvard, I do trust you. I think I trust you more than anyone I've ever met."

"Okay," I said.

"Okay what?"

"Okay, we're going to find out if that's true."

Novack now knew what he was looking for, and how to find it. That is why it took him less than four hours to determine that the other fake IDs Charlie Harrison had in the safe-deposit box were much like William Beverly. That is, they had lives clearly represented in cyberspace, but in reality never existed.

Less than one hour after that he was meeting with Captain James Donovan, his boss. They had an interesting dynamic in their relationship. Novack knew he was full of shit, yet at the same time he liked him. He was probably the only person Novack ever met who he could say that about.

The reason, both men knew, was that Donovan never tried to hide who he was, at least from Novack. Donovan was more politician than cop; a descendant of a long line of high-ranking police officials, he knew he was going upward from the moment he joined the force. It is unlikely there was ever a person less inclined to make waves.

Their relationship was established the first time they met. Donovan was brought in from another precinct, in what was to be a key rung on the climb to the top of the department. He called his direct reports in for individual meetings, just to get to know one another, and to establish ground rules for going forward.

When Novack got into the office, they shook hands and Donovan said, "I've heard a lot about you."

"I've heard a lot about you, too."

"What did you hear?" Donovan asked.

"That you want to be commissioner, and you'll kiss any ass necessary to make that happen."

Donovan waited a beat and said, "That about sums it up." And from that moment forward, Novack liked him.

He was not a third of the cop Novack was, but some leaders would try to compensate for such a deficiency by exercising tight control. Not Donovan; he gave Novack a great deal of autonomy, except of course when it had the potential to make him look bad.

The situation with Sheryl Harrison did carry such danger, but not the traditional kind. Certainly, no department likes to be revealed as having put an innocent person behind bars, but it really wasn't police work that led to Sheryl Harrison's incarceration. Her confession took care of that quite nicely.

But Donovan was still very concerned about where Novack might be going with this. This was an incredibly politically charged issue, national in scope, and anything that the department did to influence it would be seen through a political prism. Which meant that enemies would be made, no matter which way things went.

For Novack, the issue was a simple one, and he laid it straight out. "I don't think she's guilty," he said.

"She confessed, Novack," Donovan said. "That's a pretty significant piece, don't you think?"

"In some cases it would be. But I think she lied. I think she's still lying."

"Why?"

"I don't know. She's scared of something."

Donovan was factoring in the fact that if progress was

made, then it would seem as if the department had come down on the side of Sheryl Harrison. That was simply because if Novack got nowhere in his investigation, then no one would need to know the investigation had taken place at all. But if he succeeded in casting doubts on Sheryl's guilt, it would be seen nationally as an effort to let her commit suicide.

"Have you seen the national polls on this?" Donovan asked. "Thirty-five percent of the people are opposed to her; they don't want to let her kill herself. Fifty-two percent are on her side."

Novack couldn't have cared less about the polls, but it seemed as if Donovan was making Novack's point. "So you'll be a national hero," he said.

"That ain't how it works," Donovan said. "These are people who have never heard of me. We do this, and thirty-five percent of the people in America will hate me. That's got to be over a hundred million people. By definition, if a hundred million people hate me, it's a bad thing."

Novack tried to bring Donovan back to discussing the specifics of the case. He laid out all that he had learned to that point, which was considerable. As he reached the end, he said, "I've got a feeling that Charlie died before he could cash in on the death of Beverly's brother; I should say his fake brother. What we need to find out is if big money changed hands involving these other identities, the ones that were in the safe-deposit box."

Donovan nodded, seeing a chance to delay a decision. "Why don't we meet again after you check that out?"

Novack shook his head. "No, Captain, it can't work like that. This has to become a department investigation, not me tinkering around on my vacation. I need help; I don't know what I'm doing with all this computer stuff. We need to bring the fraud and cyber-crime people in. And we need to do it in a hurry."

"What's the rush? The murder is six years old, and he obviously faked these identities before that. So why are we all of a sudden in such a big hurry? Sheryl Harrison?"

Novack hit it straight on. "Right. Sheryl Harrison. And I'm not just talking about the thing with her daughter. She's been in prison for six years, and I put her there. Even if she planned to retire in Miami Beach when she gets out, I don't want her to spend another day in prison . . . not if she didn't kill him."

"What about jurisdiction? None of these other crimes, if that's what they were, happened here."

Novack was getting annoyed, and he showed it. "Why the hell would that matter? We're reopening the Harrison murder. That's been ours from day one."

Donovan basically had nowhere to go with his argument, but if he was going to go down, he'd go down flailing. "I don't like you working so closely with this lawyer, Wagner. We don't know anything about him; we could wake up one morning and find out he's sandbagged us with the press."

"He's okay," Novack said, one of the very few times he had said that about an attorney. "And she trusts him; he's our link to her."

By that point, Donovan knew he would have to cave. Novack would never let it drop; he'd plant a story in the press if he had to, or let the lawyer plant it. Donovan also knew that giving Novack what he wanted was the right thing to do. Of course the fact that it was the right thing to do played no factor in his decision.

"All right. Open the investigation. But nothing is said to the press until it's cleared through me."

That was fine with Novack; he basically didn't trust or want to have anything to do with media people. "No problem," he said. "As long as I get my week's vacation back."

"You're an irritating pain in the ass," Donovan said.

"You sound like Cindy."

They were the three most intimidating people I had ever seen. This was true even though none of them was under sixty years old and I had no doubt I could beat up any of them, and probably all three together.

Their names were Robert Hudson, Sofia Hernandez, and Alexander Minter, and they made up the three-judge panel that I was hoping to successfully persuade.

My opponent in this action, representing the state of New Jersey, was Lydia Aguirre. I had done some quick research on her when I found out she had the assignment, and learned to my dismay that she was considered whip-smart, and a rising star in state legal circles.

What my research didn't tell me, but which I believed, was that she was chosen at least partially because she was a woman. Surveys showed that women were particularly partial toward Sheryl's position, and I'm sure it was believed by the powers that be that a woman arguing against her would be more palatable.

We each were to have an opportunity to give short presentations, which would support the written briefs we had already filed. There would then be time for questions, which we would answer together. However, I knew from my research into court procedures that my presentation would be interrupted constantly by questions from all three of the judges, so I prepared myself for that.

The reputations of the judges, honed by thousands of opinions that they had collectively written, told me what I needed to know. Judge Hudson was a staunch, pro-life conservative, and Judge Hernandez was an equally staunch, pro-choice liberal. While this was not an abortion case, polls showed that opinions on this broke down in a reasonably similar fashion.

In the middle was Judge Minter, and that was a position the moderate jurist was used to. His opinions were far less predictable, and there was no doubt that his was the vote we were fighting for.

It was fair to say that I was petrified. Just coming to the courthouse, through the mobs outside conducting their demonstrations, was an intimidating experience. And the idea that I was going to argue my first case, in this setting and on a matter of such importance, left me weak in the knees.

I barely had time to clear my throat before the first question was fired at me, by Judge Hernandez. I had started talking about the rights of prisoners, and how Sheryl was being unfairly treated, when held up to that standard.

"What prisoner has ever been granted the right to commit suicide?" Judge Hernandez asked. So much for thinking I had a friend on this bench.

"Explicitly? None," I said. "But with respect, that is not the relevant question, since that is not the right Sheryl Harrison is seeking."

"I would suggest playing word games with this court might not be the best approach, Mr. Wagner," she said. "Giving away her heart would cause her death, more surely than if she jumped off the Empire State Building."

"Certainly, but she is not asking for any special consideration from the Department of Corrections. No surgery, no assisted suicide, nothing like that at all. But she does not want to be persecuted, to be put on suicide watch and subjected to unfair and unwarranted invasions of her privacy, and deprivations of her rights."

Minter jumped in. "She has not requested that the state allow her to die?"

I shook my head. "She has not, your Honor. I had a conversation with an executive in the Department of Corrections, but it was an informal exploration of options. I made no official request on Ms. Harrison's behalf, despite the department's mischaracterization of it in the press immediately thereafter."

"So she does not want to give her daughter her heart?" Judge Hudson asked, obviously skeptical.

"Certainly she does, your Honor. She loves her daughter, and the fact that she is dying causes Ms. Harrison a horrible grief, as I'm certain you can imagine. But the simple fact is that she is entitled to her wishes, providing she doesn't ask the state to assist in attaining them. It is not the province of the state to anticipate or imagine what she might secretly wish, and take preemptive measures to deny them, depriving Ms. Harrison of her rights in the process."

It was an unusual tactic that I took, but the only one which I felt had any chance of succeeding. The law was firmly against Sheryl, and there was simply no possibility that the state of New Jersey was going to assist in her death.

The best we could hope for was a restoration of her rights, and a removal of the suicide watch. Then she would be relatively free to attempt suicide. If she succeeded, I would be there to intervene, and demand that as she was a registered organ donor, her organs should be harvested. As she was a perfect match for Karen, who was certainly near the top of the list, there should be no problem arranging the transplant.

It was all way, way beyond a long shot. Even if we won, the state would likely appeal, and we would have to go through this all over again. By then I would need a new heart, since the one I had could not take the pressure.

I finally got through my presentation, battered and bruised, and Ms. Aguirre took her turn. She for the most part ignored my arguments, and instead made a boilerplate speech against assisted suicide. Of course, she included a number of obligatory references to the sympathy everyone felt for Sheryl in her plight. She said that everyone was praying for Karen, though it didn't seem that everyone included her or the three judges.

She seemed not to be subject to the rigorous questioning that I was, though perhaps I couldn't be an impartial judge of that. But in my estimation she emerged relatively unscathed.

When the court adjourned, I saw on the way out that my uncle Reggie had been in the gallery. "Good job, son," he said. "I'm proud of you. Come on, I'll buy you a beer."

"You think we've got a chance?"

"Zero."

I didn't bother answering; I could do that over the beers. But he was wrong; we had one chance.

Novack.

"Did you ever think I might have a date?" Cindy asked. Novack had come straight to her house, after working in the office until almost nine o'clock.

"I wish you did," said Novack. "I'm in the mood to kill somebody. Your date would make a perfect candidate."

"What's the matter?" she asked.

"I keep turning over rocks and finding things I should have found six years ago."

"I want to hear all about it," she said. "Are you hungry?"

He shrugged. "Don't worry about it. I ate yesterday."

She laughed. "Come on, I'll make you something."

"Have you had dinner already?" he asked, sounding surprised.

"Yes. Two hours ago."

He looked at his watch. "Boy, time flies when you're turning over rocks."

Cindy made him a delicious dinner, out of basically what she had hanging around in the refrigerator. It was a talent of hers, and he had benefitted from it many, many times. They talked about the case, and she made Novack feel somewhat better. It wasn't so much what she said as it was the fact that she was the one saying it.

After dinner they went upstairs and made love. It left him happily exhausted, as always, and he was very relieved when she invited him to spend the night. But as he was dozing off, he realized that she was no longer in bed with him.

He looked up, and saw her sitting on a chair, dressed and putting on her shoes. "What is going on?" he asked.

"I just realized I'm out of coffee for the morning."

"Don't worry about it," he said.

"Oh, I'm going to worry about it. I've seen you in the morning without coffee."

"You're worse than me," he said.

"No, but I am bad," she admitted.

"I'll go," he said, but made no apparent move to get up.

"No, I'll be right back, but I'll take your car. Mine's in the garage."

"Keys are in my pants."

She took them and went downstairs, then out the front door to the car. She got in, put the key in, and started it.

The car seemed to be racing a little as it sat there, as if she were giving it too much gas, when in fact she wasn't giving it any gas at all. Thinking that the gas pedal might be slightly stuck, she pumped it once, but it seemed to have no effect, either way.

And without her doing anything, the racing got much greater, until the car was shaking and straining, while simply sitting there. Cindy was by now frightened, and turned the key to the off position.

That also had no effect. And the racing got greater.

She started to get out of the car, to get Novack to help, and saw that the doors were locked. She didn't remember locking them, but soon discovered that she could not release the lock. Neither the automatic lock on the door or the key worked, and she could not pull up the button on the driver's side door.

Her fear turned to full-fledged panic when she started to detect a burning smell. The incredible power of the engine had long caused the car to overheat, and had burned up the available oil. She started screaming, as loud as she could, but with the window closed and the car's engine so loud, there was little chance that Novack could hear her.

But he heard the car. Just slightly at first, barely piercing the oncoming sleep, but finally enough to rouse himself to look outside. He saw the car still sitting there when he opened the window and heard the noise. And saw the flames.

He ran downstairs and out the door toward the car. He took in the situation: Cindy screaming in the front seat, the flames by now engulfing the engine, soon to reach the driver.

He tried to open the door, and called to her to unlock it. She finally realized he was there, turning and making what seemed like a silent scream. The flames were reaching for her.

Novack had nothing to use to knock through the window. He was trained in the martial arts, but never had bothered to master things like breaking bricks.

Or car windows.

Letting out a scream of his own, he smashed in the driver's side window with the side of his hand. It did not create nearly enough room for her to get out, so he kept hitting it, again and again, clearing away all the glass.

He reached in to grab her, his bloody hand brushing against the steering wheel, and getting burned by the searing heat. If she had her seat belt on he never could have gotten her out, but she hadn't put it on yet, and with another scream he pulled her through the window and out.

They landed together on the grass adjacent to the sidewalk. He quickly got up and dragged her away as the car became completely engulfed in flames, and exploded when it reached the gas tank.

She looked at him and held on to his neck, sobbing, and he held her until she slowly calmed down. All this as her neighbors, with a car on fire on their street, watched as if mesmerized.

Finally, when she was quiet but still holding him, he said, "We can do without coffee; I think I saw some tea in the cabinet."

It was one of those weird coincidences that happen in life. I was home going over my written replies to some follow-up questions that the court had given me when I decided to take a break and watch some TV. Skimming through the stations, I hit upon the local news, and my friend Mitch Allen.

Mitch and I went to high school together, and we still played tennis with each other at least once a month. He was an attorney with a small firm in Newark, but liked it even less than I did. The difference was that he wouldn't quit and walk away, at least not until he found another job. I was still sticking to my decision to leave when the case was over, and the way I threatened Timmerman would ensure my demise at the firm even if I changed my mind.

Mitch was being interviewed, but it had nothing to do with his profession. He was on a suburban street in what looked like the neighborhood where he lived. Behind him, over his right shoulder as if the shot were framed to be that way, was a car that appeared to be totally burned. Firefighters were still hosing it down, though it appeared that while they won the battle against the flames, they lost the war. The car was a smoldering shell.

"I ran out when I heard this noise; it sounded like an airplane engine or something," Mitch said. "I saw this car with the whole front end on fire. At first I couldn't tell if there was anybody inside, but this guy was standing by the driver's side door, yelling like crazy."

"That was Detective Novack," the interviewer pointed out.

"Right. I've seen him around a lot. Anyway, he does like a karate chop, and smashes the window. Then he does it a few more times, and reaches in and pulls Cindy . . . she's my neighbor . . . out of the driver's seat and away from the car, just before it explodes. It was unbelievable."

They then cut back to the studio, where they had Novack's picture on the screen and they were talking about him. I don't know what they said, because within ten seconds I was out the door and on the way to New Jersey.

It was past ten o'clock, so there was very little traffic in or out of the city. I knew the way because I had picked Mitch up a few times to go play tennis, and I was at the street in Fair Lawn in a half hour.

The problem was that I was late for the party. The car shell had been removed, the spectators and media trucks were gone, and all that was left to indicate that something might have happened was a single police car parked in the driveway of one of the houses.

I approached the car, which had two officers inside. They saw me and came out to meet me. They did not look terribly friendly.

"I'm looking for Detective Novack," I said.

"What about?"

"I'd rather not say. We're working together on something."

"He's not here. Call the precinct in the morning."

"Is there any way to reach him? I really want—"

I was interrupted by a woman's voice that said, "It's all right, Officer." I turned and saw her, standing on the porch.

"I'm Jamie Wagner," I said to her.

"I know who you are. Come in."

I followed her into the house, where she introduced herself and poured me a cup of tea. We sat in the den as she told me what happened, crying frequently through what was likely the first time she had verbalized it.

"It wasn't an accident," she said. "Someone tried to kill me. It was as if the car had a mind of its own, and it was intent on killing me."

"It was your car?"

It seemed as if the question jolted her, as if she had just realized what should have been obvious. "No . . . it was his. It was John they were trying to kill."

She said that Novack was wherever they took the car; he had insisted that it be examined immediately, to determine how it happened. "When John demands something, it's tough to refuse."

"I picked up on that," I said.

She invited me to wait for Novack to come back. I got the feeling that she didn't want to be alone, not even with two police officers standing guard in front of the house. If she thought my being there made her safer, her terrifying experience had rendered her temporarily delusional.

We moved from coffee to wine, and she seemed to get more comfortable in the process. It was almost two hours until Novack got back, which made it past one o'clock.

He opened the front door, came in, and saw Cindy and me sitting in the den. He walked over to her, kissed her on the head, and said, "You okay?"

"Yes," she said, "thanks to you."

"I'm sorry I got you into this," I said, to Novack.

"That's bullshit."

I nodded. "Yes, it is."

"I need to talk to the lawyer," he said to Cindy.

"Anything I can't hear?" she asked.

He thought for a moment and said, "Of course not." Then, to me, "I talked to the top auto guy in the department; he looked at what was left of the car."

"Could he tell what happened?" I asked.

"Not from looking at it; there was basically nothing left. But he had no doubt how it went down. It was the computer in the car."

"I'm sorry, I don't understand," Cindy said. "There was a computer in the car?"

Novack nodded. "Most people don't realize it, but for a while now, cars have been run by computers. They're fairly sophisticated."

"Could someone have hacked into it?" I asked.

"Apparently so. They would have had to have access at first, but then could have operated it remotely. It's like those commercials you see on television, where people are opening their cars, or starting them, using their cell phone. So it could have been done."

"By people who really knew what they were doing," I said. "I don't know that much about computers, but they really must be good."

He nodded. "Good enough to turn a car into a killer. And good enough to create people that don't exist."

"And bad enough to be willing to burn someone alive in a car," I said. "Sheryl Harrison isn't a killer. These are the people she's afraid of."

We were back at the prison at 9:00 A.M. When Sheryl saw it was both Novack and I, she said, "I think I've seen this movie already."

"Not this one," I said. "This one ends differently."

"What does that mean?"

"Someone tried to kill me last night," Novack said. Sheryl of course had no idea what had happened, so Novack told her. I think I heard his voice crack when he talked about how Cindy was seconds from burning alive, but he covered it quickly, and he'd certainly never admit to it.

When he was finished, Sheryl looked stunned. "I'm sorry," she said. "I'm so sorry."

"It's not your fault," I said, surprised at how protective of her I felt.

"Yes, it is," said Novack. "It's your fault because you haven't told us the truth. But what you don't understand is that it's not going to matter."

"What do you mean?"

"Because if they're trying to kill me, then it's because they know I'm after them. And they know I'm talking to you; they probably followed me here today. So whatever you're afraid might happen if you talk is going to happen anyway, because they think you're talking. And if we don't know what it is, we can't stop it."

"Sheryl, Charlie was involved in a conspiracy," I said. "The fake IDs in the safe-deposit box were of people that profited from someone's death, and those people had died of apparent malfunctions of some type of computer. The same thing would have been done with the ID in his wallet, had Charlie lived."

"I'm not sure why this matters," Sheryl said.

"I'll tell you why," I said. "All of this had to be the most important thing in his life for at least the last six months. From what I've learned about him, he was not the shy, retiring type. He must have talked about it."

"You're double-teaming me, Harvard? You're playing bad cop, bad lawyer?"

"We're not playing games, Sheryl, no strategy, no manipulations. I wouldn't do that to you. But the time to tell us what you know is now. For a lot of reasons, later may be too late."

She was silent for a few moments, which became a full minute. Her lower lip was quivering, and I thought she was going to cry. But she was not any more likely to do that than Novack; she was one tough lady.

"Will you protect Karen?" she asked. It struck me that it was the same concern she had six years earlier, when Novack came to the house to find Charlie and arrest her. She had made sure that Karen was met at school, and taken to Terry's.

"Absolutely," Novack said, without any hesitation at all.

She nodded. "I didn't kill Charlie. I wanted to many times, but I didn't kill him."

I wanted to ask, "Who did?" but a look from Novack silenced me. I figured he had considerably more experience than me in getting witnesses to talk, so I took his lead and kept my mouth shut.

"Those last few months, Charlie would brag about these new people he was working with. He was really proud of it, like he was on the inside of something, and how it was going to make him rich.

"One night, when he was drunk and hit me, he told me that he could have me killed, that he could tell his people, that's how he put it, 'tell my people,' and he could have anyone killed."

As I listened to her say this, it made me want to resurrect Charlie and slit his throat myself. But Novack just nodded encouragement; there was no way he was going to say anything and interrupt the flow.

"Then it seemed to change. A couple of times he referred to them as stupid, and if he was in charge things would be better all around. It was typical Charlie, thinking he was more than he was, and everybody else was less. Well, these people were more than he could handle.

"There's a man . . . his name is Hennessey . . . he doesn't know I know his name. He came to our house that day, to talk to Charlie. He was much bigger than Charlie; I could tell that Charlie was afraid of him.

"I left them alone and was upstairs in the bedroom when Hennessey came in. He raped me, and then he brought me downstairs to the den. Charlie was lying on the couch, and there was blood everywhere. Then he picked up the knife and put it in my hand, so my fingerprints would be on it.

"He told me that with my history, and with me being in the room with Charlie, and my prints on the knife, the police would know that I did it. That nothing I could say could ever convince anyone otherwise. But if I denied it, or told anyone about him . . ."

She took a few moments to compose herself, then took

a deep breath and continued. ". . . then he would do to Karen what he did to me, and then he would do to her what he did to Charlie. But that if I did what I was told, he wouldn't hurt her, and she would have plenty of money to live."

I couldn't resist jumping in. "He gave you money?"

She nodded. "My mother gets money every month. It's the only way she and Karen have survived."

"We're going to have to talk to your mother," Novack said. "And we're going to need your help identifying Hennessey."

"You said you'd protect Karen."

Novack nodded. "And we will. It will be the first call I make when I leave here."

"Then leave here now," she said.

He did, and I stayed behind to talk to her. "I know, Harvard, I should have told you earlier."

"It took a lot of courage to tell us now."

She smiled. "You know, I think I might double your fee."

"I'm worth it."

One hand was handcuffed to the table, but she grabbed my arm with the other. To my recollection, it was the first time she had ever touched me, or I her. "I'm scared, Harvard," she said. "Isn't that ridiculous? I'm trying to die, and I'm scared."

I put my arm around her to comfort her, and I have no idea how this happened, but I kissed her. Or she kissed me; I'm still not sure. It was brief, but it wasn't a kiss of understanding, or friendship, or compassion, or pity.

We broke it off quickly, and just looked at each other, not knowing what to say. She thought of something first, which was just as well, since it would have taken me years to come up with something.

"You going to invite me to the senior prom?" she asked.

The call came in to Agent Charlie Ammerman in the Charlotte Bureau office. Ammerman was assigned to the task force, working under Mike Janssen on the plane crash investigation. On the line was the receptionist, Judy Clifford.

"Charlie, I've got a bit of a weird call on the line. It's a little girl, asking to speak to Mike Janssen."

Ammerman literally jumped out of his chair, walking with the cordless phone toward Janssen's office as he continued to talk. "What's her name?"

"Tammy. She said she has to talk to Janssen, or people will die. Then she said, 'Just like on that plane.' "

So closely guarded was the Tammy secret that there was no way that even a receptionist in the Bureau office would be aware of it, but Ammerman knew it all too well. "Tell her you're trying to find Agent Janssen, but that he'll be right with her."

"She's pretty insistent," Clifford said. "She's getting upset."

"Just don't lose her. If you think she might hang up, tell her you're putting it through, and do so."

Ammerman went past Janssen's assistant's desk without pausing, opened the door, and entered the office. Janssen was in a meeting with four other agents, and they looked up, surprised at the unusual interruption.

"Tammy's on the phone," Ammerman said, and the group sprung into action, going to their respective work areas, from where they would each monitor the call. A trace was put on the call, though based on their last experience with Tammy, no one had any real hope it would yield useful information.

Before Ammerman could tell the receptionist to put the call through, she did so. That likely meant that she thought Tammy was getting upset to the point that she might hang up.

"This is Janssen," he said as he picked up the phone.

"This is Tammy. Hi." Nolan Murray sat in his office, his two colleagues watching and listening, and loving every minute of it. One of them, Peter Lampley, sat in front of his computer, ready to execute the plan.

Even though Janssen knew exactly what the voice would sound like from listening to the air controller's conversation, it was still jarring and incongruous to hear it.

"What can I do for you, Tammy?"

"Give me two million dollars."

"Only if you stop hurting people."

She laughed a little girl's laugh. "They were more than hurt."

"Let's meet and talk about it," he said.

"Can I have my money?"

"If we meet."

"I think you're trying to fool me," she said. "So I'll just crash a train instead." Nolan Murray was having a great time with this; the feeling of power at being able to humiliate so powerful an entity as the FBI, as the U.S. government, was intoxicating.

"There's no reason for you to do that. We can get you the money."

"You're trying to fool me. My mommy was right."

Janssen was growing more and more furious, but kept himself under control. "How can we get you the money?" He had neither the intention nor the authority to pay any money. He just wanted to keep the conversation going, trying to find an opening or goad Tammy into a verbal mistake.

"Never mind, I'm going to crash a train. Good-bye."

"Wait!" Janssen yelled. "Where is the train?"

"Oops." Tammy giggled. "Los Angeles."

The agents came back into Janssen's office the moment that Tammy hung up the phone. There had been plenty of time to trace the call, and it showed that it had originated in Omaha, Nebraska. Agents were quickly sent to the location, but Janssen knew there was no possibility of it paying off.

Ammerman had spent the time that Janssen was on the phone alerting Homeland Security to an impending emergency, and the assistant director, Cody Schumacher, was on the phone with Janssen within seconds after Tammy's call.

"We need to stop every train in southern California, right now," Janssen said.

"I need to understand the situation before I can order that," Schumacher said.

"Here's the situation. A train is going to crash in the Los Angeles area; it could be crashing while we're talking. If a train is stopped, it can't crash. So stop the fucking trains, or don't and send a truckload of body bags to L.A."

Homeland Security has awesome power in an emergency, and is well set up to communicate with and direct local agencies when an extraordinary event has taken place or is about to. The rail system fits very comfortably into their domain; trains have long been considered likely targets of attacks, as they have been in Europe.

So remarkably, within ten minutes, every train in southern California was stopped, literally, in its tracks. Passengers were told over loudspeakers that there was nothing to worry about, just a mechanical failure that would soon be corrected. The people talking on those loudspeakers did not have the slightest idea why they were directed to stop.

Communications in the form of an open, secure line were set up between Janssen, Schumacher, the FBI director, the secretary of transportation, and the White House chief of staff. All except Janssen were relieved when Schumacher reported that the trains were by then halted and "no incidents of any kind have been reported."

Attention turned to how to now deal with the stationary trains; since they were packed with people, they could not sit there for any great length of time.

Janssen was adamant. "Get the people off the trains," he said. "Bring buses in; I don't care what you have to do. But this was no false alarm."

The transportation secretary was uneasy with this. "It will be a mess. L.A. is a mess on a normal day."

"People will be inconvenienced," Janssen said. "Take a poll. Ask them if they would rather be inconvenienced or dead."

No one on the call wanted to be responsible for the carnage that Janssen was envisaging, so the decision was made to get the people off the trains and do intense inspections on each. No train would be put back into service until it was cleared, which meant that the next day's morning commute would be a nightmare, even by L.A. standards.

While the others on the call were worrying about outraged commuters, meaning outraged voters, all but Janssen thought they had successfully dodged a terrorist bullet. He didn't know where it was coming from, or why it hadn't been fired already, but he believed they still were in the crosshairs.

One of the many trains in southern California that was stopped was Rolling Thunder, the wild railroad ride at Disneyland. The only difference between that and the others was that Homeland Security had nothing to do with stopping it; that task was accomplished by Peter Lampley, at the direction of Nolan Murray.

The twenty-eight passengers on the stopped train looked around in vain for someone to help them. There were no small children on the ride, since the high speed and sharp turns dictated a height requirement. So they were mostly teenagers and adults, and they calmly waited for the ride to start up again.

That particular ride has two trains, and they run one minute and ten seconds apart. At that moment, the passengers on the second train were having a very different experience. They were traveling at an incredible speed, such that if they were not securely belted in, they would be thrown from the train. Those who had been on the ride previously knew that something was wrong; it was not meant to travel this fast. Everyone, whether a frequent rider or a first-timer, was panicked by what they were experiencing.

Under Lampley's computer direction, the second car rammed into the stationary one. Nineteen people were killed, seventeen critically injured, and many others badly hurt.

Tammy had crashed her train, just like she promised.

I did not want to have dinner with my parents. That would be a true statement pretty much every day since I was six years old, but on this particular night I was dreading it even more than usual.

They live less than forty-five minutes from the city, and are there all the time, but once a month they have what they call their "New York vacation weekend." That consists of checking into an exclusive hotel, they rotate among six of them, and doing New York things like taking in a show, going to fine restaurants, et cetera. All the things that they do almost every weekend, but this somehow feels different to them.

Whenever we are going to have dinner, I invite them to my place so that I can cook a meal for them. I do this even though there is never the slightest chance that they would ever accept, or that I would ever want them to. But by making the offer, I'm able to amuse myself by imagining them working their way up my elevator-less building to my third-floor apartment.

My mother once again declined the invitation, chuckling slightly at the prospect. Instead she chose Le Bernardin, a Midtown French restaurant specializing in seafood. It is widely considered among the best restaurants in New York, in fact in the world. And it is priced accordingly; four people could have dinner there with one of the better bottles of wine, or they could use that money to buy something with bucket seats.

Restaurants like it are said to cater to the rich and famous, though I'd been there four times without actually seeing anyone I recognized. Then the weird realization hit me that to most Americans, I was the most famous person in the place.

Once we were finished with the obligatory chitchat about what was going on in their lives, their work, their charities, and their friends, it was my turn. "Tell us all about this exciting case," my mother said.

I had absolutely no desire to do that. "I really can't talk about it; it's confidential." When my mother looked wounded, I said, "Attorney-client privilege. Pretty much all I can say is what's being reported in the press."

"Is your firm willing to lose you for this long?" my father asked.

"I think they'll get by."

It was Mom's turn. "I think this could be good for your career, especially if you win. Though I have to say, based on the people I have spoken with, it seems as if you're in a difficult legal position."

I nodded. "Very difficult."

They asked me to tell them what Sheryl was like, and I said that she was the strongest woman, actually the strongest person, I'd ever met.

"But she committed a murder," my mother pointed out, and I didn't correct her.

For some reason I was interested in knowing their opinion. "If you were in charge," I said, "if you could make a ruling and that would be the end of it, would you let her give her heart to her daughter?"

"I would," my mother said instantly, surprising the hell out of me. "She's stuck in that prison, and her daughter has a whole life that could be ahead of her. It's her body, it's her choice, and I think she should be allowed to make it."

"I would tend to agree," my father said. "But as a doctor I would never participate in it, and I doubt you'd find a doctor who would."

"But once she had died, even by suicide, there are doctors that would perform the transplant. Right?"

He nodded. "Without a doubt. And they should; at that point there would be a life to save."

"Would they stand by, passively, while she took her own life? Maybe with her daughter already there, prepped for the transplant?"

"I don't think so," he said. "That's coming too close to the line." Then he laughed. "Although Bud Jenkins probably would."

"Who's Bud Jenkins?"

My mother answered the question. "He's a colleague of your father's, a heart surgeon, very talented. But very opinionated."

My parents thinking someone else was opinionated was chock-full of its own ironies, but I avoided pointing them out. The rest of the dinner was fairly uneventful, actually borderline pleasant. I even let them order me a brandy that they described as their favorite, and which probably cost more than my monthly rent.

It was delicious, burning a very pleasant path straight down to my core. I ordered another, which my parents seemed to note with delight, as if the brandy was the long sought after tool they could use to transform me into someone of whom they could heartily approve.

I got up to leave before they were ready, mainly because if I stayed I would order another brandy and be too drunk to work and think about Sheryl's case when I got home.

I apologized for my abrupt departure, and shook hands with my father and kissed my mother on the cheek. I said truthfully that I had work to do, and that I had to drive to the prison early in the morning to see my client.

"I'll bet she's always happy to see you," my mother said. "She's completely dependent on you."

Her comment sort of stopped me in my tracks, and it took me a moment to answer. "In some ways I'm dependent on her," I said. "Actually, I think I'm falling in love with her. Good night."

I wish there was a way that I could have both left and heard the rest of their conversation. I'm sure they were stunned by what I said. Hell, I was stunned by what I said, and even more by the realization that it was true.

I was falling in love with my client, whose death I was trying to arrange.

Just another day at the office.

The only thing Sheryl was certain of was that she was not certain of anything.

That was what she told the prison chaplain when he came to see her, asking if she wanted to talk.

He nodded and smiled, as if that made perfect sense and was all part of some grand plan. "Certainty. That's a tough one," he said. He was probably younger than Sheryl, so she thought that being wise beyond his years wouldn't be that difficult.

"What are you grappling with?" he asked.

"Two things," she said. "I don't want to die, and I want my daughter to live. Not necessarily in that order."

She felt some relief in showing her weakness and vacillation to this man. She felt it was safer doing so with him than with her mother, or Jamie Wagner. She didn't want them to hone in on it, feeding her doubts and pressuring her to change her mind. Because she wasn't going to change her mind, no matter what anyone said.

They talked some more, and Sheryl admitted that she had put herself in this position. "I've made bad choices in my life," she said. "Pretty much every one I've ever made was wrong." Which of course, led to an ironic question, which he asked.

"If you are so poor at making choices, what makes you think that this one is right?"

She wouldn't answer that, couldn't answer that, and extricated herself from the conversation. But after he left she thought about how she had never really believed in God, never thought much about the concept either way. But some really smart people, much smarter than her, did.

She couldn't really figure out where He would come down on it, though if He existed she guessed she'd know soon enough. She just figured that what she was going to do was good, and right, and if there was a God He'd probably approve of it for just those reasons.

Of course, if there was a God, He just demonstrated a hell of a sense of humor in sending Jamie Wagner. He was everything Sheryl never wanted, everything she always scorned. A Harvard guy, rich family, probably went to operas and played touch football at family outings in Connecticut.

But scorning didn't seem to cut it anymore, or get her anywhere she wanted to be. She liked him; he was funny and smart and he understood her. She even thought she understood him, and she liked to keep him off balance.

He made her feel like she hadn't felt since high school, or maybe ever. And maybe it was just a coincidence that he showed up, or maybe God had sent him to test her, or just play with her mind a little.

That God must be a funny guy.

The meeting was held at 8:00 A.M. at the Department of Homeland Security. Present were the directors of both Homeland Security and the FBI, the White House chief of staff, a total of nine staff members under those three men, and Mike Janssen.

Janssen hated attending meetings like this; he would much prefer to have been video-conferenced in, since by definition coming to Washington was taking time away from doing his job.

The reason he came was that not being present in the room would make his job harder. Janssen felt that stupid decisions often came out of meetings among panicked people, especially those not out in the field. He saw himself as a counterbalance, someone who could bring reason to the process.

Reason-bringing, in Janssen's experience, was far more effective when done in person. It was a dynamic that Janssen couldn't fully explain, but which he had seen time and again. Someone physically present in the room had far more influence over the process than someone brought in through technology.

Since he was the one that was going to have to live with the decisions that were made, it seemed easily worth his time to make the trip to Washington. And the traveling itself was not exactly a major inconvenience; an Air Force jet was dispatched to bring him to Reagan International, from where a helicopter brought him to the meeting.

It was left to Janssen to bring everyone up to date on the investigation's progress, which he was unfortunately able to do in a brief presentation. "We're nowhere," is how he candidly began, much to the consternation of his direct boss, FBI director Edgar Barone.

"We have conclusively determined that the voice has gone through a synthesizer, but common sense told us that anyway. We have traced each call, but not only has the caller successfully hidden his tracks, he has sent us on a wild-goose chase to places from which the calls did not originate.

"In both cases, the plane and the amusement ride, the perpetrators have penetrated the computer systems that operated them. They were essentially hacked into, but in an ingenious way that gave the hackers total control. Our experts think it is possible that the control could have been regained, but not nearly within the time frame we were given. In fact, as you know, we were given no time at all on the amusement park ride; we didn't know the target until it was hit."

The White House chief of staff was the first to interrupt. "So they're demanding money, and then not giving anyone an opportunity to pay."

Janssen nodded. "That's one of the many puzzling aspects of this. My view on it, and psy-ops agrees, is that they're demonstrating their power and their ruthlessness. Probably setting us up for the big one."

The Homeland Security director asked, "And what might that be?"

"There is absolutely no way to know that, and the possibilities are limitless. When it comes to computer crime of this type, it's fair to say that the United States is a target-rich environment. The country is run by computers. All of our mass transit, many of our weapons systems, our dams, power plants of all kinds, you name it."

Everyone in the room was stunned by the implications of this statement, even though they had all been briefed on most of this before the meeting. The Homeland Security director then took the floor, and outlined emergency measures that were already being taken to ensure security of computer systems throughout the country, starting with what were considered the most vulnerable, and most devastating if compromised, targets.

"As I'm sure you understand, a project of this magnitude can take months, if not years. Even then, our cyber-security people tell us there's no guarantee that we can effectively stop them, even on a system that we recheck. These guys are beyond good, and if they've penetrated a system, they could most likely stay hidden in there as long as they want."

Janssen nodded. "They could have been preparing this for years, and they can sit back now and hit us wherever and whenever they choose. And make no mistake, they will hit us again. I understand that we need to play defense, to make the systems as secure as possible, but if we're going to stop them, it will be by catching them."

"And we have no suspects?"

Janssen shook his head. "No. We've been identifying and investigating everybody we can find that is known to have extraordinary capabilities in this area. But while probably less than half the people in this country can point to North America on a map, computer geniuses are on every street corner."

Until that point the meeting was just a briefing; law enforcement and security efforts were already well under way, and not waiting for any decisions to be made by this group. The real purpose of the gathering was to contemplate a key decision, how to deal with the public.

This was the White House chief of staff's area, because this was a presidential decision. Until that point the public was in the dark. While there was rampant speculation that the airplane crash was a terrorist incident, it had not been confirmed by anybody of authority. The amusement ride was viewed as a tragic accident, and the two tragedies were not considered connected by the public.

As the conversation began, Janssen could smell the whiff of politics in the air. He jumped in, though he was not expected to; this was definitely not his domain or responsibility. "You need to tell people," he said. "They have a right to know, and to protect themselves as best they can."

The Homeland Security director said, "Protect themselves against what? We can't even tell them where the danger is. How can they protect themselves?"

"Let me ask you something," Janssen said. "Are you going to put your son on a plane this week to go down to Florida and visit Grandma? Of course not, because as little as we know, you're in on it, so you know better."

The chief of staff said, "The country will grind to a halt. It would do more damage to the economic underpinnings of this country than fifty terrorist attacks."

Janssen nodded. "I'm sure the people on that plane gave a major shit about economic underpinnings."

"That's bullshit, Janssen. If the economy goes in the tank, people suffer. They lose their jobs, and they can't pay for heat, and they can't feed their families, and they can't go to doctors, and some of them die."

"But it's their decision," Janssen said. "We are their government, not their parents. And there is something else to consider. If we go public with this, we'll have three hundred million pairs of eyes looking for the bad guys. We've got no tips coming in; if we spread this word we'll be swimming in them. It would increase our chances of catching the bad guys a hundredfold."

The meeting continued for another half hour, but the main points had been made. The chief of staff said that all views would be presented to the president, who would make the decision. He then pointedly added, "Which we will all support."

It was almost two o'clock in the afternoon before Janssen got back to his office, and by then he decided that not only had he accomplished nothing, but he had been wrong.

Video-conferencing would have worked just as well.

The good news was that Novack knew what he was looking for . . . hackers. He had thought as much from his investigation of William Beverly and his brother. It seemed certain that those people, as well as the others whose IDs Charlie Harrison had in the safe-deposit box, never existed. The police department experts in the field agreed that only tremendously accomplished hackers could have pulled off such a feat.

But those hackers had stepped it up a terrifying notch with the attempt on Novack's life. They had hacked into his car, and nearly succeeded in turning it into a murder weapon.

Novack asked his computer fraud people for a list of everyone they ever had in their sights who might have the capability to pull off an operation like this. He realized that those names would be mostly in the metropolitan area, yet by its very nature the masterminds could be anywhere there was a computer and modem. They could have sent someone in to deal with Novack's car; that by no means meant that the top person lived around there. He could be in Pakistan, for all Novack knew.

At that point, Novack had two things to go on, Charlie Harrison and Hennessey, the person Sheryl named as the real murderer.

There was no way that Charlie could have been the center of the operation, or crucial to it. If the people employing Charlie needed him, they wouldn't have killed him off.

There could be ten Charlies, or a hundred, or a thousand, spread out like a virus across the country. There was no way to know, and putting out the word looking for similar crimes would be unlikely to yield positive results. Entities like insurance companies that had paid off on these kinds of bogus claims would be unaware that they were swindled; surely no one had any idea that the beneficiary they paid money to did not really exist.

Hennessey provided more opportunities for Novack to go after. Assuming Sheryl was telling the truth, and every instinct Novack had made him believe she was, then Hennessey was also probably an employee of the people behind this. He seemed more like traditional muscle, the type that the hackers would have relied on for their more conventional needs. He would be the means by which they would avoid getting their hands dirty.

Novack and Captain Donovan considered going to the FBI with the information they had accumulated, but decided to hold off for the time being. They had very little concrete to go on, and the Bureau would at that point be likely to shrug them off. Either that, or move in on their case, claiming it was their domain under the interstate commerce clause of the Constitution. Both of those results were unacceptable, so Donovan rejected the idea.

Novack had arranged for round-the-clock protection for Karen Harrison at the hospital, and had suggested that her grandmother move in there as well. Terry Aimonetti was fine with that; she hated leaving her granddaughter anyway.

With that accomplished, for the time being there was

little Novack could do but wait for the detectives working the case to come up with some leads, something he could dig his teeth into. And that's what Lieutenant Steve Emerson brought with him when he came into Novack's office . . . a lead. Not the case-breaking, earth-shattering kind, but a lead nonetheless.

Emerson was in charge of the Computer Crime Division, a position he had sought even though he readily admitted he knew almost as little about computers as Novack. But it was a career path that included the rank of Lieutenant, so he decided to just surround himself with enough computer geeks to get the job done.

The head geek was Andrew Garrett, who was in charge of the technological end of the division, and who counted as one of his job responsibilities to make Emerson look good. He did that quite effectively, which was why Emerson brought him to meetings like this one with Novack.

"We've talked to ninety-one people already, and we're just scratching the surface," Emerson said. "All computer hacker types. The nerd population is exploding." He turned to Garrett. "No offense."

Garrett smiled. "None taken."

"It's the geeks' world," Novack said. "We're just living in it. What did you find out?"

"There are a lot of people who can hack into stuff, change records, steal identities, that kind of stuff," Garrett said. "Some of them do it to profit from it, but most just to show they can. Like a badge of honor, or something.

"But they all see themselves, and the other people like them, as basically decent people. They sit in little rooms, peering at their screens, and doing what they do. And they go mostly at businesses, government agencies, that kind of thing. It rarely gets personal, and it never gets physical."

"You going to get to the point in my lifetime?" Novack asked.

Emerson took over. "Let me take it. One name came up that is interesting. He's supposed to be sort of a hacker legend. People have crossed him, and he ruined their lives, just ruined them, all with his computer."

"I hope there's more," Novack said.

Emerson nodded. "There is. The informant told a story about a guy named Clemens. The story is that this computer guy ruined Clemens, raided his bank account or something. Anyway, Clemens somehow found the guy and confronted him, threatened him. The story goes that the computer guy killed Clemens, and left his body in the gutter."

"You checked into it yet?"

"Yeah. Little over a year ago Victor Clemens was found dead in an alley in Passaic. His throat was slit ear to ear. It's an open case; no leads."

"This person you talked to . . . how did you find him?"

Garrett spoke up, concisely so that Novack wouldn't jump on him again. "The hacking community is small, and fairly close. Everybody knows everybody else. They compete with each other."

"I want to talk to the informant," Novack said, now fully interested.

Emerson nodded. "I told him we'd be back. But there's one thing I had to promise, that we'd keep his name out of it. They're all scared shitless of this guy."

"What's his name?"

"The informant?"

"No. The killer."

"Nolan Murray."

"Listen, about what happened the other day, Sheryl . . . I'm sorry." I hadn't seen her since we kissed, and I wanted to clear the air right away, and I was nervous about seeing her. So I said it as soon as I was brought into the room.

She looked surprised. "I thought it was my fault."

"I think it was mine. So I'm sorry, it was completely unprofessional and can only get in the way."

"So you're not going to take me to the fraternity formal?" she asked. "Or the homecoming dance?"

"No, I'm taking one of the rich country club girls."

"I'm not surprised. But listen, Harvard?"

"Yes?"

"Just do your job and make sure you and I don't have a future."

I wanted to argue with her, to plead the case for a future that actually could hold incredible promise, but I didn't. Nor did I tell her how I felt about her; to do so would have been unfair and counterproductive to her future plans for her daughter.

Instead I smiled and updated her on what I knew, which was not a hell of a lot. She had a ravenous appetite for information about the case, which I could understand completely.

"Novack will be all over this," I said. "After what happened to his ex-wife, he'll be relentless."

"What about Karen?"

"I called the hospital and spoke with your mother. She said she and Karen are fine, and that there are police everywhere. Karen is feeling stronger and is anxious to leave, but your mother understands that it's safer for them to stay there. She's a strong lady."

"You have no idea."

"It runs in the family."

She deflected that, and I mentioned that I needed to go see her mother.

"Why?"

"She's been receiving money from the people who killed Charlie. There might be a way to track that down."

"So you're a cop now? I thought you were just a lawyer."

"Novack asked me to do it; he thought she'd be more likely to talk to me. I guess he also figured that if she hit me, I'd already be in a hospital, so I'd survive."

"Okay."

I was surprised; I thought she'd fight me on it, but she didn't. "Can you call her and tell her it's okay to talk to me?"

"You won't have a problem, believe me. She's been wanting to talk about it for six years. What's happening with the court case?"

I shrugged. "No word yet, but you shouldn't read that as positive or negative. They don't give updates along the way; they'll issue a ruling when they're ready. But the higher court recognized the urgency, so they should be quick about it."

"All right," she said, with apparent resignation.

"What's the matter?"

"The waiting is hard, that's all. The waiting is hard and that's the only thing that I do."

"I can only imagine what it's like," I said, lamely.

"You probably can't, and I hope you never have to."

"Sheryl, if at any point you change your mind about this, or start to have doubts, it's okay. I'll understand. Everyone, including Karen, will understand."

"Thanks a lot," she said with obvious sarcasm. Then, "I'm not changing my mind."

I nodded. "Then there's something else we probably should talk about."

"You do a lot of talking."

"I'm a lawyer; that's what we do. In the unlikely event that we win, or that we get you out of here some other way, have you given any thought as to how you're going to accomplish your goal?" It was a cowardly way to put it, but at the moment I just couldn't seem to bring myself to say "kill yourself."

"Of course."

"And what have you come up with?"

"I want a doctor to do it, with Karen in a bed in the next room, so there can't be too much of a delay."

"No doctor is going to kill you, Sheryl. That's unrealistic; it's just not going to happen. The best you can hope for is to have a doctor standing by."

"You're full of good news today. Didn't any of your fraternity brothers go on to med school?"

"Probably half of them, but we're out of touch. However, there is someone I could talk to." I had been kicking the idea around in my head, but only in the moment decided to mention it to her.

"Good idea, lawyer. Go talk."

Things were going fast now for Nolan Murray and his team. Faster than he would like or felt completely comfortable with, yet he was the one putting his foot on the gas pedal. Speed was a necessity; it would not let the opposition have a chance to collect themselves. Besides, the sooner the goal was accomplished, the less time there was for something to go wrong.

The fast pace did not really fit Murray's style; his preference would have been to relax and enjoy himself as it all slowly unfolded. But he had to adapt himself to the circumstances, and it was a small price to pay for the reward that was coming.

The opposition was coming after him on two fronts, and after the train crash they were coming hard. There was the FBI and Homeland Security, headed by Janssen. Murray had checked him out and knew him to be a formidable adversary; he would handle him, but he wouldn't underestimate him.

The federal side was where the danger, such as it was, would come from. The other front was the local police, in the person of Novack. Murray had tried to eliminate that concern by hacking into his car computer.

Murray knew that was a mistake, and that it was a failure of his own personality. He could just as easily, even more easily, have had Churchill rig an explosive to go off when the car started. But the fire was more dramatic, and Murray had a weakness for the dramatic.

Of course, it wouldn't have mattered anyway, since as it turned out, even a successful explosion would have only killed Novack's ex-wife. That would have represented insignificant collateral damage, but it wouldn't have put Novack in the ground, as was the goal.

So Murray had adapted again, and characteristically would take a negative and turn it into a positive. He was aware that Novack was ramping up his efforts, and had officers scouring the hacker community. He also knew that he had been implicated, and that Novack would soon be convinced he had a name to put on his quarry.

It wouldn't matter at all; in fact, Murray would turn it to his advantage, when he was ready to.

The one surprise so far in the operation was the government's ability to conceal from the public the terrorist aspect to the two operations. Of course, Murray could break the story whenever he wanted, but there was no hurry. At whatever point the public found out, there would be widespread panic. But this way, if they simultaneously found out that they had been deceived and the truth had been withheld, that panic would be coupled with extreme anger.

That would work to Murray's benefit.

Everything always worked to Murray's benefit.

At some point, fairly soon, the landscape would change, and Murray would do the changing. The public would know what was going on, and they would be aware of the pathetic failure of their government to protect them. Novack and the Feds would join together, and they would believe that in tandem they would be able to close in and capture their prey.

They would be very wrong, and it would cost them, big time.

For now, Murray had to decide whether his opponents had learned how serious he was, and how he was not to be trifled with. The question was whether another lesson was necessary, or not.

He decided there was no downside to another lesson, except to the people that would be killed.

Kevin Laufer moaned when Emerson, Novack, and I entered through the back of the room. He caught himself and tried to cover it, but his junior high school students picked up on it and turned around to see the cause of Laufer's discomfort. He tried to continue with the class, but there was no way he could concentrate. Since the period was five minutes from the end anyway, he let them out early. None of them complained.

Once they had cleared out, we walked toward the front of the room, where Laufer was still standing in front of the blackboard. On it were written a bunch of what I assumed to be computer symbols; if it were written in Martian, I would have understood it just as well.

"Come on, man. I told you I would only talk to you if you kept it quiet. So you come in here while I'm teaching a class?"

"This is Lieutenant Novack," Emerson said, not bothering to introduce me. Emerson wasn't pleased that I was there at all, but Novack had promised to include me on some things, and this probably seemed to him like a situation where I'd be unlikely to do much damage.

"I'm supposed to be impressed?"

"What's the name of this class?"

"Introduction to Computing. What are you doing here?"

"Detective Novack wants to talk to you about Nolan Murray."

Laufer looked around, as if worried that he would be overheard. "Will you keep it down?" He shook his head. "I never should have said anything."

"How'd you get this job?" Novack asked. "I mean, you've only been out eighteen months, right? They hire ex-cons to teach impressionable kids? Although, a private school like this, maybe they didn't check that carefully."

It was obvious to me that Novack was threatening to reveal Laufer's criminal record to the school administration if he didn't cooperate, and it turned out not to be too subtle for Laufer, either.

"Don't hassle me, okay?" Laufer said. "I need this job. And I was in for hacking, not assault or murder. I'm not a danger to anyone."

Novack nodded. "Tell me about Nolan Murray."

Laufer pointed to Emerson. "I told him everything I know, which ain't a hell of a lot."

"So tell it again."

Laufer looked at me, as if noticing me for the first time. "Who's he?" he said, meaning me.

"Your worst nightmare. Now tell it again."

Laufer started to argue, but finally nodded in resignation. "Okay. How much do you know about hackers?"

"I prefer that we do the questioning, and you do the answering," Novack said.

"Okay, well, we get a bad rap . . . hackers, I mean. Most of us are really smart, or we couldn't do what we do. And we're curious; we want to see what's out there, and how much we can test ourselves."

Novack turned to Emerson and said, "He sounds like

Garrett." Then, to Laufer, "You're all wonderful people; the world needs more of you. We know the story. You want to get to the point?"

"We break the law sometimes, but that's not the purpose, is what I'm trying to say. We're not bad people, and we're not trying to hurt anybody. We want to see how far we can go, what we can get away with. It's an ego thing."

Emerson cut in. "Nolan Murray."

"Right. Nolan Murray is smarter than any of us; he can get to places I wouldn't even try to go. But he's not curious, and he doesn't want to test himself. And he does want to hurt people. Nolan Murray is a mean son of a bitch."

"You've met him?" Novack asked.

Laufer cast a quick glance at Emerson before answering. "Yeah. I've met him. I was there the night he killed that Clemens guy."

"How did you happen to be there?"

"I was at a bar at like two in the morning, hanging out with some guys. One of them was friends with Murray, I guess, because he was there as well. I didn't even know his name at the time; didn't even talk to him. I saw Clemens come in and go over to Murray. I don't know how he knew him, but I saw Murray nod and get up, and they went out the back door into the alley.

"Anyway, it looked a little strange to me, so I went out near the back door to check it out. They were talking, and Clemens sort of pushed him, nothing hard. Next thing I know Murray goes like to slap him, but I saw some light off a blade. All of a sudden Clemens is grabbing for his throat, but he can't stop the blood going through his fingers. He goes down to his knees, and then falls over."

"What did you do?" Novack asked.

"I went back in the bar and minded my own business," he said, and then laughed. "What the hell should I have done, make a citizen's arrest?"

"So you don't know where Murray went?" Novack asked.

"Yeah, I know where he went. He went back into the bar and finished his beer. And then he ordered two more after that. The guy is an ice-cold prick, I'm telling you."

"Where does he live?"

"How do I know? You think he sends me a Christmas card every year?"

"Where does he live?" Novack asked again.

"Last I heard he lived in the city. Soho, or the Village, or something. And somebody said he was from Maine . . . I think . . . it could have been Montana, but I think it was Maine."

"We need more than that," Novack said.

"What do I look like? Google?" Laufer asked. Then, "Come on, I can't have Murray finding out I've been asking around about him."

"You can do it quietly."

"No, I can't."

Novack nodded and stood up. "Okay, forget about it. We're going to be interviewing quite a few of your fellow hackers. You've got a fairly small community, right? So we'll just tell people that you ID'd Murray as a suspect, and ask if they know where we can find him."

Emerson nodded. "That works."

Laufer was scared, and he was beaten. "I'll see what I can find out. Just don't mention my name to anyone."

Novack and Emerson both agreed to that, and then Novack asked, "Does the name Hennessey mean anything to you?"

"No," Laufer said. "Who is he?"

Novack didn't bother answering, he just told Laufer that they would be in touch.

We left, and when we got outside, I tried to talk to Novack and tell him my impressions of the interrogation. He seemed completely uninterested in hearing them, and he and Emerson left me to drive home alone, talking to my-self.

I was pretty impressed by what I would have had to say.

Karen Harrison's medical condition was as cruel as it was deadly. There were times when Karen would feel better, experience a renewed energy and stamina that surprised and delighted her. It would give her a burst of hope that she had turned the corner, that the nightmare would give way to a normal life.

But that's not how it worked; that's not how it ever worked. She was in fact getting worse, inexorably moving toward a time when her heart simply could not keep her body going. And anything different that Karen felt was an illusion.

The good times were always followed by a descent, and it seemed as if each time Karen fell farther than the time before. This episode was a perfect example of that. Karen had felt better for twenty-four hours, and even though she had learned not to trust the highs, she couldn't help herself.

"I want to go see Mom," she said.

Terry knew that Karen wasn't strong enough to leave the hospital, especially for something as stressful as a visit to her mother at the prison. And the police wanted her to stay where she was, where she could be protected.

Karen wasn't even aware that she was being guarded, or that she was in danger, and Terry saw no reason to burden her further with that.

"I'm not sure that's a good idea, sweetheart. At least right now."

"Why not? I feel good, and I haven't seen her in so long."

"Let me see what I can arrange," Terry said, floundering for a way to deflect the request. "Your mother had said that the visiting hours there—"

She stopped in midsentence, because Karen wasn't listening. She had gone completely pale, her eyes rolled up in her head, and she slumped back. He head lolled back on her neck, and Terry immediately screamed.

She thought her granddaughter had died.

The doctors and nurses rushed in, ushering Terry out of the room. They, too, thought they might lose Karen, but after a very nervous half hour she was stabilized.

Later that day she rallied, and was resting comfortably, while her doctors met for more than an hour to talk about her condition.

They finally called an anxious Terry into the room to tell her their recommendation. Karen needed a VAD, which was short for "ventricular assist device." It was an implant, the sole purpose of which was to support the heart while a patient was waiting for a transplant.

Karen's heart could fail at any time, the doctors said, and resuscitation was far from a guarantee. A VAD implant also was not a guarantee, or a long-term solution, but it was the best chance she had until a donor organ was found.

But the implantation itself was a surgical procedure, and there was no certainty that Karen would get through it. The doctors felt that it was likely she would survive, and they strongly recommended it as the only viable option.

It was not a decision that Terry wanted to make alone. She called the prison, and after waiting twenty minutes, and having the surgeon speak to the prison authorities, she got Sheryl on the phone.

She told Sheryl what was going on, and then put the surgeon on to tell her in more detail. Sheryl kept him on the phone for fifteen minutes, peppering him with questions, questions that Terry hadn't even thought to ask.

He finally handed the phone back to Terry. "Do it, Ma. It's her only chance."

"That's what I think, too," Terry said. "Honey, I am so scared. I don't want to lose her, but she's so weak."

"We won't lose her, Ma. She's going to keep fighting and winning until we can get her help. We won't lose her, and we will get her help."

After promising to do whatever was necessary to reach Sheryl after the procedure, Terry got off the phone and signed the necessary papers.

The medical team immediately went to work, not wanting to waste a second. Within thirty minutes, Karen was under anesthesia, prepped, and in the operating room. The procedure itself was a quick thirty minutes, and was instantly judged a success.

The surgeon came out to talk to Terry. "It went well," he said. "We bought some time."

Terry cried a bit, and then went to call Sheryl with the news. Sheryl would ask how much time Karen had, but Terry wouldn't know. She hadn't asked the doctor that question.

She was afraid to hear the answer.

The ruling came down at two o'clock in the afternoon. There had been no indication that it was coming, and I first heard about it from a New York *Daily News* reporter, who called to ask me my reaction to the total loss that we suffered.

I told him that I wouldn't comment on the opinion until I had a chance to read it, though the truth was I had absolutely no desire at all to read it. He had told me all I needed to know.

I forced myself to go to the court website to read the opinion. They had rejected every one of our arguments, and had done so unanimously.

They even ruled against us on things we didn't argue, saying that "were the Department of Corrections to facilitate a suicide, no matter what terminology is used to hide the reality, it would itself be in violation of the law. Such a decision would require a legislative act, not an arbitrary decision by the Department."

They went on, stating unequivocally that the prison authorities had every right to put Sheryl under a suicide watch. "The evidence shows it to be completely consistent with their actions with other inmates. They have a right and obligation to ensure the safety of inmates within their control, whether or not those inmates might desire such protection."

The opinion went on in that fashion, getting even worse as it went along. They went so far as to comment on the lawsuit itself, doubting its merits but allowing it to proceed, at least for the time being.

I would appeal the ruling; that was a foregone conclusion. But another foregone conclusion was that we would lose the appeal. The law, whether one agreed with it or not, was simply against us.

I wanted to go to the prison and tell Sheryl the bad news in person; she deserved that much and more. But I needed to get to the hospital to meet with Terry Aimonetti. Novack and I were hoping that she would have some information that could help the investigation, an investigation that now represented Sheryl's only hope of prevailing.

I got to the hospital, and found Terry sitting alone in Karen's room. It surprised me how young she was; she didn't look like she was even fifty years old. Obviously she and Sheryl had both had their children at a very young age. She was crying, and for a brief moment I thought that Karen might have died.

I have very little understanding of women under any circumstances, and when they are crying I find them even more bewildering. But I came to realize that Terry was crying from happiness, and she explained about the procedure Karen had just undergone, and that she had just learned that it was a success.

She called Sheryl to tell her the news, and after a ten-minute wait got her on the phone. I could hear Sheryl crying through the phone, and the two of them went on that way for three or four minutes. Three or four minutes of listening to two women cry feels a lot longer.

Finally, Terry put me on, and I told her straight out that

we lost the court case. "I'm sorry, Sheryl. It wasn't even close."

"I understand, Harvard," she said. "And as phone calls go, this is still a good one."

"The parole board is our best shot now." I could have substituted "only" for "best" in that sentence, but I didn't.

"How is that going?"

"I spoke to Novack a little while ago; he says he's making progress. That's the first time he's said that, so maybe it means something. I'm meeting with him later; I'll let you know what I find out."

"Come here if you can," she said.

"I will."

I had questions for Terry, but before I could get to them I had to answer a bunch of hers.

"Are you making progress on getting Sheryl what she wants?"

It seemed like she couldn't bring herself to verbalize what it was that Sheryl wanted, and I understood that completely. "It's very difficult," I said. "We are making progress, but partial progress isn't enough. It's all or nothing, and I honestly don't know how it's going to come out."

She nodded. "I don't even know what I want. It seems that either way I lose my little girl."

I then asked her about Hennessey, but she claimed to have no idea who or what I was talking about.

"Sheryl told us the truth about the day that Charlie died."

"Thank God," she said. "I've wanted to tell someone for so long."

She had not known Hennessey's name, and certainly had no idea how we could find him. She was happy to sign a power of attorney, allowing me to get her bank records, in the unlikely event that the money she had been receiving could be traced. Novack could have gotten a court order to get the records, but this was easier and quicker.

Other than the access to the financial records, Terry really had nothing else to offer. I had hoped to talk to Karen, but she was still in the recovery room, and in any event should not be exposed to the stress my questioning might cause.

Unfortunately, spreading stress seemed to be all I did.

Novack was in his precinct office when I got there. Actually, he was in the front lobby, talking to a uniformed officer, a conversation that was breaking up as I walked in.

"You're here," I said.

"Wow, you don't miss a thing," he said. "It's like Sherlock Holmes became a hack lawyer."

"Sorry, I guess I expected you to be out actually doing something."

"How's your client's daughter feeling?" he asked, knowing I had been to the hospital to talk to Terry.

"Not good. She just had a surgery to implant a device that can keep her alive for a while, but not long term."

He shook his head. "Shit." It was an unlikely one-word sentence to show a soft side of someone, but he had just pulled it off. Then, "Come on back."

Once we were in his office, I told him that I brought Terry Aimonetti's power of attorney with me, that would allow her financial records to be examined.

He nodded. "Good. Give it to me."

I ignored the request. "What did you think of Laufer?"

I asked. He hadn't given me a chance to talk about Laufer after the interrogation, and I still wanted to.

"I thought he was a sniveling, chickenshit nerd. Other than that, I liked him."

"You want to know what I thought?" I asked.

"Not even a little bit. But I've got a feeling you're going to tell me anyway, so make it quick. There's no jury here."

"I thought he was lying."

"About what?"

"Everything he said. I think it was all bullshit."

"Well, since you lawyers wrote the book on bullshit, you might know it when you hear it. Tell me why."

"A few reasons. First of all, he talked too much. He told you much more than he had to; you just weren't that scary. He didn't have to describe to Emerson or to you what happened at the bar that night; you would have no way of knowing that he was there. If he was so scared of Murray that he looked around in a panic when you mentioned his name, you guys would be the last people he'd tell it to."

"He was afraid of losing his job," Novack said.

I shook my head. "I don't buy it. I checked into his job; he teaches two courses, an hour a week for each, at that junior high. Makes maybe six grand total. If he loses that job, he can go work at McDonald's and step up an economic class."

"Keep going," Novack said.

"Okay. Then there was the story itself. I don't believe that Murray would have knifed the guy, come back into the bar, and finished his beer. But maybe he would have; maybe he's a ruthless sociopath who operates illogically."

"I've seen killers who would do exactly that."

I nodded. "I believe it, and maybe Murray stayed there. But Laufer didn't."

"What do you mean?"

"Laufer said he saw Murray come back into the bar, finish his beer, and then order two more. There is no way that a—I believe you used the term 'chickenshit'—guy like Laufer watches a murder, and then sits around drinking beers in the same room with the guy who did it. Especially since that guy still has a knife, and had no qualms about using it."

Novack looked interested, and it was more than two minutes since he had insulted me. I was enjoying having the floor, a lot more than I had enjoyed talking to that three-judge panel.

"There's one more thing," I said. "I'm not sure if it meant anything, but I noticed it, and it's worth mentioning."

"What's that?"

"You asked Laufer if the name Hennessey meant anything to him, and he said, 'No. Who is he?' Well, how did he know Hennessey was a male?"

Novack didn't say anything for a while, then finally told me he didn't agree with what I had said. "Which part?" I asked.

"Starting with when you opened your mouth."

I wasn't in the mood to be put off, so I pressed him to explain himself.

He nodded. "Okay, he gave up the information fairly easily. Maybe the job was important to him. Maybe he wants to have it on his résumé. Or maybe there's a female student in the class that he has the hots for. Or maybe he needs the money. The point is that he's teaching the class, so for whatever reason he wants to be there."

He continued. "Or maybe it's not the job at all. Maybe he wants to see a cold-blooded killer put behind bars. He could have been scared to say something all these years, and we gave him the chance to unburden himself. You ever see someone sliced to death?"

"No," I said.

"Good. If you have the chance to see it someday, don't.

As far as Laufer coming back into the bar and watching Murray drink three beers, maybe he was stunned and afraid to leave, because Murray might suspect that he saw too much. Or maybe he is lying about that; maybe he took off and ran, but is embarrassed to tell us. Doesn't much matter either way."

"He knew Hennessey was a male," I said.

Novack shook his head. "When I asked him if he heard of Hennessey, he said, 'No, who is he?' What should he have said, 'Who is he or she?' Or, 'Who is it?' Sorry, Jamie, but people don't talk like that. I was a cop investigating a murder; it was natural for him to assume I was asking him about a male. He'd be right ninety-nine percent of the time."

"Okay, I've heard enough," I said.

"Don't stop me, I'm on a roll, and I haven't got to the important part yet. Why would he lie?"

"To get revenge on Murray for something."

"So he took a job he didn't want, for no money, in the hope that the cops would show up and ask him something that would give him a chance to get revenge? Don't forget, he didn't come to us. We went to him."

I could have pushed it further, but I wasn't going to get him to agree with me, and I was no longer sure that I agreed with me. He had given me a good lesson in police work, should I ever decide to become a cop. And since I was about to become an unemployed lawyer, that might not be a bad idea. Except for the part about the danger involved.

"Where do you stand on finding Nolan Murray?" If Novack believed Laufer, then I assumed he was out there looking for Murray.

"I'm getting a report from the computer crimes people this afternoon," he said.

Novack reached into his desk drawer and took out a photograph. It looked like a mug shot of a very scary guy.

"This is Raymond Hennessey. Show it to your client, and see if she ID's him."

"What have you learned about him?"

"He was a hit man; one of the best. Worked mostly out of Chicago, but would go anywhere if the price was right."

"What do you mean 'was' a hit man? Is he dead?"

Novack nodded. "More than six years ago. He died a month before Charlie Harrison." Then he paused. "At least that's what the computer says."

Nolan Murray thought of it as a field trip . . . a class outing. Of course, he was the only member of the class, or at least the only person there to learn.

He was on the public tour conducted at the Limerick power plant in Montgomery County, Pennsylvania, about thirty miles northwest of Philadelphia. It was less than a three-hour drive for Murray, well worth his time.

Nolan had been there before, when he was deciding whether to put the grand plan into operation. He had seen what he needed to see then, but felt a refresher course couldn't hurt. It was unlikely that there had been major structural changes, but as someone who would soon be in charge of the plant, Nolan felt he should check it out again, just in case.

He wore a disguise of sorts, a mustache and a baseball cap pulled down fairly low. Nothing fancy or elaborate, but it would suffice, since nobody would have any idea that's how he would be spending his day off from his regular job, anyway.

There were seventeen people with him on the one-hour tour, and Nolan amused himself by listening in on their conversations, to try and determine why they were there, and more important, where they were from.

By the end of the tour, he figured that eleven were tourists, though why anyone would want to visit a nuclear power plant on their vacation eluded him. The other six, the ones that might be dead or dying in a couple of weeks, were local.

There had been some minor changes in the place, but nothing that would influence Nolan's plan. What Nolan really cared about was the computer system and its security, and he already knew all he needed to know about it. He couldn't help smiling when the tour guide talked about the new state-of-the-art computer systems that were put in just eighteen months before. That system made all of what would happen possible, and soon Nolan would be giving the FBI a demonstration in how it worked.

Peter Lampley was waiting for him when he got back. Having him teach those classes at the school under his real name, Kevin Laufer, had paid off. Novack had paid him a visit, as Nolan knew he would, and Laufer had done his job.

"What did you learn, Peter?" Nolan asked, following the rule he had set to always use the assumed names.

"Novack knows about Hennessey," Lampley said. "He asked me if I had ever heard of him."

"How did you respond?"

"I told him I never heard the name."

Nolan had been surprised that Sheryl knew Hennessey's name. Charlie must have ignored his instructions and mentioned it, but it was too late to make him pay for his indiscretion. There was unfortunately a one-time limit to how often somebody could be killed.

But this represented a problem, at a time when Nolan didn't need any. Hennessey was an important part of the operation, a problem solver in the physical world that Nolan did not have a backup for. It was unlikely that Novack would find him, at least not in the next two weeks, but it was always possible.

It was also very unlikely that, if found, Hennessey would talk. For one thing, that would run counter to his attitude and reputation. For another, Hennessey was unaware of Nolan's identity, or the location of his operation, so he couldn't put Novack on the right track even if he wanted to.

Or so Nolan thought. But he recognized that if he could be wrong about Sheryl Harrison knowing Hennessey's name he could be just as wrong about Hennessey knowing nothing about Nolan's operation; and that could be a disaster.

Nolan made a quick decision; he would call Hennessey in, thus taking him out of Novack's reach.

Of course, Nolan was not the type to call Hennessey up and say, "Hey, Ray, come on over and we'll hang out." Instead he contacted him as he always had, through his computer, and the message was, *Follow the GPS in your phone. Leave at 5:45 P.M.*

Hennessey was not a tech guy; he actually doubted he would even own a computer if not for his job, and the messages he received through it. He had bought the cell phone that his employer told him to buy, but never used it for anything other than phone calls.

He was sitting in a diner on Route 46, having coffee and a burger, when he felt the phone vibrate in his pocket. He reflexively ate another large mouthful, since he had a feeling that whatever the message was, it was going to interrupt his dinner.

He hadn't even known the phone had a GPS, but when he looked at it, there it was, a single destination in Garfield that had been inserted into the memory. He ate another couple of bites, left some cash on the table, and went to his car.

Hennessey basically knew where the address was, but he decided to let the GPS guide him there, in case his boss had programmed it in a way that the real destination was different than the one listed.

Hennessey had no idea what this could be about; it was the first time he had ever received instructions like this. He assumed it was in some way connected to his employer's recent comment that the operation was approaching a "sensitive time," but there was no way to be sure of that, or what it meant if true. All he could do was follow the instructions he was given; doing so had always proved profitable in the past.

The other possibility was that it was somehow tied into Novack, and his conversations with Sheryl Harrison and that lawyer. But he basically discounted that; after what he had done to her, and threatened to do to her daughter, he doubted that Sheryl would break her six-year silence.

In terms of what was going on, he would know when he would know. Hennessey wasn't the type to worry very much; he would wait for his boss to give him the lay of the land. If there was trouble, he knew how to handle it.

The GPS took Hennessey on a twenty-minute ride, ending at a small strip mall in a run-down area. Three of the stores in it were closed, with FOR LEASE signs covering the windows. Hennessey had a hunch that there was not exactly a bidding war going on for the locations.

The specific address was one of the empty stores, and the outline of the removed sign above the door identified it as having been a pizzeria. There seemed to be no one inside, and for a moment Hennessey thought that the address might be a mistake. He rejected that notion quickly enough, though; if they made a mistake, it would be the first he was aware of.

He knocked on the door and got no answer, then tried it and found out it was open. He went inside and looked around, confirming that there was nobody there. He would just have to wait.

Then Hennessey saw, on the counter, a cell phone. It looked exactly like his own, so much so that he felt for his pocket to make sure he hadn't placed it on the counter and forgotten. He hadn't; this was a different phone, but identical to his.

He walked over to it, and was startled when it started to ring. Certain that his employer had left it there for him as the way to deliver another message, he waited two rings and then picked it up to answer it.

He pressed the button to answer the call, and was dead before the connection was made. The explosion was sufficient to destroy the place, as well as the adjacent store on each side.

If Mike Janssen had ever felt this helpless, he couldn't remember when. He was essentially tied to his desk, waiting for his army of agents to come up with promising leads. But they simply were not coming in, and Janssen was beyond frustrated.

Janssen had always been more comfortable out in the field, and that's where he wanted to be for this investigation. And he would go out there, if something would materialize that was worth his time.

In his mind, the failure to go public with the danger was not only immoral, but was crippling the investigation. A huge portion of crimes are solved by tips from the general public. In this case the public would be highly motivated, and they would inundate the Bureau with information. And information was something that Janssen knew was in short supply.

So all he could do was sit in his office and sift through reports that told him nothing. That's when he wasn't fielding calls from his bosses, all the way up to the White House, inquiring as to what progress was being made.

As time went on, those "inquiries" became more demanding, and the people doing the inquiring became more agitated. There were many lives at stake, and many political careers. And Janssen couldn't tell which was causing more agitation.

Tammy, or whoever it was that was utilizing the little girl's voice, was not going away. She seemed to be motivated by money, yet so far hadn't received a dime. There hadn't even been a real effort to get any money; the acts so far were set up as demonstrations. The real monetary demand was still to come, which meant that the threatened act accompanying it would be much bigger and much deadlier.

And if by some chance money wasn't the goal, if perhaps it was the power that the acts provided her, there was still no reason to stop.

Because so far Tammy was undefeated.

Sheryl physically pulled back when I put the photograph on the table. She recoiled, like I would do if I came upon a spider, or a snake. For a moment I thought she was going to cry, but she held it together, showing incredible courage.

Like always.

I wanted to hold her, but I didn't. I missed the moment, the chance to be more than observer and actually help.

Like always.

"You found him?" she asked, after a short while.

"No. But Novack has identified him. The computers show that he died a short while before Charlie."

She looked at me strangely, and then shook her head. "He didn't."

"I know. Novack will find him."

"And Karen is protected?"

"Yes. I was there. There are police everywhere."

"Did you see Karen? Did you talk to her?"

"No, she had just come out of surgery. They wouldn't let me go in. But they assured me she's fine."

"She's beautiful," Sheryl said.

"I know. I've seen her picture. And I've seen her mother."

Sheryl smiled. "I was going to get my hair done before you came, but who has time?"

"You definitely should do it before the parole hearing, and maybe a manicure and pedicure." I smiled to show her I was joking, in case she didn't know. Nothing like a good solitary confinement prison joke to lighten a mood.

"We have a chance in the hearing?" she asked.

"I don't know yet; it really depends on what Novack comes up with."

"It's a week away."

I nodded. "Believe me, I know." Then I added, "We'll be ready," although I had no idea if we would or not.

"Don't bullshit me, Harvard."

I smiled. "I don't usually. It was just a weak moment."

"Harvard, if anything happens to me, you know what to do, right?"

"Nothing is going to happen to you until we're ready for it to happen, Sheryl."

"But if it does, you know what to do, right?"

She was telling me that she might have a way to kill herself, even in her current circumstances. "Don't do anything, Sheryl."

"Okay," she said, "I won't."

"And don't bullshit me."

She smiled. "I don't usually. It was just a weak moment."

I didn't know where to go with it; she obviously had some plan she was working on, and I had neither the power to find out what it was, nor to stop it. Her ability to die was what I had been fighting for all this time, yet hearing that it was possible scared the shit out of me.

I assume she was reading my mind, because she put her hand on mine and said, "You can't fix this, Jamie. Don't use up your energy trying."

I wanted to tell her how hard all of this was for me, but it would have sounded stupid and self-centered, because it was. When all of this was finally over, either she or her daughter would have died, and my biggest problem would be where to work.

But I knew one thing; wherever I worked, I was going to refuse pro-bono cases. Give me a boring contract law case where nobody I cared about died, any day of the week.

"Mr. Wagner? Can you come with me, please?" It was the guard, standing at the door.

"What's the matter?"

"You have an urgent call from Lieutenant Novack."

"Maybe he found Hennessey," Sheryl said.

I nodded, and told her I'd be back to tell her whatever I learned.

The guard led me down one hallway, and then another, finally pointing at a room with the door open. I went in, and saw that the hold button on the phone was flashing. I closed the door behind me, and picked up the phone.

"Novack?"

"Yeah. There was an explosion in Garfield this morning, in a strip mall."

"I heard about it," I said. "They said on the radio that it was a gas leak, and that one person was killed."

"It wasn't a leak," he said. "And the dead guy was Hennessey."

The Predator drone was not exactly a secret weapon. Any casual reader of newspapers knew that these unmanned aerial vehicles were widely used in the wars in Iraq and Afghanistan to locate the enemy and often attack them with deadly munitions.

Less commonly known, but also far from a secret, was the fact that the same drones, minus the armaments, were used to help patrol the U.S. border with Mexico. They dramatically reduced the amount of border guards necessary to do the job, and acted quite literally as the eyes of the border patrol. A lone border agent, sitting at a terminal, could watch the images fed in by the drones' cameras, and dispatch patrols where needed.

But what most people didn't have any sense of was their size. The common perception was that they were very small, almost like toy planes. It was this size, most believed, that allowed them to fly relatively undetected, just another bird in the sky.

The truth was that the Predator B, a common model, had a wingspan of sixty-six feet, was thirty-six feet long, and weighed ten thousand pounds. It was an amazing engineering feat that this five-ton vehicle was as mobile and agile as it was.

But it was not without its deficiencies. When it was far from its base, the terrain often caused it to lose direct contact with its operator. It compensated for this by bouncing its signals off a satellite.

Also, when the Predator communicated with the ground, its signals were not encrypted. This was a flaw in the design, an inexcusable one, since encryption was so common. Every financial website, for example, and most online retailers, used encryption for security. An engineering marvel like the Predator should certainly have had it.

Both of these flaws left the Predator vulnerable to hackers. Our enemies in Iraq, for instance, had success in hacking into the systems, thereby sometimes enabling them to know where the Predators were, and what they were watching.

If the relatively unsophisticated Iraqi insurgents had that kind of success, it was a piece of cake for Nolan Murray and his team. And the Predator B, serial number A256489, became the vehicle through which Nolan Murray would impart his next lesson.

This time there was no difficulty in Tammy getting the call through to Mike Janssen. Janssen was waiting for it, had been waiting for days, and his team was prepared to deal with whatever emergency arose, no matter where.

"Hi, it's me, Tammy."

The Bureau psy-ops people had not come up with any way that Janssen could effectively deal with the situation, no way of talking that could likely influence the outcome. What Tammy had to say was preordained, as if part of a play. She was delivering a message, the content of which Janssen was believed to have no chance of influencing.

So they told him to keep his voice cold, measured, aloof. If the caller's goal was to get enjoyment out of toying with

Janssen, with exercising power over him, that would be the best way to keep that enjoyment to a minimum.

"What do you want?" Janssen asked.

"Are you mad at me?" The little girl's voice was petulant, hurt.

"What do you want?" he repeated.

"You know what I want, silly. I want money."

"We're prepared to talk about that."

"All you want to do is talk," Tammy said. "Ooh, you make me so mad. It makes me want to crash another plane."

"That's not necessary," Janssen said.

"Is too. Is too! I'm gonna crash one. That'll show you."

"Where?"

"Texas. Oh, and Mr. Janssen?" Tammy said, her voice softening.

"What?"

Suddenly it wasn't Tammy's voice anymore, but that of a man speaking in a tough no-nonsense manner. It was filtered through a synthesizer, and sounded nothing like Nolan Murray. "This will give you something to remember, but next time it will be for real."

The call was disconnected, and the government apparatus swung swiftly and efficiently into action. All planes still on the ground in Texas, as well as those preparing to take off for there from airports in other states, were not allowed to take to the air.

There were sixty-eight flights airborne at that moment in the air over Texas, forty-three were commercial flights, eleven were private, and fourteen were military aircraft. All were ordered to immediately land, and within a half hour all were safely on the ground.

All Janssen could then do was wait. After the crash on the amusement park ride, he had no illusions that disaster had been diverted. He knew better than to think there was any chance that Tammy's plan had been thwarted that easily.

At that moment, the Predator B, serial number A256489, had finished its run over the border, and was on its way back to base. It was currently five miles south of Crystal City, about a hundred and twenty miles from San Antonio.

At a 135 miles an hour top speed, it would take under an hour to get to its destination. The operator on the ground, watching the computer, believed that it was on course back to base. After twenty-five minutes, he finally realized that the pictures it was sending back were inconsistent with the route it should have been on.

It took another seventeen minutes for the word to get to the command center, and another five before anyone connected the off-course drone with the Homeland Security emergency that had grounded airplanes throughout the state.

The only option at that point would have been to shoot it down, but the Army had no way of doing that. Not considering its location, and the fact that all of its airborne assets were grounded.

The operator could only watch the pictures the drone was sending back. They were crystal clear, in high definition, and he could actually see the horrified, panic-stricken faces of the tourists at the Alamo as the drone bore down on them, and crashed in their midst.

Forty-one people died, and another twenty-eight were injured in varying degrees, eleven of them critical.

The man's voice that replaced Tammy had told Janssen that he would give him something to remember, but Janssen had not made the connection.

Until it was too late.

And now the entire country would again remember the Alamo.

"My fellow Americans, I come before you tonight to tell you that we are under attack." With those words from the president of the United States, in a national address to the nation, any chance Jamie Wagner had of maintaining press coverage of Sheryl's case came to an end.

"It has been an insidious form of attack, technological in nature, but deadly in its result. When I campaigned for this office, I promised that I would always be straight with you, and that's what I'm going to be tonight."

He proceeded to explain the origins of the three incidents, the Charlotte plane crash, the Disneyland ride crash, and the Predator drone crash, and to show that the three were the work of a single entity. He didn't mention the childlike Tammy voice, and he withheld some other facts as well, as Janssen thought it would be wise to keep those things known only to the investigators.

Also at Janssen's suggestion, the president talked of the need for the public to get involved and to report any suspicions they might have to a special number that the FBI had set up. He talked about the way Americans come together in a crisis to defeat whatever enemy was before them, and this time would be no exception.

And then he talked about our technological strengths, saying that our expertise in this area was second to none. He said extraordinary measures were being taken to ensure that our computers were secure, and he was confident that those efforts would be successful.

He was lying. He knew as he was speaking that the military had tested the security of not only its aircraft, but also its Predator drones. They had done this before the attack in Texas, and had specifically tested Predator B, serial number A256489. It had been judged secure, and then within days had been coopted by the terrorists.

The implications of that were chilling, so much so that the president felt it exceeded the limit of what his "straight talk" might include. Because in the drone case, we assumed they were coming, we took defensive measures, and the enemy still prevailed.

How, then, could we stop it next time?

Janssen watched the speech with mixed feelings. On the one hand, he was glad that his advice was finally being heeded, albeit mostly for the wrong reasons. The president and his team felt that the lid could not be successfully kept on the secret for much longer, and that it was far better politically to be the ones to tell the American people, rather than have it come out through the press.

In fact, in the hours before the president spoke, there was rampant speculation as to what he was going to say, and much of it was fairly accurate. The press was on the story, far too late for them to take any bows, but the administration wanted to come out ahead of it, to the extent that they still could.

Janssen was also glad that the public would now be a source of investigative tips. Someone, somewhere, knew the perpetrators, and if they could connect the dots and come forward, the chances of arrests grew exponentially.

But there would be a negative component to the revelations, Janssen knew. When people get scared, they get irrational, and things can turn ugly very easily. Especially when more attacks follow.

And that was the other part of this that made Janssen uneasy, and a little scared himself. There was always the chance that the public exposure could speed up the timetable of the perpetrators. Janssen had long felt that there was something big coming, something which the killers hoped would net them far more than the money they had so far been leaving on the table.

And the truth was that Janssen and his team had no idea where the attack would come from, what it would be directed against, or how to stop it.

After the speech, the administration sent a small army of people out to deal with the media, to supply the details that the president had not gone into. The story they told made the situation seem that much more dire, because of the lack of specificity as to how people could protect themselves.

If computers were not safe, and computers were everywhere, then how could anyone hope to stay safe?

Novack and Captain Donovan had no illusions about getting federal help. While they originally rejected the idea of going to the FBI and trying to take advantage of their cybercrime capabilities, they hadn't taken the idea off the table.

Now, with a declared national emergency totally relying on those same capabilities, there was not a big enough table in the world to accommodate the requests of a local police department. The FBI had one mission, and one only, and that was to catch the hackers that were killing and terrorizing people.

Even Donovan, who had been less than eager for his department to even peripherally get involved in the Sheryl Harrison situation, was aware that the investigation had increased dramatically in importance.

Hennessey's murder, plus the discovery that Charlie Harrison had participated in other frauds in the same jurisdiction, using the IDs in the safe-deposit box, had upped the ante considerably. Donovan did not have to be coaxed into putting more resources into the investigation. Anders, Novack's partner, was now assigned to the case exclusively, as were two other teams, who would work under Novack's direction.

Most important, Donovan gave instructions to Emerson that the Computer Crime Division was to drop anything that wasn't an emergency and devote itself to the case. Local police departments are not exactly overstaffed in this area, so it put considerable pressure on Emerson, Andrew Garrett, and their small team.

The decision was made not to go public with Hennessey's identity or murder, at least not at that point. It would give them something to hold back in the investigation, and with all that was going on in the news, it wouldn't get the notice they would have wanted anyway. There was time for that later, if they chose to release it.

Novack met with Emerson and Garrett to get an update on the computer search for Nolan Murray. An old schooler, Novack believed that Murray would be found by old-fashioned street work, but he looked to Emerson and Garrett to give him a head start.

He invited Jamie Wagner to sit in on the meeting, though it was clear that both Emerson and Anders considered it inappropriate to have an outsider there. Novack was sticking to his promise to keep Wagner as involved as possible, in return for access to Sheryl Harrison. That access had already paid off by getting Hennessey's name, and entry into the safe-deposit box.

Novack would never have admitted it, but another motivation for having Wagner there was the parole hearing, which was less than a week away. He had come to like Sheryl, and to sympathize with her plight. Even more important, he was now positive she was innocent, and he had helped to put her behind bars. It was an error that needed to be rectified, regardless of the situation with her daughter.

"Nolan Murray barely exists," said Emerson, starting the presentation. "He has no driver's license, no home, no birth or death records. He has not filed tax returns, or worked at a job. He has not received medical care, been married, or ever gotten so much as a traffic ticket."

"So no Nolan Murray exists anywhere?" Wagner asked, instantly breaking his promise to Novack that he would just listen and not ask questions. "It can't be that uncommon a name."

Nobody seemed to mind, probably because the question was logical, and Garrett answered it. "We're going by Laufer's estimate of Murray's age, and the fact that he thought he might be from Maine. It's very inexact, but that doesn't really matter, because we have the right guy."

"How do you know that?" Novack asked.

"Because, as I said, he 'barely' exists. We found a Nolan Murray who has no record of himself anywhere, except in one place. He took a class at Bowdoin College in advanced computer science eleven years ago. He wasn't a student there, and in his record it shows that the grade was sent to the University of Maine, to fulfill a graduation requirement."

"You checked with the University of Maine?" Novack asked.

Emerson nodded. "Yes, they have no record of a Nolan Murray ever going there, and also no record of having received the grade that Bowdoin sent."

Garrett jumped back in. "So it has to be our guy. He has systematically erased his own existence. Just like he created people online, he's made himself disappear. Except he made that one mistake; he missed the Bowdoin grade."

"Does the Bowdoin record give an address? Any personal information at all?"

Emerson nodded. "There's a form that Murray filled out, showing personal information. The Social Security number he gave doesn't exist; either he provided a false number, or he's since erased it. I suspect it was the latter, since he probably didn't have all this planned that far back. But maybe he did; this is a smart guy. There's an address as well, in Damariscotta, Maine."

"We checked," Garrett said, anticipating the question. "He doesn't live there now."

Novack turned to Wagner. "You ever been to Maine?"

"Yes," Wagner said. "I went to camp there as a kid."

"Good. You can show me around."

I have to admit I was a little nervous about the trip to Maine. We were flying from LaGuardia to Portland, an hour-long trip that I had made a number of times. But I had never made it after the president of the United States said that terrorists could take over the plane's computer.

One thing was for sure; getting a seat would be no problem. Airline traffic in the immediate aftermath of the president's address had dropped 71 percent. It was just one part of an economic downturn that was sure to get much worse.

No one knew what to be afraid of, so people made the logical decision to do as little as possible. And when people do nothing, they don't spend money. Businesses then cut back or shut down, laying off employees, so people don't earn money to spend anyway. The situation had economists predicting a deep recession, perhaps even a depression, if it was not resolved quickly.

The political repercussions were coming fast and furious as well. While there was some banding together of politicians and citizens to unite and fight the common enemy, the fact that it was an unseen enemy made that difficult.

There was also a sense of outrage that the secret had

been withheld from the public for so long. Families of victims of both the Disneyland tragedy and the drone crash at the Alamo were coming forward, furious that their loved ones were sacrificed in this manner. Had they been armed with the information they should have had, they would not have gone on their vacations, and they would be alive and safe.

Ethnic and political groups were being scapegoated, aided and abetted by the Internet. Outlandish speculation and conspiracy theories would appear and then spread like wildfire online. The authorities would rebut them, but ineffectively, since no one trusted the authorities.

It seemed to me that pretty much the only two people in America that weren't in a state of panic over the terrorist danger were Sheryl and Novack. Sheryl, of course, had a mounting panic of her own. The word from Terry at the hospital about Karen was not great; while the new device was doing its job, it was a short-term fix. Of course, nobody could say exactly what "short term" meant.

Novack just seemed oblivious to the danger. He had a job to do and he was going to do it. If something happened to prevent that, like his plane crashing, then there was nothing he could do about it. But he was not about to stop himself out of fear.

My natural reaction would be to curl up in the fetal position in my apartment with headphones on, not to listen to music, but to drown out the world. But something prevented me from doing that. I don't think it was courage; it's more likely it was potential guilt. Sheryl was depending on me to be ready for the parole hearing, and I simply wasn't going to abandon her.

We met at the mostly empty airport at eight in the morning. I had come up with another legal Hail Mary pass to throw, and I would work on it on the plane. Hopefully it would distract me and make me less scared.

I was going to petition the governor for a commutation of Sheryl's sentence. Before the president's address, when the last poll about Sheryl's situation was conducted, a healthy majority felt she should have the right to give her heart to Karen.

In New Jersey the majority was even greater, and I figured it would be a natural thing for a politician like the governor to try and do something popular with the voters. But in any event, just like with the parole board, Novack and I would have to come up with evidence that could provide a political cover for him to act.

Which was why I was on the plane to Portland, and why I didn't take a normal breath until the wheels touched down. We rented a car, and made the one hour and ten minute drive to Damariscotta. There was almost no traffic along the route; it seemed as if the entire country had shut down.

I had actually visited Damariscotta once; we had stopped there for lunch after a camp whitewater rafting trip. It's not the quintessential New England town; it's not pristine, with the smell of potpourri in the air. But it has more than its share of charm, sitting on the water in a beautiful setting, and it feels more real than most similarly sized towns.

We went straight to the address listed as Murray's home on his Bowdoin transcript. It was on Route 215, about five minutes from the heart of town. The house was large, with probably ten more rooms than needed, unless the inhabitants included the Maine National Guard. It sat on at least twenty acres, which did not seem unusual for the surroundings. Were I in the mood for irony, I would have reflected on the glee with which New Yorkers reacted to getting an apartment with a three-by-six-foot balcony.

The woman who answered the door identified herself as Mrs. Danforth, and was probably in her late sixties. She had lived in that house for just three years, having moved to the town to be near her children, once her husband died.

She believed that the previous owner had also only lived there a short time, but she wasn't sure. She had never heard of Nolan Murray, but said that we should ask her daughter, who had lived in the town for fifteen years.

Her daughter Julie was at work, but Mrs. Danforth said we could talk to her there, and she offered to call her and arrange it. We expressed our appreciation, turned down a second offer of tea, and were on our way.

Julie Danforth worked as a waitress at the King Elder's Pub, on Main Street, a two story pub-restaurant with a look and a menu so appealing that I decided I could eat every meal for the rest of my life there. She was expecting us and didn't even ask to see Novack's identification. If her mother said we were okay, that was clearly good enough for her. Of course, her mother hadn't asked for ID either.

These were trusting people.

She yelled out to a guy I assumed was her boss, telling him that she was taking us upstairs to talk. She led us to a second-floor room, and we sat in a booth. Another waitress brought us coffee and assorted pastries, and I decided that maybe I was cut out for police work after all.

"We're looking for a man named Nolan Murray," Novack said. "We believe he used to live around here."

Julie thought for a few moments, and then brightened. "Nolan! Sure, I remember him. Strange guy . . . what ever happened to him?"

"That's what we're trying to find out. What can you tell us?"

"Well, I'd have to think about it; it's been a while. But he used to come in here. He'd have coffee, or a beer, and read."

"What did he read?" Novack asked.

"I think some kind of textbooks, but I'm not really sure. We sort of let people be around here, you know?"

"Did he have family here?" I asked.

"I really didn't know him very well, but now that I think of it, I think he lived with his mother, no, it was his father. He died, and Nolan must have moved away, because he stopped coming by."

"And you have no idea where he went?" Novack asked.

"No, I really don't. Sorry."

"Could you describe him for us?"

She said she'd try, and proceeded to do so. Unfortunately, it was a fairly generic description that could have fit a half dozen people in the room, including me.

But it seemed clear that the person who lived here was the Nolan Murray that we were looking for. The person who had effectively erased his entire personal, online history.

Except the course at Bowdoin.

As far as we knew it was the first mistake he had made, maybe the only one. We just had to figure out a way to take advantage of it.

Darren Seibert's dread was about to become his reality. Seibert was the CEO of ITC, short for Inter-Technology Corporation, a service organization that provided computer and network service and troubleshooting to a large number of clients, big and small.

Many of these companies had their own, substantial IT departments, but still found it cost-effective to hire ITC on a consultancy basis, mostly for troubleshooting. Seibert's company had a well-deserved outstanding reputation, and a long list of satisfied clients.

When Seibert heard the president's speech to the nation, he was one of many Americans who felt fear, but his was for a very different reason. Two of the companies hit by the terrorist attack, Southern Airlines and the Disney theme park company, were clients of ITC. More specifically, an invasion of the computers of those two companies had resulted in tragic loss of life, and Inter-Technology provided computer service to both companies.

That in itself was not proof of any connection between ITC and the attacks, since they were just two of many clients. But it was extraordinarily worrisome; if ITC were to be implicated in any way, even indirectly, if would be a disaster for the company, as clients would leave them in droves.

There was danger even if no connection was made. If the public simply became aware of the fact that both attacked companies were ITC clients, that perception alone could be catastrophic.

So Seibert set out to preempt the issue, by checking everything there was to be checked, and thereby arming himself with the facts, should the issue ever be raised by anyone. It would not be easy, since he would essentially be trying to prove a negative, but he would leave no stone unturned.

With that in mind, he put one of his top analysts, Sean Camby, on the project. Camby had been with ITC for all fifteen years of its existence, and he had Seibert's complete trust. He could be counted on to do a thorough and complete analysis, and to do so in total secrecy. Seibert was so worried about word of the issue leaking out that he felt it necessary to conceal it from his own employees.

Seibert was in a meeting with his executive committee when his assistant came in and placed a note in front of him. It simply said, "Camby must see you. Urgent."

He quickly ended the meeting, trying to conceal the turmoil raging inside him. Camby would not have sent such a message if he had not found something, and if he had discovered something important, it would by definition have the potential to destroy the business that Seibert had spent fifteen years building.

He had Camby come up immediately, then closed the door and steeled himself for what he was about to hear.

"Remember about five months ago, when the big crunch hit?"

Seibert nodded. Around that time there had been a perfect storm of computer problems for ITC's clients. Some of them were normal in nature, system glitches that all seemed to happen at once. There was also a virus going around that caused havoc with some of the systems, and some treacherous weather in the Southeast, which caused further problems.

Camby continued. "We were overloaded, and put on some temporary help, I think it was fourteen people. Just for about three weeks."

"I remember," Seibert said.

"One of them was a guy who came highly recommended from Bill Sherman over at Cyber-Systems. Had a terrific résumé, completely knew what he was doing, so we put him on. We were just using him to assist an exec engineer, Collins, and he was overqualified for that."

Seibert wanted to hear all of it; he needed to know every aspect of what Camby was about to tell him. He just wished Camby were telling it faster. "What was the guy's name?"

"Murray. Nolan Murray," Seibert said. "Anyway, things were so crazed that we were putting these temps on, and rechecking their background on the fly. It turned out that Murray's résumé didn't check out; we couldn't find any trace of him when we tried. And the Sherman reco was a fake; Sherman said he never heard of the guy."

"So we fired him, or at least we would have if he hadn't stopped showing up. I wasn't privy to all of this at the time, but Collins figured he had learned that we were on to him and split. And that was that."

"That wasn't that," Seibert said.

"I'm afraid it may not have been," Camby said. "He was on two pieces of business in the week he was here. Southern Airlines and Disney."

Camby had placed the bomb on the desk, and now Seibert had to decide whether to detonate it. There was a chance, in fact a reasonable one, that this was just a coincidence. Certainly there was no evidence that this Murray guy was the killer, or that he had access to the computers that were invaded.

ITC could do some investigating on their own, hire outside investigators and counsel, and dig deeply into the situation and Murray's background. Perhaps they would come up with proof that Murray was not involved in the terrorism, that he was just a guy willing to tell lies about his background to get a job.

But many people had already died, and many more could die in the future if the terrorists were not caught. It was a situation that was being referred to as the greatest threat to national security since World War II, and it was already swallowing the economy.

If there was any chance at all that Murray was responsible, and if Seibert had kept the information secret, then Seibert would stand alongside Murray as two of the greatest villains in American history. That simply could not be allowed to happen.

"We need to call the FBI," Seibert said.

Sheryl hung on every word I said. I was telling her about the trip to Maine, and what we were learning about Nolan Murray, and I could see the excitement building in her mind. She had accepted the possible way to win this thing was to prove her innocence, at least to the parole board's standard, and we were making progress in that direction.

The big step that allowed her to finally tell the truth was the same thing that caused her to withhold that truth all those years. She had kept silent to protect Karen, but now the simple fact was that unless she left prison, Karen was going to die. So telling the truth became the only way she could protect her daughter, which was all she ever wanted to do in the first place.

I found myself getting excited as well, so much so that I hadn't even been nervous on the plane ride back. If we had more time, I would think we really had a chance.

As always in these situations, the dynamic with Sheryl was a weird one. We were sharing the excitement; in a different setting we'd be giving each other high-fives. But at the end of the day, if our hopes were realized, she was going to die. And while I fully understood the situation intellectually, I simply did not want that to happen.

I had come to that realization when I began to understand my feelings for Sheryl. It's stating the obvious that you don't want someone you love to die. The irony here was that love was also the same reason that Sheryl wanted to die, since doing so would save her daughter.

As I was telling her the news, I was very careful about the emphasis I put on it. If I built up the positives, then she'd be hopeful and less inclined to preemptively take her own life, in whatever way she had alluded to. But then I might be unfairly raising those hopes, only to be dashed later.

The stakes had escalated, even if she didn't see it that way. This had started as a woman trying to save her daughter by giving up her own life. But at that point she was giving up a life that was going to be spent behind bars. Now, if we succeeded and she went through with her plan, she'd be giving up a life that could be spent in freedom.

The difference could not be overstated.

Of course, I didn't have the guts to state it at all.

She must have been aware of it, but if it gave her pause, she certainly didn't show it.

I left Sheryl, after promising to keep her informed of everything on as timely a basis as I could. Once I was outside, I called Columbia Presbyterian Hospital, and asked to be connected to Dr. Bud Jenkins's office.

Much to my surprise, I was talking to Dr. Jenkins himself within thirty seconds. "Hello, Jamie. I expected to hear from you sooner than this."

"Why?"

"Your mother said you'd be calling."

My parents had mentioned at dinner that Dr. Jenkins, who they described as a talented heart surgeon, would be the type to help Sheryl on the medical side of her quest.

I thought it was a casual mention, but it clearly wasn't. My mother knew I'd pick up on it, and she paved the way.

Thanks, Mom.

"Did she tell you why I'd be calling?" I asked.

"In general terms. Come on in and let's talk about it."

"When?"

"Now is good. Later not so good."

I drove straight to Columbia Presbyterian, which is located on West 168th Street in Manhattan, an easy drive down from the George Washington Bridge, and not too far from my apartment.

Once again there was very little traffic; people were staying inside and hunkering down. As media outlets were falling all over themselves to list the things that were run by computer, and the disastrous things that could happen from those computers being compromised, it just seemed safer not to be out and about.

Even the hospital seemed mostly empty when I got there, and parking spaces were plentiful. When I got to Dr. Jenkins's office, his assistant said that he was in a consultation, but would be with me shortly.

It took only ten minutes, and I was ushered in to see him. We introduced ourselves, and I said, "Seems kind of slow today."

"Not for me," he said. "I have my third surgery coming up." He then explained, "Computers run everything around here, so people are putting off elective surgeries, and any procedures that aren't completely necessary. Heart surgery doesn't fall into that category."

"Have you done heart transplants?" I asked.

He smiled. "Are you interviewing me?"

"I guess we're interviewing each other."

He nodded. "Thirty-eight. Thirty-nine tomorrow. Tell me exactly what you would want me to do."

"The same thing you've done thirty-eight other times, thirty-nine tomorrow."

"Too cryptic," he said, and then repeated, "Tell me exactly what you would want me to do."

I nodded. "The recipient of the transplant would be in a room in this hospital. Somewhere else in the hospital, hopefully in an adjoining room, a donor heart that is a perfect match would become available."

"I would not assist it in becoming available," he said. "I need to be clear about that."

"I wouldn't ask you to," I said. "But purely as a hypothetical, I would like you to help me in some research. I would like to know what causes of death could render a heart unfit for transplant."

He nodded. "There's plenty of information on that on the web. I can direct you to it, to help with your hypothetical research."

"So you'll help, if it comes to that?"

"Where is the potential recipient now?"

"Hackensack University hospital," I said.

"She would have to be transferred here, at least two days before the operation, sooner if possible. I will have to clear it with the hospital administration, but so far there is nothing you have said that would be illegal, and I would think that would be the standard they'd apply."

"Thank you."

"What are the chances this is going to happen?" he asked.

"Right now, slim. But we're making progress."

"I'll be here."

"We caught a break," Emerson said when Novack picked up the phone. "You got a minute?"

"We'll come to you," Novack said, on his feet before hanging up the phone. Anders was across the room at his desk. "Let's go."

When they got to Emerson's office, he was sitting with Andrew Garrett, who had papers spread out in front of him.

"I said it was a break," Emerson said, "but it wasn't. It was great police work. Andy?"

Garrett seemed embarrassed by the praise, and said, "I don't know about great police work, all we did was trace the money.

"Not the money that was paid off in the deaths that Charlie Harrison was involved in, the ones that related to his fake IDs. As you know, the money didn't go to him; he just got the fifty-grand installments from the fictitious foreign company. That was a dead end.

"So I'm talking about the money that was paid by the insurance companies. And like in everything else we've seen, our perpetrator was good, actually extraordinary. There were no similarities in the paths of the monies, and it all went through four different banks. This money wasn't just laundered, it was dry cleaned and martinized."

"So what did you come up with?" Novack asked.

"I'm getting there," Garrett said, seeming to relish the moment.

"I checked all other settlements for negligent deaths in the year after Charlie Harrison died. I figured they wouldn't have iced Charlie without having someone to take his place. For screening criteria I only used settlements over a million dollars, in the metropolitan area. There were seventeen such cases, but ten of them were clearly legitimate. Three others appeared to be good, but four could easily have fit the MO of our guy."

"And?" Anders asked. He was by nature even more impatient than Novack.

"And two of them had money paths that were mostly dissimilar to each other, and to Charlie's. But when you follow them, all four wind up in the same place."

"In the same account?" Novack asked.

"You got it," Emerson said, jumping in. "The names on the account are all different, and none is Nolan Murray, but guess what? We've got an address off the bank records."

"It could be fake," Novack said. "It could be a delicatessen. It could be a nursery school."

Garrett shook his head. "No, it's a house in Montvale. Registered to an Alan Mitchell. I've checked into Mitchell; I think he's one of Murray's creations." He paused for effect. "I think we may know where Murray lives."

"Good work," Novack said grudgingly. He wasn't prepared to believe that this was going to get them to Murray, but clearly Garrett and Emerson had accomplished more than the rest of the department, Novack and Anders included.

"I really can't take the credit; it was mostly the state police," Garrett said. "They have better and faster access to banking records than we do." He held up a piece of paper. "They even e-mailed me the address."

"Okay," Novack said. "We've got work to do."

Captain Donovan insisted on convening the meeting in which the operation would be planned. He, Novack, Anders, and Emerson were included, and all recognized the need to move cautiously but quickly. They also knew that before they could come close to finalizing a plan, they needed a lay of the land.

As the relative newcomer to the investigation, and therefore not likely to be recognized, Anders would do the reconnaissance. He would drive through the Montvale neighborhood and by the address in question, to get a sense of the area. Mounted on the car would be hidden, miniature video cameras, which would give them a clear understanding of what they were dealing with.

Within an hour, Anders was on the way to Montvale, and he was back two hours after that. Donovan, Novack, and Emerson had already seen the video fed back from the car, but Anders still described what he saw.

"It's a tough one," he said. "The house is on a hill, near the top, with one other house below it on one side, and two on the other side. You can get to the house from either side of the hill, but anyone in the house would see us coming. On the positive side, we could easily seal off the hill, and no one could get out."

"Could you tell if anyone was in the house?" Novack asked.

"I can't be sure, but I don't think so. There were no cars in the driveway, and no lights on inside, at least that I could see, although it was obviously daytime. The exterior was a little shabby, the grass hadn't been mowed in a while. I'm guessing it's empty, but it's just a guess."

All of this presented a dilemma; they needed to know if

there was someone in that house before they approached it. Donovan once again called on the state police capabilities. They would use a device that could sense body heat, and that way determine if there was anyone alive in the house.

By that morning they had their answer; the house was unoccupied. Sentries were placed inconspicuously near the bottom of both sides of the hill; if someone approached the house, they would know it.

The final preparatory step was securing a court order to enter and search the premises. This they obtained easily; there was well more than probable cause to believe that crimes had been committed. The operation was set for 5:00 P.M. that afternoon; there would be at least some traffic in the area at that time, and their movements would therefore be slightly less conspicuous.

Continued surveillance indicated that no one had come to the house in the interim, and that it was still unoccupied. A SWAT team would be in position, ready to move in if called upon, an insurance policy that no one really thought would be necessary.

Once again it would be Anders who would be the point man. He would approach the house casually, map in hand, as if lost and looking for directions. He'd ring the bell, and if, as expected, no one answered, he'd call in the rest of the search team.

They went over the plan at least three more times, poking and prodding for flaws. High secrecy was maintained, only the four principals, Garrett, and the SWAT team leader knew all the specifics. At 4:00 P.M. they set out for Montvale. Novack expected it to be relatively uneventful, except for the fact that these kinds of operations were never uneventful.

At exactly 5:30 they were all in position and ready to move in. The SWAT team was there to back up Anders should he have any difficulty at all. A forensics team was following in a van, and the secrecy was so tight that they did not even know where it was they were going.

Anders parked in front of the house, looked around as if confused by his whereabouts, and then ambled up to the house. "Hello?" he called out, but did not get a response. He called out again, and again was met with silence.

He reached the front door and rang the bell, but it made no sound. The fact that it was not working seemed consistent with the general run-down appearance of the house; from up close it looked even more dilapidated to Anders than it had from a distance.

He tried the bell again, but it was clearly not working. Then Anders noticed that the door was ajar, open about two inches. He called out again, but there was still no answer.

Proper protocol called for Anders to step back and call in the search team, but the open door was too enticing. He decided to push it open a few more inches, and look inside.

It was the last decision, and the last mistake, he ever made. The explosion came from under the porch, below Anders, and tore him apart. Secondary explosions came moments later in various areas of the house, reducing it to rubble.

Novack called in the SWAT team, but by that point there was no one to save, and no one to kill.

It came as no surprise to Mike Janssen when he was fired. Somebody had to go. It wasn't going to be the president, though in light of what was happening people would be lining up to run against him in the next election. And it wasn't the FBI director, at least not yet.

But when pressure builds up as it was doing, it spits somebody out, and the exit door is usually as low as the top people can get away with. In this case it was at Mike Janssen's level.

Janssen wasn't fired in the way it's done in the real world. No two weeks severance and "clean out your desk." That's not how the Bureau operated, and certainly not in the intense glare of this publicity.

The announcement was so filled with praise for Janssen that it sounded like a promotion. It portrayed him as the world's leading expert on aviation terrorism, which was why he got the job after the Southern crash. The investigation had expanded dramatically after the other two incidents, which moved it somewhat out of Janssen's area of expertise. Which was why, the bullshit announcement continued, Janssen had requested the reassignment. He wanted to get back into the field, to dig his teeth into the Southern crash.

In that capacity, it went on, Janssen would continue to be an integral part of the terrorist investigation, reporting to the FBI director, Edgar Barone, who would assume overall command.

The last part was true; Janssen would continue to work on the investigation, focusing on the Southern crash. But in the real world, as he knew all too well, the upward trajectory of his Bureau career was over. When you're held out as a failure on an assignment with great public exposure, you're not going any higher. And there had never been public exposure as great as this.

Also left out of the announcement was Janssen's anger at the bureaucrats who effectively sent him out to pasture. He would not go quietly, nor would he go privately, but retribution would have to wait. As pissed off at his "superiors" as he was, he was more pissed off at the person or people committing these horrible acts.

He was going to get them, no matter what it took.

The number of tips called in by Americans to the FBI was by this point numbering in the hundreds of thousands, and even in crisis mode, there was simply not enough manpower to handle it.

Janssen, in his former role, was completely reliant on those under him to analyze even the most promising leads. Once he was demoted and able to focus on the Southern crash, he became as hands-on as possible, familiarizing himself with as many of the tips as possible.

The tips were graded on five levels, according to their potential reliability and significance. One was the highest, and only three and a half percent of the candidates were graded at that level. Janssen set out to familiarize himself with as many of these as time permitted.

So it was that Janssen became aware of the report that a former employee of ITC, Nolan Murray, at one point possibly had access to the computer systems of both Southern Airlines and Disneyland. Not only that, but suspicions about the employee's background had led to his termination, or at least would have had he not left abruptly on his own.

Janssen was not familiar with ITC or CEO Darren Seibert, but a quick Google search showed him to be a formidable businessman, running a large operation. The tip had already been sent to an agent for follow-up, but Janssen circumvented the process and called Seibert directly.

He introduced himself and asked if Seibert had developed any follow-up information since the initial report.

"Some. We've tried to identify everywhere Murray was while in our employ, and how long he was in each place. We've also tried to assess how much access he had."

"Do you have all this documented?" Janssen asked.

"I do. I also have documentation of his falsified personnel records."

"Good. E-mail it to me, and then wait for my call."

Janssen had the documents in hand within a few minutes, and shared it with members of his team on the technical side of things. Their opinion was that, while it was promising, it was unlikely that Murray's limited access could have resulted in total security system failures, as happened in the airplane and at the amusement park.

The caveat, however, was that none of them knew Murray, or how good he was. But for him to have infiltrated and controlled the systems in these situations, he would have to be beyond extraordinary.

Of course, Janssen knew all too well that was exactly who they were dealing with, someone beyond extraordinary. He assigned a team of agents to focus exclusively on

Nolan Murray. They would interview everyone at the ITC offices, as well as the people that Nolan Murray dealt with at the two targeted companies.

The only thing Janssen hadn't nailed down was a connection between Murray and the military that would explain his taking over the Predator drone.

But he would find it, and he would find Murray. He would take the son of a bitch down.

I tried to reach Novack when I heard about Anders's death. It was the previous night, maybe an hour after the news reports said it had happened. He wasn't answering his phone, or at least he wasn't when he saw it was me calling. On some level I couldn't have blamed him, since I entered his life his partner was killed and his ex-wife nearly incinerated.

I was positive the operation that led to the tragedy had something to do with going after Murray. Novack had told me that morning that they had a promising lead, though he wouldn't tell me what it was. I didn't see anything in the media about arrests being made, and there was no information about what the police were attempting to do in entering the Montvale home.

I tried to put it out of my mind; I would eventually speak to Novack and find out what had happened, and what the status of the investigation was. I had to spend the night preparing for the parole hearing, just five days away.

I had another reason to speak to Novack that day besides getting an update on what had happened. I had petitioned the parole board for the right to call witnesses; it is sometimes, but not always, allowed. Permission to do so was granted, as I suspected it would be.

Most parole hearings do not attract much attention, but this one certainly would. Even with the national crisis that had unfolded, Sheryl's case stayed in the news. The publicity would have been much greater if the world were not coming to an end, but the parole board had to know that this particular hearing would garner a great deal of scrutiny. They would try to bend over backward to appear fair, and not granting us the right to call witnesses could have cast them in a negative light.

Novack was to be my key witness, a fact I had not yet shared with him. I needed to lock that in, and though he'd give me a hard time, I was confident he'd come through.

I had an idea for a much needed second witness, and that was Kevin Laufer, the part-time computer teacher who had implicated Nolan Murray. My instinct was that Laufer had been lying, for a reason I could not pinpoint. Novack disagreed, and presented an annoyingly coherent case for his point of view.

I was sure that Laufer would resist testifying. He was petrified of Murray, and insisted that his talking to us be kept in the strictest confidence. The idea of going to the parole board and saying the same things would probably be far too frightening for him to contemplate.

I was quite sure that I could get the parole board to take his testimony in a closed session, with Laufer's name redacted from all public transcripts and pronouncements. I doubted it would be enough to make him speak willingly, and I considered threatening him with revealing him as an ex-con to his employers, as Novack did. It would not be my proudest moment, but I'd handle the guilt.

I had started calling the hospital every day, to speak to Terry Aimonetti and get information on how Karen was doing. This time Terry sounded more worried than usual; Karen was running a low-grade fever. Nothing severe, but health issues of any kind could impact or prevent transplant surgery.

I talked to Terry about wanting to move Karen to Columbia Presbyterian, to go under Dr. Jenkins's care. She seemed willing to do so, and also asked that I set up a meeting for her with him. She wanted to understand everything that was going on, as it related to the health of both her daughter and granddaughter.

She also asked anxiously if the police detail providing protection would be going with them. I assured her that they would.

Once I got off the phone, I called Dr. Jenkins, who was quite willing to meet with Terry, and promised to do so as soon as she and Karen arrived at the hospital.

I took my morning drive out to the prison, something I found myself looking forward to each day. I enjoyed seeing Sheryl; there was no denying it. She was hoping to die, and failing that would spend most of her life in prison, and I was relying on her to be upbeat and brighten my day. I wasn't sure what that said about me, and really didn't want to figure it out.

But on this day, if I was looking for cheering up, she didn't provide it. She was very upset when I told her about Anders dying. She had never met him, and certainly didn't send him to that house, but she blamed herself nonetheless.

"I was quiet for six years, and everything was fine," she said. "Then I opened my mouth, and all these terrible things are happening."

"Things were not fine, Sheryl. You've been locked in a cage for something you didn't do."

"I was glad he was dead," she said, so softly that I could barely hear her.

"You didn't kill him."

"I wanted to."

"Doesn't matter, Sheryl. The thought police didn't put you in here."

"Are you a ladies' man, Harvard?" She had an annoying, charming habit of changing subjects on less than a moment's notice.

"I used to do okay," I said, smiling.

"I bet you did. But not anymore?"

"Let's just say I'm reassessing my priorities." I didn't want to tell her how I felt. I just didn't think it was fair to dump that on her, even though I was pretty sure she already knew.

She did. "I'm the last one you should be falling for, Harvard."

"Now you tell me."

"If it's any consolation, I'm right there with you."

"It is," I said.

"Hey, when this is all behind you, you'll start having fun again," she said.

At that moment, having fun did not seem like something that would happen again in this lifetime. "That will give me something to look forward to."

"While you're having fun, will you look out for Karen?"

"How's that?" I asked.

"I know it's a lot to ask, but my mother won't be around forever, and Karen doesn't have anyone else. I would just appreciate it if you would look out for her. You know, take an interest. Call her once in a while, take her to dinner, give her away at her wedding. That kind of thing."

I had a lump in my throat. I had never before realized a throat could actually get lumps; I always considered it a mythical conceit of fictional tearjerkers. "I'll get to know her, and I'll watch out for her, Sheryl."

"Thanks, Harvard. I know you will."

And then we stopped talking about the stuff that hurt, which at this point didn't leave much else. And I realized that I used to think of Harvard as the school I went to. Now it will be the name that Sheryl called me.

"Novack's going to be coming to see you again," Murray said. He was talking to Peter Lampley, who while using his real name of Kevin Laufer had pointed the finger at Murray. It was, of course, done under Murray's direction.

Everything was done under Murray's direction.

Lampley, Murray, and Daniel Churchill were in their daily, one-hour meeting. Murray found it a wise practice to find time for the meeting each day, no matter what else was going on. It wasn't so much that he needed or valued their input, and especially not Lampley's, but he wanted to know everything that was going on. If they knew it, Murray insisted on knowing it as well.

"Why do you say that?" Lampley asked.

"Because you told Novack that you'd ask around about me." Murray was annoyed that Lampley could forget something so obvious and important. "You tried to avoid it, and he threatened to spread the word that you had implicated me."

Lampley nodded. "Right. So I'll just tell him I've talked to people, and nobody has seen you. But I'm still working on it."

Churchill, pacing the room as he frequently did, shook his head. Lampley couldn't see him do it, because he was sitting near the center of the room, facing Murray. "No, that doesn't move the ball," Churchill said.

Murray had a rule that he insisted they live by; every move they made as part of the operation had to "move the ball," that is, bring them closer to their goal.

"Right," Murray said. "Telling him that gets us nowhere." Murray already knew what he wanted to do, but he was waiting to reveal it. Timing was everything.

Lampley had long ago accepted his position as number-three man in the hierarchy, and it had never bothered him. He felt lucky to be there at all; it was going to make him rich beyond his wildest dreams. Beyond anybody's wildest dreams.

"Okay," Lampley said, nodding. "I hear you. What do you want me to tell him? But Novack is no dope; it needs to be something believable. Tell you the truth, the guy scares the shit out of me."

"You did well with him last time," Murray said.

Lampley nodded, but a bit uncertainly. "Yeah, I just wish we had gotten rid of him when we had the chance."

"We turned it to our advantage," Murray said, and Churchill agreed.

"Okay," said Murray, "we need to keep him motivated to come after me. Something to make him think I'm smart, and dangerous, and ruthless."

Churchill was still pacing around the room, but he was now holding a handgun. "I haven't thought this through yet, but I have an idea . . ."

Novack was working on four hours sleep. He and Cindy had visited with Danielle Anders until almost midnight, and then Cindy wound up sleeping there, when Danielle didn't want to be alone. It seemed comforting for Danielle to have them there, though that was a concept that Novack had trouble grasping. At the saddest times in his life, he always wanted to be alone.

This was one of those times; any time a fellow cop went down, Novack took it hard. And Anders was more than a fellow cop, he was a partner and a friend. But being alone was not a luxury Novack could afford, not now.

He called a meeting for eight o'clock in the morning in Captain Donovan's office. It was not correct protocol for a lieutenant to be calling a meeting in a captain's office, particularly at that hour, but Novack really wasn't in a "protocol" mood.

He told Emerson to come to the meeting as well, and insisted that he bring Andrew Garrett. Everyone was there on time, and Novack noticed that the rest of the precinct cops, on duty and off, were around and waiting for assignments. One of their own was down, and they were going to make good on it.

Novack wasted no time. "They knew we were coming, and they didn't find out at the last minute. They had this set up before Anders checked out the place the first time. They knew we were coming before we did."

"You think Murray has someone on the inside?" Emerson asked, meaning within the department.

Novack nodded. "I do."

Emerson didn't like where this was going, and didn't back down. "Like somebody in this room?"

"Yeah," Novack said. "And every other room in the precinct. I think he's in the computers. I think he has access."

"Did we put the operation at the house into the system?" Donovan asked. "I don't think so."

"I don't either," Emerson said.

Garrett nodded slowly. "It was in there. Maybe not the time we were going in, or the specifics, but we got the address from the state police through the computer. That's how we corresponded. They even put it in an e-mail. If he were able to read it, he'd have had time to set up the explosives. But . . ."

"Bingo," Novack said.

But Garrett was shaking his head. "No, I think that's wrong. I was worried about the same thing, so I've been checking it out. If he had access, I'd have found it. He would have to leave prints."

"I don't buy it," Novack said. "He's been tracking us all along. He knew I was after him; that's why he went after me with the car."

"From this point on, nothing about this operation goes on the computer," Donovan said. "If we have something to say to each other, walk down the hall and say it. Like the old days."

They agreed, and then Novack said, "We need to go

public with Murray's name. We've got nothing on this guy; he's been pulling our chain from the beginning. We don't know what he looks like, where he lives, who his friends are. Nothing. But somebody out there does."

"I'm not so sure," Donovan said.

"If Laufer knew him, other people knew him. Laufer said that the night he committed the murder, he was hanging out in a bar, drinking beer with his friends. Well, those friends have to be out there. If we can't find Murray, let's find them."

"The entire country is already out there looking for a computer geek," Emerson said.

"Well, now they'll be looking for another one," Novack said.

"We don't need the whole country looking," Garrett said. "The guy is local. I think he's strictly local."

"What does that mean?"

"Remember I told you that I was looking at insurance settlements over a million dollars, and I found a bunch of them in this area that were suspicious? Well, I've been doing the same thing in other areas of the country. I took the seven leading metropolitan areas after New York, and used the same criteria."

"And?"

"And it's not there. This area has an entirely different pattern. I could show you the data, but believe me, it's clear. This guy is not operating anywhere else, or at least not in those areas. He's local."

"He doesn't have to be physically here," Donovan said. "Just because the frauds were being done here."

"Somebody planted the explosives," Novack said. "And it wasn't Hennessey."

"He could have a new Hennessey," Emerson said. "At the prices he was willing to pay, he could have ten Hennesseys."

"Maybe, but I don't think so. I think Garrett's right; I think Murray's local. So let's find the son of a bitch."

Fame has its advantages. I went to the junior high school in an effort to talk to Laufer, but I hadn't known his schedule, and it apparently was not at a time that he was scheduled to teach. I needed to ask, and coerce if necessary, him to testify at Sheryl's parole hearing.

I went to the principal's office, and his administrative assistant immediately recognized me from my television appearances. She was so impressed that I was there that if somebody were already in with the principal, I think she would have dragged that person out by his or her ear.

The principal, a beleaguered-looking man who introduced himself as Mr. Richardson, shook my hand unenthusiastically. "I understand you're looking for Mr. Laufer." Unlike the firm of Carlson, Miller, and Timmerman, first names at this school were apparently discouraged.

"Yes," I said.

"Well, join the club. He failed to appear for his last two classes."

"And didn't call in?"

"Correct. Which is inexcusable, because it left us unprepared, without a substitute teacher. I had to fill in, not the best fit for a computer class. I can barely open my e-mail."

"You've tried to contact him?" I asked.

He nodded. "Without success. At this point the only reason to speak with him would be to terminate him."

I hoped that was just a poor choice of words, but Laufer had been outspoken about his fear of Murray coming after him, describing Murray as a cold-blooded killer. "Do you have an address for him?" I asked.

"I'm certain that we must. Mrs. Simon will provide it for you, though she may ask for an autograph in return."

Mrs. Simon did in fact provide me the address, but resisted asking for my autograph. That disappointed me a little.

As I was leaving the school, Novack called on my cell phone. "You were trying to reach me?" he asked, in lieu of "hello."

"I was calling to say that I'm sorry about Anders."

"Yeah," he said. "Me too."

He didn't sound like he was in an accommodating mood, but then again he never did, so I decided to push ahead. "I also wanted to ask if you would testify at Sheryl's parole hearing."

"With pleasure," he said. The man provided one surprise after another.

"Thanks. Have you been in touch with Laufer?"

"No, I'm on the way over to the school now."

"That's where I am," I said. "Laufer hasn't shown up for work in two days, and they haven't been able to reach him."

"You know where he lives?"

"I do."

"Stay there; I'll pick you up."

It took Novack twenty minutes to show up, during which time teachers and students wandered out to gawk at me. Apparently Mrs. Simon had spread the word that there was a celebrity in their midst. Three girls, no more than thirteen years old, summoned up the courage to come talk to me and ask me what it was like to be on television.

Novack saw this, and when I got in the car, he said, "Did you get their phone numbers?"

I ignored that, and gave him Laufer's address, which was in a building called Royal Towers in Hasbrouck Heights. With Novack driving like a maniac, we were there in ten minutes.

The way to get into the building was to have the tenant buzz the visitor in, but instead of pressing the button for Laufer's apartment, Novack buzzed for the super instead.

The super, who told us his name was Benny, had to be at least seventy-five years old, and took what seemed like twenty minutes to walk us to the elevator, and then down a long corridor to Laufer's apartment. I thought Novack was going to go insane at the pace, and finally he demanded the key and the apartment number, and we walked on ahead.

We got to the door, and Novack rang the bell a couple of times, without getting an answer. Before he put the key in the door, he turned to me and said, "Based on Laufer's fear of Murray and his not showing up for work, we have reason to believe that he is in danger or was the victim of violence."

I nodded. "Probable cause." He was giving me our reasons for not needing a search warrant to enter.

"Wow. Perry Mason lives."

Novack took out his gun, and my immediate reaction was to pull back in cowardly alarm. I hoped Novack didn't notice it, but of course he did, and said, "Wow. Davy Crockett lives."

Then he said, "Wait here," which I was happy to do. At that point the super finally joined me, and we waited in the hall as Novack opened the door and went in. About twenty seconds later, he closed the door, leaving us in the hall.

Another three or four minutes went by, which felt much longer. Worried about what might be going on, I yelled into the door, "Novack, are you all right?"

Maybe thirty seconds later the door opened again. He said to the super, "Go downstairs, open the door, and leave it open. Hurry up." To me he said, "Come on in. Don't touch anything."

I went in, and Novack closed the door behind us. Sitting on a chair in the middle of the room was the obviously dead body of Kevin Laufer. There was a bullet hole in his forehead, and a white towel tied around his neck like a bib, that said in red, "Talking is deadly." "Oh, man . . . ," I said, and tried really hard not to be sick.

I walked around the body, so as not to have to see the bloody bullet hole, only to discover a bigger one in the back of his head. It seemed to me that he had been shot there, and that it traveled through to the front, though fortunately that was not my area of expertise.

"You okay, Wagner?" Novack asked.

"I think so. You ever get used to things like this?"

Novack shook his head. "Not so far."

Within ten minutes the place was swarming with police and forensics people. The only one of them that I recognized was Emerson, but he had as little to do as I did. I assumed that was because he was in computer crime and was just here because he was involved in the investigation.

He came over to me at one point and said, "Are you okay?" Apparently my stability was something the local police had high up on their list of concerns.

I nodded. "Yeah. Just weird that we're talking to a guy one day and then he's dead."

"I know. Let me tell you, there's a switch you have to be able to turn off. Especially cops."

"What do you mean?" I asked.

"Well, Laufer is a perfect example. I brought him into

this; if I hadn't talked to him in the first place, he'd be at the junior high writing on the blackboard. So if I focus on that, if I don't turn off that switch, it could drive me crazy. You have to turn off that switch and move on."

"Makes sense, but probably not so easy to actually do."

"You'd better learn quick," he said.

"Why?"

"That client of yours. If it doesn't work out, or even if it does, you've got to deal with it and put it behind you."

"And then what?" I asked, but I didn't ask it of Emerson, and I didn't ask it out loud. I asked it silently, of myself, and I didn't get an answer.

"This you're not going to believe." The speaker was FBI Agent Carlos Vazquez, and he had just barged into Mike Janssen's office unannounced. Since Janssen was his boss, the abrupt entry was not commonplace.

"What are you talking about?" Janssen asked. Vazquez had worked for Janssen a very long time, joining him on each of his assignments, so Janssen gave him more latitude than he would ordinarily give more junior agents.

"Get up for a second."

"Excuse me?" Janssen was sitting at his desk, but Vazquez was already walking toward him.

"Come on, Mike. Just listen to me, okay? Let me sit at your desk. I promise, it will be worth it."

Janssen got up and watched as Vazquez sat in his chair and started typing into his computer.

As he was typing, Vazquez said, "So I went online to check out the *New York Post,* you know, the sports section." As Janssen was aware, Vazquez was an ex–New Yorker still devoted to New York teams.

"You got nothing better to do?" Janssen asked.

"Come on, that's how I relax. Anyway, at the top of the

home page they have these short topics, and one of them caught my eye, so I hit on it, like I'm doing now, and . . ." He stood up to let Janssen sit down. "Take a look at this."

Janssen sat down and looked at a story about New Jersey police looking for Nolan Murray, suspected of two murders in a case that began with computer fraud. One of the murders was that of David Anders, the police officer who died in a recent house explosion.

There was not much identifying information about Murray, nor was there a picture, but the story did quote Lieutenant John Novack as saying that Murray should be considered armed and dangerous.

Janssen was momentarily annoyed that they had to learn about this in the newspaper, but he soon realized that the local cops would have no idea he was also looking for Nolan Murray. Therefore, there would have been no reason for them to contact the Bureau.

Janssen stood up and started heading for the door. "You packed?"

"Always," Vazquez said, following him out.

It was three and a half hours later that Novack was called into Captain Donovan's office, where Janssen and Vazquez were waiting. Donovan did the introductions, and then said, "It seems our friend Nolan Murray is a main suspect in the three terrorist incidents that have taken place."

"Whoa," Emerson said.

"What do you have on him?" asked Novack.

"We know he had possible access to two of the systems that were compromised," Janssen said. "Or at least the systems of the companies involved."

"Possible access to two of the systems of the companies involved?" Novack repeated. "That makes him a main suspect?"

Janssen nodded. "There isn't a lot of competition for the title of 'main suspect.' "

"He's not easy to pin down. What else do you have on him?"

"I'm waiting for you to tell us that," Janssen said.

The five men spent the next three hours going over everything that Novack and Emerson had learned about Murray, taking him through every step of the investigation, starting with Sheryl Harrison.

Donovan had little to add, but was relieved that things were going smoothly. Novack famously had little tolerance for other investigators getting in his way, especially if they were of the federal variety. But he and Janssen seemed to develop an easy relationship and early respect, which would make Donovan's life infinitely easier.

At one point Janssen went to the restroom, and Donovan said to Novack, "Thanks. I was sure you were going to be a pain in the ass about this."

"Why?" Novack asked.

"Because you're a pain in the ass about everything. Especially when the Feds are involved."

"Their case is more important than ours," Novack said. "It's more important than every case we will ever have put together. Besides, if we didn't cooperate, they'd put so much pressure on, you'd fold up like an accordion."

Donovan nodded. "You got that right."

As the meeting resumed, the more Janssen heard, the more enthusiastic he got about Murray as a suspect. It was clear from what Emerson had to say that Murray was brilliant with the computer, possessing an astonishing ability to hack into systems and make them bend to his will.

And with all that Murray was doing locally, it seemed way too much of a coincidence that he would suddenly drop everything and take a temp job that would provide access to the two targeted systems.

Janssen always got a feeling, a gut instinct, when he

was ready to close in, when he knew exactly who he was after. And he had that feeling now.

"If it's all right with you, Captain, Agent Vazquez and I will work out of these offices."

Donovan was surprised. "Don't you need to be at the Bureau offices in Newark?"

"As far as the Bureau is concerned, I don't even need to be on the planet."

"Ah, the scapegoat," Novack said.

Janssen nodded. "In the flesh. Can you give me an office?"

"Of course," Donovan said.

Emerson left to get all the documents related to the case for Emerson and Vazquez to go over with Novack over dinner later that night. It was decided that a lid would be kept on the developments, that only the five men in the meeting would be aware of the possible connection of Murray to the national situation. The only exception to this would be Andrew Garrett, since he had the computer knowledge and access that they would need to rely on.

Janssen was under an obligation to tell his FBI bosses what was going on, and he intended to do that. But he would not call special attention to it; he would put it through normal channels, and it would get lost in the chaos.

When and if he was ready to declare that this was for real, he would make sure that the full resources of the government were brought to bear on it.

And he had a feeling that time was coming.

I would describe my emotions as somewhere between dread and terror. The parole hearing was thirty-six hours away, and to say I was floundering was giving me an enormous benefit of the doubt.

I had planned on calling two witnesses that would be crucial to making our case. The first, Kevin Laufer, was lying in a drawer at the coroner's office, which would likely hurt his effectiveness as a witness. The second, Novack, had just called to cancel our meeting that night, which was when I'd planned to go over his testimony with him.

When I asked why he was canceling, he said that "something came up." He wouldn't say what that was, except to say "sort of" when I asked if it was related to our case. He didn't answer any more of my questions, probably because he had already hung up.

The difference between having Novack at the hearing and not having him there could not be overstated. The case was the same, but the messenger was all important. As Sheryl's lawyer, her advocate, my version of events would be expected to be biased in her favor.

But as the arresting officer, for Novack to be taking her side and agreeing with my point of view would be enormous. He was Sheryl's natural adversary, and for him to reverse that role and testify on her behalf would increase her chances many times over.

Additionally, our evidentiary case itself was something of a mess. Having lived it, Novack and I had no doubt that Sheryl did not murder Charlie Harrison, that she was telling the truth in her new version of events.

Her implicating Hennessey was the key that opened up everything. Hennessey's murder, Laufer's accusing Murray, Laufer's murder . . . it could all be traced back to Sheryl's naming Hennessey.

But that was the basis of the problem; it was Sheryl that named Hennessey. Her word was all that made Hennessey relevant to this case, and if the parole board disbelieved her, then everything that flowed from her Hennessey accusation would become irrelevant.

Besides her having an obvious self-interest in blaming someone else for the murder she was convicted of committing, there was also the little matter of Sheryl's having confessed to the crime herself. Not only that, but she had spent six years in prison without having recanted that confession.

Only now, when she wanted to save her daughter, was she changing her story. Why should the parole board believe her? I wouldn't believe her.

Boy, did I need Novack.

The other question I had, besides what the hell to do if Novack didn't show up, was the question of whether I should have Sheryl speak on her own behalf. Even though I was not a criminal defense attorney, I was well aware of the great risk in having the defendant testify. It is rarely done, mainly because defendants generally do themselves more harm than good. It's much better if anything they would have to say could be brought in through other witnesses, so that the defendant would not be subject to a potentially devastating cross-examination.

In truth, there were a number of differences here. For one thing, there would be no cross-examination; there was no prosecution to conduct it. The members of the board would be doing the questioning, and they were supposed to be unbiased, and didn't have as their mission to show Sheryl to be guilty or a liar by trapping her.

Technically speaking, Sheryl wasn't even a defendant. She was a petitioner, which cut both ways. The positive was that it was not an adversarial proceeding, with no prosecutor on the other side of the table. The negative was that she had the burden of proof. In a trial, the prosecutor has that burden; he or she must prove guilt beyond a reasonable doubt. Here the burden was Sheryl's, and mine, to prove that she was worthy of parole.

But the trickiest area of all was the question of Sheryl's desire to save her daughter. Parole boards are not there to judge guilt or innocence, in the minds of the system the jury has done that long ago. They are there to judge worthiness for early release, and they weigh two factors in doing that.

One of them is the convict's behavior and comportment while imprisoned. We're fine in that regard; Sheryl has by all accounts been a model prisoner.

The other consideration was far more problematic for us. The board is supposed to consider most carefully whether the petitioner will be a danger to society once released, whether or not he or she can be expected to repeat criminal behavior.

There was no secret as to what Sheryl wanted to do. It would be a huge stretch to argue that taking her own life could be considered a danger to society, but it would be equally hard for us to argue that it was not criminal behavior.

My plan was to spend the night preparing, and then go over all these factors with Sheryl the next morning.

But if we didn't have Novack, none of it would matter.

It was a dinner that Stanley Breslin was not looking forward to. And it certainly was not the kind of situation he was expecting when he took the job as commissioner of the New Jersey State Board of Parole.

Breslin only got the job in the first place because his brother Alan was the finance chairman of Governor Scott Patterson's campaign committee. Not that Breslin wasn't qualified; he spent thirty years as a prosecutor and then defense attorney, and was highly regarded. He was capable of doing the parole board job in his sleep, and for eighteen months, that was pretty much how he did it.

Not that the operation that he headed was a small one, far from it. They conducted more than twenty thousand hearings a year, and supervised well over a hundred thousand already paroled felons. But Breslin had many trained professionals under him who actually did all that work, while he concentrated on the political and social end of things.

Breslin had spent considerable time with Governor Patterson, but it was only at campaign events with hundreds of people, all of whom were there to write checks. In fact,

Breslin wondered with some amusement if Patterson would even recognize him without a check in his hand.

But this particular dinner was going to be different. Breslin was invited to the governor's mansion for dinner. His wife was not part of the invitation, since it was to be a "working dinner." Breslin knew all too well that he was the one that was going to be "worked," and the working topic was going to be Sheryl Harrison's parole hearing.

Patterson welcomed him graciously, and the two had a very pleasant dinner. Breslin had always found him to be an affable guy, tough but fair, and the dinner did nothing to change that opinion. Both men shared a love for sports, the New York Giants in particular, and they spent a lot of time analyzing their roster and coaching staff.

After dinner they went into the den for coffee, at which point Patterson said, "Big day, Thursday."

"How do you mean, Governor?" Breslin asked, though he knew damn well what Patterson meant.

"You know damn well what I mean," Patterson said, smiling. "The Harrison parole hearing is Thursday."

"Yes, it is."

"I want you there," Patterson said.

"We conduct two-person panels," Breslin said, already not pleased with the way this was going. "The two people have already been assigned. And I have not sat on a panel all year."

"The number is up to you; there's no law that you have to follow. And you being part of it shows the importance with which we are viewing it." Then, "It's important to me, Stanley."

"What else is important to you?" Breslin said, cutting straight to the chase.

"You mean how do I want it to come out? That depends on the case that they make."

"Suppose it's a strong one."

Patterson thought for a moment. "Well, let me tell you the situation I find myself in. I've received a prepetition requesting a commutation of her sentence. The evidentiary brief is going to follow, simultaneous with the presentation to you and your panel."

Breslin didn't say anything, though he noticed that Patterson had already assumed Breslin would cave and be part of the hearing.

Patterson continued, "I don't want to have to rule on it, one way or the other. There's no upside for me. Whichever way I go, a whole bunch of people will hate me for it."

"That's why you get to live in this big house," Breslin said.

Patterson shook his head. "No, it isn't. I get to live in this big house because I've managed to not get a lot of people hating me. And I'm comfortable here; I want to stay awhile."

"You need to spell this out for me, Governor."

"Okay. I wouldn't presume to tell you how to rule. Certainly, if they don't make a compelling case, you have to turn her down. But here's the thing: If you parole her, then I don't have to make a decision. If you turn her down, then it comes to me."

Breslin finally understood; the governor wanted to get out of sticking his neck out by having Breslin parole Sheryl Harrison.

"Here's the problem as I see it," Breslin said. "We are not there to decide if she committed the murder. We are there to decide if she deserves to be paroled. The main factor to consider is whether she will commit crimes in the future, and she already has said she will. She'll kill herself. That gives her a steep hill to climb in a parole setting."

"Hills are there to be climbed."

"Forget the politics of it for a second," Breslin said. "If you were not involved, not the governor . . . how would you want it to come out?"

"I'd want her to be allowed to save her daughter."

Breslin nodded. "Me too."

"Give her a fair hearing; that's all I ask," said Patterson, though both men knew he was asking much more.

"That I can promise. But I'm sorry, Governor, you can't count on me to provide your way out of this."

Livan Figueroa did not want to be at work. A computer technician at the Limerick nuclear power plant, Figueroa had put in for that week as a vacation week months ago, and his supervisor had approved it. He and the family were going to drive to Ocean City; they had wanted to go to Disneyland, but Figueroa's wife was too freaked out by what had happened on that ride in California.

But if someone wanted to take a vacation at that time, it was not a good idea to be a computer technician at an installation that was considered a prime terrorist target. The word came down immediately; all vacations were off, and all employees should be ready to work overtime hours if called upon to do so.

Figueroa had told his wife to take the kids and drive down to their rented house, and he would try and join them on the weekend. The fact that she was willing to do so eased his guilt somewhat, and also it would allow him to head to the bar with his buddies after work to drink beer and watch sports.

Work itself had been uneventful, as always. It was basically Figueroa's job to monitor the computer systems, and troubleshoot if anything minor went wrong. If a major problem should arise, he had only to make one phone call, really just press one button, and an army of technicians would descend on the place. Nuclear power plants were prepared for all eventualities.

Of course, Figueroa had been there for eleven years, and the next serious thing to go wrong would be the first. In the year and a half since the new computer system had been put in, there hadn't even been a minor glitch. The thing could pretty much run itself, as Figueroa's supervisor mentioned every time he went in to ask for a raise.

But Figueroa was buttoned down on his job, and he dutifully checked the computer systems every twenty minutes. He paid special attention to the systems controlling the fuel rods, since this was the area of greatest danger in a nuclear plant.

The fuel rods generated the heat, and that heat had to be controlled, since that was the key to averting a meltdown. The rods were in a large containment area, and the heat was controlled by lowering covers onto the rods. Lifting the covers meant that the heat would build up, lowering them reduced the heat.

The entire containment area that the rods and covers were in was kept from overheating by a coolant, which was fed into the tank and surrounded them. The coolant then came out the other side as steam, was recooled, and circulated back in. All of this was done to keep the temperature down.

But on this day, as on every day, all systems were checking out fine, and Figueroa's mind wandered to how much traffic he might hit driving to Ocean City on Friday evening.

Combining resources didn't get them any closer to Nolan Murray. Novack and his team basically had no idea where Murray was or what he looked like, and Janssen had little to add. The fact that their separate investigations each led to Murray was a comfort in that it made them more confident they had their sights set on the right guy, but it didn't constitute any real progress toward catching him.

They met in the morning to map out their strategies, though their operations would remain separate. Janssen was there with two members of his team, while Novack was there with Donovan, Emerson, and Andrew Garrett.

Janssen and Novack were clearly the two decision makers, while Donovan seemed to recognize the reality of their respective abilities and mostly deferred to Novack.

"We're still going after him through ITC," Janssen said. "It will come as no surprise that he covered his tracks very effectively. But we still believe that's how he connected to the attacked computer systems, so we've got a bunch of agents and an army of nerds going after it."

Novack nodded, though Janssen was not looking for any

kind of assent or permission. "Our best lead is still through Charlie Harrison," he said. "It's obvious that Murray was directing those financial frauds, before he worked his way up to mass murderer."

Novack continued, "Emerson, using his knowledge and connections in the local hacking community, will investigate the Laufer killing, trying to find people who knew something about the circumstances under which Laufer died. Garrett will man the inside computer operation while Emerson is out in the field, but will venture out if there is a need for him to do so."

Both Emerson and Garrett nodded; their roles had been established before the meeting.

"Okay, good," Janssen said. "The key thing is that we communicate. I don't think there's any doubt that Murray is the guy we've both been after. Something might come up that seems inconsequential to you, but could fit neatly into something we've been developing."

"And vice versa," Novack pointed out.

Janssen nodded. "Absolutely."

Everybody left the room, leaving just Novack and Janssen. They agreed to meet briefly every half hour to consult.

"Garrett gave you an internal department e-mail address," Novack said. "I'll have him go over it with you. You can communicate through that to any of us."

Novack left the office to get back to work, but took the time to call Jamie Wagner. "Sorry about not coming by last night," Novack said. "It couldn't be helped."

Jamie, who was relying heavily on Novack, wasn't quite satisfied with that. "What happened? What's going on?"

"Let's just say that things took a surprising turn."

"No, let's say more than that."

"Okay. Things took a very surprising turn," Novack said. "I need you at that hearing."

"I'll do my best," Novack said. "But if something happens and I'm not there, you can be sure there's a damn good reason."

"No reason could be good enough."

"I'll keep you posted," Novack said, and extricated himself from the call. He and Wagner had a deal, he knew that and intended to keep it, but there was no telling what events might transpire in the next twenty-four hours.

Emerson called in to say that he had found someone who knew Laufer, and was with him at a bar the night he died. He said that Laufer got a phone call that upset him, and he left the bar moments later. Novack told him to get Laufer's cell phone records, in the hope of finding out who made that call.

Novack went into Janssen's office to update him on this news, and waited a few moments because Janssen was on the phone.

"Yes, I understand. Of course I will," Janssen said, and then hung up.

"I just heard from Emerson. He said—"

He didn't get a chance to finish the sentence, because Janssen interrupted him. "We got another call," he said.

The look on his face told Novack what he meant. "Another attack?" Novack asked.

"Most likely. They called with the little girl's voice to get right through, then dropped that. The caller said that playtime was over, and that the price has gone up to five billion."

"What's the target?" Novack asked.

"He wouldn't say; he insisted on talking only to me. They couldn't convince him otherwise."

"So he hung up?"

"Yes, when they told him I was out of town. He said he'd call back in a half hour, and that if he didn't get through to me immediately, he would teach us another lesson."

"Any idea why he would he insist on talking to you?" Novack asked.

Janssen shook his head. "No, and it surprises me. This didn't feel like a one-on-one thing; there was no special relationship established. But I guess we'll find out soon enough."

Janssen spent the next twenty minutes making sure that the FBI techs could trace and monitor the call from where he was. He was assured that it would be no problem, since the call was going to come into the Bureau and be patched into Janssen.

In the interim, Homeland Security was notified and put on alert, but that was a basically empty gesture. The attack could be anywhere in the country, at any kind of facility, and all preparations that could be made had already taken place.

Now they could only wait.

"Here's the problem as I see it, Mike." Those were Murray's first words to Janssen as soon as the call was connected. Then, "It took me a half hour to get through to you, which gives you a half hour less to give me what I want."

"What is it you want?"

"I'm thinking five billion," he said, and then laughed. "That way if I invest it in four percent treasury bonds, or CDs, it will give me fifty million a year, which should provide me with a decent lifestyle, without having to dig into my savings."

"You're pretty funny, for an asshole."

Murray laughed again; he was clearly having a great time. "Whoa, a new approach. Trying to get me angry, maybe goad me into a mistake. Pathetic, but understandable. Anyway, clearly our relationship is deteriorating, so I suggest we get to it."

"I'm ready."

"I own something, and I want the United States government to buy it from me. I've already quoted you my non-negotiable price."

"What are you selling?" Janssen asked.

"The Limerick nuclear power plant. I've owned it for about a year now, but I think the market is right to sell."

Janssen knew two things. One, that the Bureau and Homeland Security people had just sprung into action, and were reaching out to the plant management immediately. And two, that this was a nightmare.

"How is it you own it?"

"First, let me tell you where things stand. I control the computer systems at the plant, which means I am running the entire facility. For the last six hours, I have been slowly draining the coolant from the fuel rod containment area. You may not know what that means, but I'll bet a lot of the other people listening in on this call do."

"I know what it means," Janssen said.

"Good, then you know that I've already triggered the first stage of a meltdown. At the current pace, it's about twelve hours until catastrophe. And the problem is, I'm the only one who can start putting the coolant back in."

He went on to warn that any attempt to enter the plant and bring in outside coolant would precipitate a disaster. At the present time the covers for the fuel rods were lowered 75 percent of the way down, keeping the heat at least somewhat manageable. If plant workers attempted to bring in coolant, Murray would have the covers lifted, exposing the rods fully, and a complete meltdown would be rapid and inevitable.

"In fact," Murray said, "you've got thirty minutes to determine that everything I said is true, and then I want everyone out of the plant. No exceptions. And remember, I control the cameras in there, so I can see everything that goes on. Call you back in thirty."

As soon as Janssen hung up, he was immediately patched into a call with FBI director Barone and the head of Homeland Security. They were joined after maybe a minute by the chief of security and the executive director of the Limerick plant.

The Limerick officials said that immediate steps were being taken to determine the veracity of all that Murray had said, but Janssen already knew that the worst would be shown to be true. Murray had previously and repeatedly demonstrated his power and ruthlessness, and there was no reason to think he'd be bluffing now.

The executive director quickly laid out the facts, and they were daunting. The plant was twenty-eight miles from Philadelphia, and the population living within fifty miles of the plant numbered in excess of eight million. He used the fifty-mile figure because that was the radius the U.S. government suggested should be evacuated during the Japanese nuclear plant crisis.

Within five minutes the report they were waiting for came in. The fuel rods in the plant were in fact already heated to unsafe levels due to a lack of coolant in the tanks. It took a manual inspection to determine that, since the computer systems were still showing no problem whatsoever.

Obviously the computers were no longer reliable, because they were compromised and being controlled from the outside.

Just as obviously, everything Murray said was true.

Novack's call did very little to relieve my anxiety. The fact that he was at least somewhat paying attention and took the time to call was a positive, but that was more than outweighed by his vaguely conditional promise to show up for the hearing and his cryptic nonanswer when I asked what was going on.

I wasn't too worried about not being able to go over his testimony with him in advance. I would lead him where I wanted him to go with my questions, and I knew what his answers would be. He was an experienced witness, having testified in many trials, and there would be no cross-examination to deal with.

If he showed up, we'd be fine. If he didn't show up, we'd be dead in the water.

My own preparation was finished, which gave me twenty-four hours to obsess and worry. Since that is probably my least favorite way to spend time, except for maybe hanging out with my parents, I decided to spend my time in a productive way, even if it didn't benefit our case.

Karen and Terry were to be transferred from the Hackensack hospital to Columbia Presbyterian that morning.

Karen would be put under Dr. Jenkins's care, and she would theoretically be ready to receive a donor heart, should by some chance we succeed with the parole board.

Transferring a weak patient like Karen always involved some stress and had to be handled very carefully, and this particular transfer's difficulty was compounded by the fact that Karen's police protectors had to move with her. If someone were going to go after her, she would be at her most vulnerable during transit.

Her contingent of police was going to be there until she was set up at Columbia Presbyterian, and then Novack had arranged for the protective detail to switch to NYPD. He had friends there, and was able to prevail on them to handle it, even though it was a manpower drain.

I was not that worried about this external danger to Karen; I thought that Hennessey's death had lessened it considerably. Besides, at this point it seemed that Murray had bigger fish to fry. Since Sheryl had clearly talked, there didn't seem much for Murray to gain by trying to break through a police protective unit to kill this young girl, but it was certainly a possibility.

I planned to get to the hospital at around ten, to make sure that Karen and Terry were settled in, and to get them anything they might need. It was an easy subway ride up from my house, especially since subway traffic was still way down due to the all-pervasive terrorist fear.

That fear seemed to be subsiding slightly, as there had been no incidents since the president's address. I didn't share the optimism, or at least reduced pessimism, since I had heard nothing from law enforcement that indicated the terrorists had been identified or stopped. If they were still out there, having operated with impunity, there was no logical reason to believe they would suddenly cease their attacks.

I was incredibly impressed when I got to Columbia Presbyterian and saw the efficiency with which they had handled the transfer. Karen and Terry were well settled in their rooms; it seemed like they had been there a long time. The NYPD guards were also in place, and blocked my entrance until Terry gave them the okay.

Terry was effusive in her praise of everybody involved, and grateful that Karen had come through it so well. She had also met with Dr. Jenkins, and said that he was completely forthcoming and cooperative, which she appreciated. My presence there was clearly not needed, a state of affairs I was starting to get used to.

According to Terry, Karen had also become aware of, and grown more comfortable with, the presence of the police security. "Ever since she saw that man who was killed, she's been pretty nervous. But knowing the police are here helps," Terry said.

"What do you mean, saw the man that was killed?" I asked.

"On television. They said it could be part of Sheryl's case. She saw you also."

I nodded, understanding. Karen's seeing talk of Hennessey's murder, and the newscasters relating it to herself and her mother, could be frightening.

"I could talk to her," I said. "Reassure her."

"Thank you, but I don't think it's necessary," Terry said. "It's just that seeing him brought back that memory. But she's over it now."

"What memory?"

"Of when she saw the man before."

Now I had no idea what she was talking about, but I wasn't going to leave there without finding out. "Terry, the man that was killed, Karen saw him before?"

"Yes. That's what she said."

"I need to talk to her."

Terry was not thrilled with the idea, protectively concerned that I would upset Karen. I assured her that I would not, but I was overstating it. I would try to be gentle, but Karen's level of stress would depend upon the memory of Hennessey that she had.

Terry excused herself and went into Karen's adjacent room, coming out a few minutes later to say that Karen would be willing to talk to me. She led me in to see Karen, who was lying in bed, no tubes or machines attached to her.

She looked so much like Sheryl in person that it was eerie. She was beautiful, but also incredibly frail, and weak, and tired, and vulnerable. She looked exhausted from fighting something she could not defeat.

She looked like she was dying.

"Hello, Karen, my name is Jamie. Jamie Wagner. I'm a friend of your mother."

"You're the man that's trying to help her."

"Yes."

"I don't want her to die."

I had no idea what to say, so I decided to go with the truth, even if it was pretty much a non sequitur. "She loves you very much."

She just nodded; I hoped she would let me off this hook, and she did. "You want to talk about that man I saw on television, the one who was killed."

"Yes. I understand you've seen him before?"

She nodded. "He was with my dad."

"Do you remember where?"

"Not really. It was like on the side of a highway or something. One of those rest areas. My dad pulled over, and this man pulled over in his car. They got out and talked."

"Did you get out as well?"

She shook her head. "My dad told me to stay in the car. He said that was important."

"What else do you remember?"

"The man looked over at me; he stared at me, and it scared me a little . . . not too bad. But they just talked for a few minutes, and the man gave my dad an envelope. Then my dad got back in the car, and we left."

"How is it you remember this?" I asked, since it was an unextraordinary event, witnessed by a seven-year-old girl more than six years ago.

"Because when my dad got back in the car, I asked him who the man was. He told me that he was the person who was going to give us everything we could ever want."

She seemed lost in thought for a few moments, and then said, "It didn't work out that way."

By the time Murray called back, a number of decisions had been made.

The top computer experts that the power company and Homeland Security had would immediately get to work trying to regain control of the Limerick systems. They thought they had a reasonable chance of success in that attempt; if they were right, the crisis would be averted.

But if they were wrong, then the United States government was prepared to pay the five billion dollars. They would do so with great reluctance, and not because of the amount of money involved. Compared to the human and economic toll that would result from a complete meltdown, five billion dollars was a rounding error.

Far more concerning than the money, or even the political implications of paying the money, was what might come next. Murray, if that's in fact who was doing this, had a seemingly endless supply of targets, and a total willingness to hit them. What would stop him from doing this again, and again? Even if they were right in identifying Murray as the perpetrator, they were not much closer to catching him than they were when he brought down the airplane.

But overriding everything was the inescapable fact that a nuclear plant, especially one near a large metropolitan area, could not be allowed to have a meltdown. The results would be so devastating and so profound that it was simply unthinkable.

The other decision that was made was to order an immediate evacuation of up to forty miles, which would include the city of Philadelphia, and to place an alert twenty miles farther in each direction, which was in effect a pre-evacuation order.

It was determined that it would not be the president who would make the announcement; they would hold him off pending subsequent events. It would be the director of Homeland Security, along with the FBI director, who would issue a statement and answer a limited number of questions.

But the press conference, and the evacuation decision, would await two things: the determination as to whether computer control could be restored at the plant, and what conditions Murray would apply when he called back.

What they didn't know was that Murray was in no hurry to call back. Time was on his side; his previous precipitous behavior in causing the disasters made him frighteningly unpredictable to the authorities. They would fear he would destroy the plant on a moment's notice, and a delay in his scheduled call would increase their panic at the prospect.

While Murray was calm and in control, his partner Daniel Churchill was less so. Churchill was almost as brilliant on the computer as Murray, which was somewhat ironic since at first Churchill had been the teacher and Murray the student.

Murray once literally saved Churchill from going to jail, and in return Churchill imparted his knowledge to him. Before long Murray had outdistanced him, and as good as Churchill was, Murray's prowess amazed him.

What Churchill also lacked was Murray's strategic thinking, and coolness under pressure. It was why Murray naturally gravitated toward the leadership role, and why Churchill never resisted it.

So Churchill sat at his computer, through which he had control of the Limerick plant, and let Murray run the operation. Murray's coolness and strategic thinking would both be tested that day, Churchill knew. No matter how prepared they were, they would run into difficulties, and unwelcome surprises.

But one thing that would not get in their way was something that neither he nor Murray possessed.

A conscience.

The call came at the fifty-one-minute mark, twenty-one minutes late.

By the time Janssen got on the phone, the bad news he was expecting had come in from Homeland Security; they were unable to regain control of the plant computer systems. Nolan Murray was right; he owned the plant, and he was already raising the temperature to dangerous levels.

The first things to melt would be the rods themselves. That is the extent of what happened at Three Mile Island, which was why it was classified as only a partial meltdown. That would be bad enough, but if the heat were allowed to keep increasing, unchecked, it would soon burn through the protective casing and then even the containment building.

That would qualify as a total meltdown.

And a total catastrophe.

There were essentially no options, or at least none that were particularly good. They could invade the plant, taking physical control, but would be unable to activate the cooling system. Bringing in outside water to act as a coolant was impractical in the time frame, particularly since it would provoke Murray into lifting the covers from the rods, which would trigger the meltdown.

Another possibility was to use helicopters to drop a mixture of elements, including boron, clay, lead, sand, and others, on top of the reactor to limit the amount of radiation that could escape into the atmosphere. That would be followed by literally encasing the plant in cement, as had been done with Chernobyl. The difference was that the Chernobyl plant had already essentially collapsed, making the burial that much easier. Whether all of this could be done at all at Limerick was very questionable, and in the required time was nearly impossible. Even if it were accomplished, it would not be without a very significant leakage of radiation.

It was a measure of the government's desperation that both ill-advised solutions were being prepared at breakneck speed. There was always the very real chance that Murray, even after the money was paid, would follow through on destroying the plant. The responses had to be ready, whatever the odds against their success.

As far as the evacuation of the people living within range of the reactor, Janssen didn't need Bureau reports to tell him what was going on. CNN on the television in his office did that quite well.

"Authorities are not even denying that the situation is chaotic," the TV reporter was saying. "There is just no easy way to move hundreds of thousands of frightened people."

Janssen then watched the report cut to a woman who was resisting efforts by the police to get her to leave. "Will we ever be back?" she cried. "This is our home!"

At that moment, the call came from the man who had caused all the fear and anguish. "I assume you've confirmed that everything I said about the plant is true," Murray said. "The payment instructions will be e-mailed to you in twenty minutes."

"Why so long?" Janssen asked. "Radiation could be leaking out of the plant already."

"Nothing compared to what will happen if you try to avoid compliance. Do you understand?"

"I understand perfectly."

"Good. The instructions will be rather complicated. Make sure you have treasury officials available to take the necessary steps. I will call back in forty-five minutes to confirm that the money has been paid."

Of all the aspects of the operation, Murray was probably most proud of the payment instructions. The wiring would go through so many steps, in so many pieces, involving so many banks and fake corporations, that it would ultimately be impossible to trace. Murray smiled at the realization that he designed it and even he probably wouldn't have been good enough to trace it.

"Why don't you lower the covers and let some coolant in?" Janssen asked. "We'll pay the money; you know we have no choice. If we don't pay, you can heat the damn thing up again."

"Gee, let me think about that," Murray said, and laughed just before he hung up.

I'm not sure I've ever heard such stunning news. I was listening to the radio on the way to the prison, and they cut in to announce that a terrorist takeover was in progress at a nuclear plant near Philadelphia. It was reported to be the same perpetrators that had committed the previous attacks, and an evacuation was under way.

But as enormous as that news was, that wasn't the stunning part. At least not to me.

The authorities had named a suspect.

Nolan Murray.

I instantly understood why Novack had become so hard to reach, why he referred to things as having taken "a surprising turn," and why there was a possibility that a "good reason" could prevent him from making the hearing. As reasons go, that was about as good as it could get.

There was nothing else for me to do but continue on to the prison to see Sheryl. I have a number of interests, but the dominant one is probably "self." So my natural inclination was to try and figure what impact this new development might have on our case.

The obvious negative was that Novack would have other

things on his mind, and certainly other demands on his time. I had to assume that he would be a key player in the national investigation; he probably knew more about Murray than the FBI would, though that wasn't much.

The positive was that Murray was going to be a key part of my case, and it wouldn't exactly now be hard to convince the board that he was capable of evil. In that regard it would seem to increase our credibility considerably, providing it didn't look as if we were just latching on to the villain of the day. Which brought us back to Novack; his saying it would have much more meaning than me saying it.

Sheryl surprised me yet again. First, because she hugged me hello. That is not something she had done before; we hadn't touched in any way since the ill-advised kiss. I hugged her back; it seemed to come naturally. Very naturally.

A more significant and revealing surprise was her reaction to the nuclear plant situation in Pennsylvania. She had heard only a sketchy report on it, and she peppered me with questions, few of which I could answer. But her interest extended well beyond the impact it might have on her case; she really cared on a human level. She was concerned about what kind of world her daughter would grow old in.

I, being considerably less focused on the future of humanity than this person who was attempting to die, related it back to our case. I went over that case in detail with Sheryl, in effect rehearsing my presentation.

"You're doing a great job," she said.

"But you've got the important role to play, not me. You are going to have be convincing in your testimony."

"I'll tell the truth," she said.

"Right. But part of that truth is admitting that you lied, when you said you killed Charlie."

She nodded. "I understand." Then, "Terry told me you met Karen."

"I did. She reminded me of you."

"Thank you. How did she look?"

"Weak. But she was hanging in there. And she told me that she had seen Hennessey, once, when she was with Charlie. I wrote out a statement about that, which she signed. It can be a helpful piece of evidence."

Sheryl smiled. "She's always had a great memory. She remembers things that I forget . . . things that we did together when she was little." She paused, seeming to let the memories come back, and then said, "The only times we had together were when she was little."

I didn't know what to say, which probably happened more in the little time I had spent with Sheryl than in the rest of my life put together. The problem was that I had no idea how I wanted this situation to end. There was simply no resolution that I could come up with that would be satisfactory.

What I did instead of saying something comforting or sensitive was continue going over the testimony with Sheryl. I didn't want to do so in too much detail, because I didn't want it to sound rehearsed.

After a half hour, I stopped it. Sheryl was going to be fine; it would be her lawyer who might be in danger of losing it.

Janssen heard the beep, which signaled that the e-mail had arrived. Novack came in and looked over his shoulder as he read it. It was a four-page set of instructions to wire the money, which was complicated beyond the ability of either man to understand.

Since it had come in on the department e-mail, Janssen forwarded it to his Bureau e-mail, which was being monitored by everyone in the operation. It was a cumbersome but unavoidable way of doing it, and Janssen even thought it might be another mind game played by Murray to keep them a little off balance. Janssen didn't know enough about how computers and e-mail operated, but he even thought it might be a way to make it harder to trace it back to the sender.

Once it was widely disseminated, the financial people set to work following the wiring instructions. Simultaneous efforts were being made to trace the money once it was sent, but that was clearly going to be difficult. Some of the pieces might be recovered, but the majority of the money was going to get to its ultimate destination, which only Murray knew.

Janssen turned up the sound on the television, which seemed to have a permanent BREAKING NEWS banner stamped across the bottom. The situation at the Limerick plant was deteriorating. The fuel rods were already melting, having reached a temperature of four thousand degrees Fahrenheit.

"How hot is too hot?" Novack asked.

"If it hits five thousand, it's over," Janssen said.

The military had been brought in to assist in the evacuation. The governor of Pennsylvania had called in the National Guard, but the president did him one better and brought in the Army and Marines. The president also declared the area an official disaster emergency, the first time in recorded American history that such a declaration was made for a disaster that hadn't really taken place yet.

Radiation emissions were being measured and breathlessly reported. At that point the leakage was not particularly significant, but that was not stopping the panic from fanning out across the country and the world. In Europe they were already talking about cutting off imports of American beef and dairy products, because of possible contamination.

The world had decided that catastrophe was imminent.

At that moment, Murray and Churchill were doing what Janssen, Novack, and everyone else in America and the world was doing; they were watching it play out on television. The difference was that they watched it in admiration of their own handiwork, while everyone else watched it in horror.

There was really nothing else for them to do, except monitor the Limerick computer system and cameras to make sure that their opposition wasn't taking countermeasures. Murray's reaction to any such move would be swift and sure, he would send the plant into total meltdown. It would mean not getting the money, but that would be a temporary setback. He had other targets waiting to be hit.

But basically they were just waiting until it was time for Murray to once again call Janssen, to confirm that the money was sent. It might not even be necessary, since their monitoring of the bank's computers would let them follow the trail. But he wanted to be able to further manipulate Janssen and the situation, and he needed to initiate contact to do that.

Ten minutes before Murray was scheduled to call Janssen, he saw the first signs of the demanded money entering the banking system. Then the rest of it was entered, and Murray knew that all the money had been sent.

He had known they would cave, but it still was exhilarating to see. He was going to be rich beyond imagination.

"The money is being sent," said Murray.

Churchill jumped out of his chair, pumping his fist. "YES!"

Murray just sat in his chair, not moving, and then said, "You feel like a pizza? I'm buying."

Churchill laughed and said, "Sure, I'm starving. But aren't you going to call them and end this?"

"Not yet," Murray said. "Let's let things heat up a little bit."

Ten minutes later, Murray made the call, and the first thing Janssen said was, "The money has been paid."

"I'll have to confirm that for myself," Murray said. "I trust you won't take offense at that?"

Silent alarm bells went off in Janssen's head. Somebody with a third the computer abilities of Murray would have already known the money was sent. "Hurry it up," he said. "Radiation is escaping. You've got what you want."

"And you'll get what you want, as soon as I confirm the money has been sent."

With that he hung up, leaving a frustrated Janssen powerless to do anything but wait and see if the lowest form of human he'd ever encountered would do the honorable thing. It was not a comfortable feeling.

Once he had hung up, Churchill said, "You want me to lower the covers and let the coolant in?"

"No."

"Why not?" asked Churchill, surprised.

"I've been thinking. If the reactor is not too badly damaged, they'll be able to get in and take the computer systems apart. They could figure out a way to track it back to us."

"You told me there was no way they could do that."

"And there probably isn't. But there's definitely no way if the entire building melts down."

"I don't think we need to do that," Churchill said.

Murray shrugged. "Maybe not. Let's drink a toast to our victory, and then talk about it some more."

Murray took two beers out of the refrigerator, and handed one to Churchill. "To five billion dollars," he said, holding up his bottle.

Churchill smiled and held up his own bottle. "To champagne instead of beer."

Churchill was unaware that his bottle contained more than just beer as they drank their toast, and as the reactor temperature continued to rise.

Andrew Garrett knew the person to call was Novack. He had tried to reach Emerson, but Emerson was also out in the field, and not answering his phone. He sent him a text, but didn't want to wait.

He called into the precinct, and was told by the desk sergeant that Novack was in Janssen's office, and was not to be disturbed. "Disturb him," Garrett said. "Now."

So in less than a minute, Novack was on the phone. "What have you got?" he asked.

"I talked to this girl . . . she was going out with Laufer . . . she's like a computer nerd groupie. Didn't know who killed him, or anything about it, but—"

"Shorthand it, Garrett. We're running out of time here."

"Okay. When I asked her if she knew Murray, she freaked. About six months ago she met him at a bar. He was drunk, and he took her home . . . he passed out, and woke up at three o'clock in the morning and freaked that she was there. Didn't remember bringing her home. She was scared stiff, so afraid he was going to kill her that she took off in her goddamn underwear."

"And?"

"And she knows where he lives. It's in Glen Rock; I'm right down the street from the house now."

"Is anyone in the house now?"

"There are lights on, but I haven't gotten close enough."

"Where's Emerson?"

"On the way here. I just texted him."

Garrett gave him the address, and Novack promised to get there right away. He quickly notified Donovan, who insisted on coming along, and then arranged for a SWAT team to meet him where Garrett was calling from. Then he went into Janssen's office.

"We've got something. Don't know how good it is; it's a possible location for Murray."

"I can get agents to meet you at the scene."

Novack shook his head. "We're on it. If it amounts to anything, I'll take you up on that. Good luck here."

Janssen nodded. "Yeah." He knew that luck was not going to be a factor. They were dependent on Murray to be satisfied with the money, and stop the attack on the reactor.

Preparations were being made to enter the reactor and attempt to flood it with coolant. Failing that, they were going to airdrop the chemicals. Neither was likely to work, but doing nothing wasn't going to do the trick either.

The address in Glen Rock was about twenty minutes away, and Novack made it in twelve. Emerson had gotten there a couple of minutes before, and the SWAT team pulled up just after Novack. The street was typical suburbia, each house on maybe half an acre, well-kept lawns, some with children's toys on them.

Garrett pointed out the house; it was fairly well suited for their purposes. They could get close without likely being seen, and the rear of the house butted up against dense woods, which would provide cover.

Novack immediately sized up the situation and laid out a plan, telling the SWAT team where to position themselves.

It wasn't ideal; he would have wanted two snipers placed high up, but the only places for that would be the upstairs of the two adjacent houses. They couldn't risk the commotion that entering those houses would cause, especially since the inhabitants of the houses might well panic.

Novack would approach from the left side, and Donovan the right. Garrett would stay back, ready to enter when the coast was clear. He was the most valuable member of the group, since if this were really where Murray was operating from, Garrett's computer expertise could be called on to stop the attack on the reactor.

As they were moving into position, Novack felt his phone vibrate. He looked at it and saw that it was Janssen, so he answered it, softly so he could not be heard in the house.

"Novack."

"Have you got anything?" Janssen asked.

"We're about to find out."

"Well, hurry the hell up. The son of a bitch turned up the heat."

Novack motioned everybody quickly into position. There would be no time to wait, no time to approach carefully, no time to make sure this wasn't really Beaver Cleaver's suburban home.

And then they heard the shots, coming from inside the house.

They had no way of knowing that the gun that fired the shots was operated remotely.

Novack gave the signal and they rushed the house, firing their weapons as they got there. Emerson got there first, followed by Novack and then the SWAT team, coming in from their position slightly farther back. In the barrage of gunfire, Daniel Churchill was shot seven times.

They had no way of knowing at that moment that he was dead from poison well before the first bullet hit him.

Novack took in the situation, saw the computer console,

and called for Andrew Garrett. Garrett raced in, ran to the console, and desperately tried to figure out how to operate the reactor coolant remotely. Emerson and Novack watched over his shoulder, as the SWAT team members made sure there was no one else in the house, and that it was secure.

Garrett expressed surprise at the ease with which he figured things out, and within ten minutes he had coolant flowing back into the chamber, and the covers lowered. They were able to watch on the monitors as the emergency workers rushed into the building, and added even more coolant manually.

That accomplished, Novack went over to the dead body, checking to see if he was carrying any identification. There was none, which was not a surprise to Novack, since by that time he had a sense of how Nolan Murray operated.

He had no way of knowing it was not Nolan Murray.

"I am here representing Sheryl Harrison, an innocent woman. You will hear from her, and you will hear from John Novack, the officer who arrested her six years ago. You also know, unless you've been living on Mars since yesterday, that he is a newly minted national hero."

Sheryl and Novack sat on each side of me while I talked. We were in a conference room at the prison, which was specifically used for hearings of this type.

I was particularly grateful to Novack; in light of everything that happened the day before, there were a million things he could have been doing, including going on every interview program in the world. But instead, he had been with me since last night, helping me implement my strategy.

Novack and I conducted an interview late the previous day with *The New York Times,* in which we laid out the entire case to be presented to the parole board. Our deal with the *Times* was that the interview would run in its entirety in the morning paper.

It was an easy deal to strike, since Novack also agreed to give a full interview about the events leading to Murray's shooting, and the defusing of the reactor. The interviewer really had his act together, and drew details out of Novack that I found surprising and interesting.

The piece ran as promised; I assumed that the three members of the board, led by Commissioner Stanley Breslin, had read it. It made our presentation to them redundant, but still worth going through with.

I also sent a copy of the presentation to the governor, in my official petition for an immediate commutation of Sheryl's sentence. I had no doubt that he would have read the piece as well, and I had more hope in winning in his "court" than with the parole board.

The governor was by definition a political animal, and there had been a lot of people on Sheryl's side since the whole matter went public. Even more important, at that moment taking a side against Novack was political folly, and Novack was squarely in Sheryl's corner.

But I was not about to put all my eggs in one basket, so we gave what I thought was a compelling and energetic presentation to the board. First I took Novack through the investigation, and he drew a straight line from Sheryl to Hennessey to Laufer and on, with the line not stopping until it led to the Limerick nuclear reactor and Nolan Murray.

The board members hung on every word; their expressions said that they were thrilled to be close-up witnesses to history.

Next I introduced Sheryl, who described in heartfelt words what happened in that room six years ago, and why she confessed to a murder she did not commit.

I asked her a bunch of questions, fleshing out the details, and she answered them simply and honestly. Then she summed up by saying, "So recently I told the truth, which I should have done many years ago. I didn't have any idea that it would ultimately lead to capturing Nolan Murray, or preventing a national disaster. I'm very grateful for that, but it's not something I can take any credit for.

"I finally told the truth for one simple reason. My daughter is very ill, and I want to be with her."

I wanted to hug her when she finished, to hold on to her and tell her how great she was, and how much I cared about her. But I don't think lawyers do that, and so I didn't.

What I did do was fill in what I thought were some slight holes in the testimony we had presented, and provide some additional evidence. Included in that was the document that Karen signed, in which she said that she had seen Hennessey with her father, before seeing him on television as a murder victim. Something was bothering me about that, but I couldn't put my finger on it.

The board members had questions for both Novack and Sheryl. The ones for Novack were somewhere between respectful and hero worship, centering mainly on the later parts of the investigation, more about Nolan Murray than Sheryl.

Then they questioned Sheryl, and they were surprisingly and disappointingly on point. They asked whether the reports of her wanting to give her heart to her daughter were true, pointing out that it was their responsibility not to release someone who they believed would go out and once again break the law.

Sheryl deflected the question as we had discussed, saying that her plans were private, but that no one would be hurt by her actions and society would not suffer.

I took it one step further. "I know you understand and are respectful of your obligations," I said, "but you also have an obligation to justice. If you have listened to this entire presentation, and I know you have, then you cannot have any doubt that Sheryl Harrison has spent six years in prison for a crime she did not commit. You also cannot have any doubt that she will be exonerated and freed by the courts, but that is a process that takes time. She wants to be with her daughter, and for that there is simply no time."

It was finally over, and we were asked to go to an adjacent room while the members discussed the case, and wait there in case they had any further questions for us.

Novack said that he had to leave, that there were "a thousand ridiculous reports to write" about the previous day's events. I shook his hand and thanked him for coming through for us, and Sheryl hugged him.

He hugged her back. "It's going to work out," he said, and then smiled. "Whatever the hell that means."

We waited in the room for a half hour, then an hour, even though they had said it would only be twenty minutes. I was getting rather annoyed, and preparing to complain, when Stanley Breslin came in.

"We have decided that releasing Ms. Harrison based on newly found evidence is outside of our province," he said. "It is a job that is rightly for the courts, and taking it upon ourselves would be setting a dangerous precedent."

I was going to argue, but it wouldn't have helped. Besides, he wasn't finished talking, and he was smiling.

"But it doesn't matter," he said, "because the governor has just commuted the sentence."

I was never really comfortable on a computer. It was ironic, because the case had been so much about computers. But what I was doing that night on my laptop was so awful that when I was finished, I was going to smash it with a hammer.

I was running computer searches for painless ways to commit suicide, ways that would not damage vital organs. I thought the answers would be plentiful, but all I did was turn up countless pleas to distraught people telling them not to die, that life was too worth living.

That's what I wanted to tell Sheryl, among a thousand other things, but there was little time left to do it. She was spending one more night at the prison, while the court reviewed the governor's commutation and processed it. The next day she would be released. She would go straight to the hospital, spend time with Karen and Terry, and then die. Dr. Jenkins was notified and ready.

So it was up to me to figure out how. I should have done it earlier, but I never wanted to acknowledge that it could happen, and I must have cut the class in law school when they taught us that killing someone you love was a lawyer's responsibility.

But there I was, searching and taking notes, when there was a knock on my door. I opened it and there were my parents, breathing heavily from the trudge up the steps. I think I would have been less surprised to see George and Martha Washington.

"Hello, Jamie," my mother said, and hugged me. My father clapped me on the shoulder, and they came in. I made coffee, and we talked for a couple of hours, though it seemed like much less.

They had read about everything in the papers, and knew what I must be going through, so they came to comfort me. My parents. Came. To. Comfort. Me.

As beyond amazing as that was, it paled in amazing-ness next to the fact that it worked. Don't get me wrong, I wasn't turning cartwheels, but it felt good that they were there, and that they understood what I was dealing with.

And when they were ready to leave, my father said, "You seem down, Jamie. Depressed and lethargic, and—"

"Yes, Dad, I—" I interrupted, but he interrupted my interruption.

"And you seem to be scratching a lot. Are your allergies bothering you?"

"Allergies? I don't have . . ."

He reached into his pocket and took out two small bottles of pills. There were no labels on the bottles. "One of these is for your depression, and one is for your allergies. But don't take too many, and don't take them together. Were you to take six of each, you would certainly not survive. Your death would be painless, but it would be certain, and very quick."

I took the bottles from his hand, and the next thing I knew I was hugging both my parents and we were all crying.

I picked Sheryl up at the prison at 10:00 A.M. Her actual release was fairly easy; the prison officials had prepared well, probably fearing the glare of the press. When she was brought out to me, we hugged briefly. "You doing okay?" I asked.

She smiled. "Best day in a while, and you made it happen."

We walked out of the building, and I saw her take a quick look up at the sky. As we made our way toward the parking lot, she saw the enormous media contingent waiting for us. "So this is real life?" she asked.

"It is for us celebrity lawyers."

As we made our way through the reporters called out questions, some of which were a little too direct and painful for my taste. Sheryl seemed not to hear them, though I knew she had to.

The forty-five-minute drive to the hospital was an uncomfortable one. We didn't talk much, although I had an endless conversation going in my head. I tested out a bunch of comments in silence, but none of them came close to accomplishing what I was trying to say.

One thing I wasn't going to do, much as I wanted to, was try to talk her out of doing what she wanted. It wouldn't be fair to her. She knew she still could change her mind, and she knew what the result of her actions would be. My pointing it all out would add nothing to the picture.

She was quiet as well, but I had no idea what she could be thinking. There were no circumstances in which I could read a woman's mind, and to hope to succeed with a woman just freed from prison after six years, about to see her daughter and mother, and about to die at her own hands, was completely out of the question.

We got to the hospital, and Dr. Jenkins was there to greet us. Before we went to see Karen, he took Sheryl and me in to talk to the executive director of the hospital, who actually read to us from a prepared statement, no doubt written by the hospital's lawyers.

The hospital was very carefully distancing themselves from anything that Sheryl was planning to do. They were telling Sheryl that they would give Karen excellent care, including a heart transplant should a donor heart become available. In that regard, they had no power and could merely wait for that possible availability, wherever it might come from.

I agreed with their approach. They were already taking a legal and public relations risk by participating in this at all, and they were demonstrating what I considered great courage by doing so. Protecting themselves in this manner was fine with me, and fine with Sheryl as well. She thanked the executive director and Dr. Jenkins, and everybody in the room knew what she was thanking them for.

Finally, Dr. Jenkins took us up to Karen's room, or at least the room they had moved Karen into. It was actually a three-room "suite," which I suspected was done to give Sheryl privacy. Karen could be in one room, Sheryl in another, and the rest of us in the third.

In the elevator, Sheryl asked how Karen was, and Jenkins said that she was very weak, and that she had very little time left. He looked at me, and I had the feeing he was trying to tell me something, but I wasn't close to figuring out what it was.

When we got there, Terry was alone with Karen, who was in bed sleeping. Terry and Sheryl hugged for a long time, and I could see them both try to keep from crying. Karen looked small and frail; I hoped she was strong enough to survive the surgery. Failing to do so would be unimaginably awful.

Everyone was counting on her to live her mother's life.

Terry went into an adjoining room; she had said her good-byes to her daughter, and it was understandable that she couldn't be there to watch her "departure." As a non-parent, I couldn't come close to imagining what she was going through.

Sheryl went over to Karen's bed, leaned over, and kissed her forehead. I wanted to leave the room, to give them privacy, but I couldn't get myself to do it. Karen opened her eyes and saw her mother standing there. She said something, so softly that it was hard for me to hear. I think it was, "Ma, don't. I can't let you."

"It's okay, sweetheart. This is the way it should be. And the truth is that nothing will change; you've always had my heart."

Then she straightened up and walked to the door to the adjoining room. She took a deep breath and said, "Jamie, can I see you for a second?"

I nodded and started to follow her into the other room. Before I could do so, Dr. Jenkins came over and blocked my path.

He spoke softly, so that only I could hear. "Don't let her do it."

"I don't understand," I said, because I didn't.

"Just don't let her do it. It's too late."

"But . . ."

"Jamie, listen to me. Do not let her do it. I am telling you that it's too late."

"Jamie . . . ," Sheryl said, with the door to the other room open. "Are you coming?"

I cast a helpless glance at Dr. Jenkins, but he was neither backing down nor further enlightening me. I followed Sheryl into the room and she closed the door behind us. She had already removed the pills I gave her, the pills my father gave me, from her bag. She pulled me toward her and pressed her head against my chest.

"You're the best, Harvard."

I couldn't talk; I literally couldn't say a word.

"Some lady is going to be lucky to get you," she said. "But don't limit yourself; give some Yale girls a chance."

She held up the pills and said, "Ten minutes, right?"

That's what my father had told me, and that's what I had already told Sheryl, so I nodded.

"Just checking," she said, then, "This is tougher than I thought it would be, and it's not like I expected a walk in the park."

I gently took the pills from her hand, which surprised her. "What are you doing?"

"I can't let you take these," I said.

"Don't go there, Harvard. We've been over this. I need you to be strong for me here, okay?"

I decided to try honesty, because I couldn't think of anything else. "Sheryl, Dr. Jenkins told me to stop you."

"Why?" She was getting annoyed. "This was all planned, okay? It's—"

I interrupted her. "He said it's too late."

She was just starting to process this in her mind when the door opened and Dr. Jenkins came in. He spoke directly to Sheryl. "You should come back in here right away."

The look of panic in Sheryl's eyes was something I'll never forget. Dr. Jenkins turned around and went back into the other room, and Sheryl rushed after him. I wanted to follow as well, but it took a few moments to get my legs to swing into action. They were having enough trouble holding me up.

It took maybe twenty seconds until I heard it, a moan, more like a wail, coming from Sheryl. I finally went back into the main room, but was surprised by what I saw, or really what I didn't see.

Karen was lying on her bed, eyes closed and peaceful. But neither Sheryl nor Dr. Jenkins was there. It wasn't until I heard Sheryl sobbing that I realized she was in the third room.

I moved to that open door, and when I got there I immediately understood what had happened. Terry was lying on her bed, also with her eyes closed and peaceful. Sheryl's head was on Terry's chest, and she was sobbing more softly now.

Dr. Jenkins saw me come in, and came over to me. All he said was, "We have a donor heart." He then picked up the phone, waited a moment, and said, "We're ready."

"Did you know, Jamie?" Sheryl was asking me if I knew in advance of Terry's plans to donate her own heart, in place of Sheryl's. It was shortly after the operation finished, and Dr. Jenkins had come in a few minutes earlier to say that it had gone very, very well.

"No," I said. "I had no idea. All I knew was that she had asked to meet with Dr. Jenkins, and did so. She said she wanted to understand everything that was going to happen. She never said she'd be the one to make it happen."

"Would you have told me if you knew?"

"I haven't really thought about it, but probably not."

"Why not?" she asked.

"I guess because it was her right to do it, just like it would have been your right. And I would think that you'd understand what she did better than anybody."

"It's not the same," she said. "I was saving someone innocent in Karen, someone who had done nothing to deserve her fate. My mother was saving me, and no one could describe me as innocent."

"The governor just did. The facts just did."

"I don't mean innocent of Charlie's murder. I mean

truly innocent. You know what my mother had to go through because of me? I took away her life long before today."

"I don't agree," I said. "But if you're right, then you need to make the most of the life she's given you."

Sheryl didn't ask me any of the details about how Terry pulled the whole thing off. She would have had to be tested, to make sure she was a match, and she would have had to have gotten the means to take her own life.

I couldn't have answered those questions anyway, but I'm sure that Dr. Jenkins was very helpful to her. He'd probably never admit it, but at this point it really didn't matter.

Sheryl planned to stay at the hospital with Karen, and in fact Dr. Jenkins said that she should be conscious and mostly alert in a relatively short time. Sheryl was getting ready to see her, and to tell her what her grandmother had done.

It would be a wrenching conversation, and not one I had any right or desire to witness. I said my good-bye, and left.

I got home and suddenly felt completely exhausted. I wanted to forget everything that had happened; I wanted to once again think about things that were of no consequence.

But I knew that was not about to happen, even if I were capable of it. It would be a long while until the media would let me forget. Sheryl's story was a media sensation. It would have been so under any circumstances, but its direct connection to the terrorist attacks made it far more so.

I turned off my phone the moment I got home; the answering machine was already full and not accepting any more messages. I listened to them, and one was from Gerard Timmerman, asking that I return the call. I had no idea why he wanted to talk to me, and the truth was that I didn't give a shit.

But to the degree that I could control it, I wanted to forget about at least the nuts and bolts of the case. So I set out to do it that very night. I had to write some final motions, some housekeeping details as Sheryl's representative.

I wanted to get it over with, so I forced myself to go through the file. When I got to the photo of Hennessey that I had shown Sheryl, I remembered her reaction recoiling from it. Then I thought about Karen, having seen him all those years before, and being told by her father that Hennessey would change their lives for the better.

I moved on, but came back to Hennessey's picture, because I realized what had been nagging at me when I presented the parole board with the document Karen signed, the one in which she said she had seen him with her father.

I called Sheryl, still at the hospital with Karen. Sheryl said that they had spoken, and that together they had a lot to deal with, but she thought Karen was going to be okay. She seemed less sure about herself.

Jenkins had also provided an additional update. The operation had gone very well; Jenkins called it a complete success. The dangerous part, dealing with the body's efforts at rejection of the foreign organ, was still to come. But for the moment all looked good.

"Sheryl, there's something I need you to ask Karen about, something that was in the file."

"Can't it wait until tomorrow?" she asked. "She's been through so much."

"Sheryl, trust me. This is one question that can't wait."

"Okay."

"Terry had said that Karen was upset, because she saw the picture on television of the man that was murdered, and she had seen him before."

"I know."

"I need to know when that was. I need to know when Karen saw the picture of the murder victim on television."

Sheryl put me on hold, and went to the next room to see

if Karen was still awake. She came back less than two minutes later. "Just a few days ago. Earlier this week."

I thanked her, said good-bye, and called Novack on his cell. He answered with, "I was just going to call you, lawyer. You okay?"

He was referring to my emotional well-being after what he knew was a difficult day. "I'm doing well," I said, even though I had no idea if I was. "But I need to talk to you."

"What about?"

"Nolan Murray."

"I'm at Cindy's. Come on over."

It took me almost an hour to get there; the traffic was backed up because of an accident on the bridge. I was getting more than a little tired of driving to New Jersey; it sort of defeated the purpose of living in New York.

I was concerned about the conversation I was about to have with Novack. He was not going to like what I had to say, that was a given. But I needed him to consider it fairly and carefully, because I needed his help if I was going to get anywhere with it.

Cindy had made sandwiches while waiting for me to get there; I was hungry but did not want to do anything to delay my conversation with Novack. "Remember the letter I presented from Karen? The one where she said she had seen Hennessey six years ago, with her father?"

"Of course."

"She said she saw Hennessey's picture on television, after he was murdered."

Novack started to nod, then stopped himself, and said, "Damn."

"Right," I said. "Hennessey's picture was never released to the media. He wasn't even named as the victim. You wanted to hold that back."

"So what did she see?"

"Well, it turns out that she saw the picture on TV earlier

this week. She didn't see Hennessey; I'm betting she saw Laufer. Which means that Laufer was with Charlie Harrison six years ago."

Novack thought about it for a few moments, and then said, "I assume you have a theory about what this means?"

"I'm working on one; you can help me flesh it out."

Novack turned to Cindy. "I think we'll hold off on the sandwiches for a while."

Novack and I agreed I should talk to Emerson, so I called him the next morning. It was Saturday, so he was off, but I left word at the precinct that it was urgent they get in touch with him, and he called me back about a half hour later.

"Listen, would you have time to talk to me for a few minutes? I've been going over my notes on the case, and there's a couple of things that don't make sense to me. I think you might be able to clear it up."

"Can't it wait until Monday?"

"It can, but I'm pretty anxious to get this off my plate. And Monday I'm going to have to start looking for a job."

"Okay, sure," he said. "Maybe an hour?"

"Great. You want to meet for coffee?"

"I'm doing some work around the house," he said. "Why don't you come over here?"

He gave me the address, and then said, "It won't take long, right?"

"I promise."

An hour later I pulled into his driveway on Thirty-eighth Street in Paterson. He came onto the porch to meet me, a smile on his face. "I don't suppose you know anything about electrical wiring?"

"You're not supposed to play with it while you're taking a bath," I said. "That's pretty much it."

He smiled again. "Thanks, that's just the kind of expertise I needed."

I followed him in and we sat in the den. "So what's on your mind?" he asked.

I came straight to the point. "My client's daughter said she saw a picture on television of a man who was murdered. It upset her because she saw the same man with her father a long time ago."

"Who was the murdered guy?"

"Well, that's what's got me stumped, and I can't ask her for a while, because she just had a major surgery. I assumed it was Hennessey, but then I realized that his picture wasn't released to the media. Based on the time frame of when she saw the picture, I'm thinking now it must have been Laufer."

He looked puzzled. "Why would Laufer have been with her father?"

"Beats me. And her father said the man was going to give them a lot of money, or something to that effect. So if it was Laufer, then it would mean he was working with Nolan Murray."

He shook his head. "Makes no sense. Laufer fingered Murray; he put us on to him in the first place."

I nodded. "Right. And if for some reason it was all a setup, and Murray wanted Laufer to put us on to him, how could he know we'd go to the school and interview Laufer?"

"He couldn't, so it falls apart."

"How did we get to Laufer in the first . . ." I caught myself in midsentence, and stopped.

"What's that?" he asked.

"Nothing, just thinking out loud," I said, then stood up. "Well, I guess with Laufer and Murray both dead, it doesn't much matter anyway. Thanks for your time."

I started for the door, but his words stopped me. "Hold it, Wagner."

I turned and saw that he had a gun in his hand, and he was pointing it at me. "Do you realize that the entire country was trying to figure it out, and you're the only one that did?"

"Right now I'm not feeling too good about that," I said.

"Everybody who knew anything is dead," he said. "Except you. And your client's daughter. I'll have to take care of her before I leave."

I knew I was talking to someone who had killed hundreds of people, and had been willing to kill hundreds of thousands. But the idea that he would kill Karen somehow seemed to cross some ridiculous line that I had in my mind, and I couldn't take it anymore. "You are a piece of shit," I said.

He laughed. "For a lawyer, you've got some guts. But unfortunately for you, I can create people, and I can make them disappear. You are going to join the disappearing group."

He started to raise the gun, and the room exploded; SWAT team members came in from everywhere. If anyone yelled "Freeze!" I sure as hell didn't hear it. Emerson turned toward one of the smashed windows, but before he could point the gun he was cut down by what seemed like a thousand bullets.

The next thing I knew, Novack was alongside me. "Well done, lawyer. You even had me believing it."

"The guy could have shot me. There had to be an easier way."

"I told you, he wasn't someone to leave a paper trail. We needed him to implicate himself, and he sure did that."

I nodded, I had known he was right, and events confirmed it. “I’m going home now,” I said.

“Nope. You need to make a statement and get debriefed. All that good stuff.”

“I’ve watched an amazing woman die, I almost got shot, and I have no job. It’s been a rough twenty-four hours. I’ll see you tomorrow,” I said, and I left.

Epilogue

I will be famous for the rest of my life. That'd become clear already. Everybody told me that the combined stories of the terrorist attacks and Sheryl Harrison were going to stretch my fifteen minutes of fame closer to fifteen decades. It was going to take some getting used to.

It'd only been a week since Nolan Murray was killed; I still found it hard to stop using his name and call him Emerson instead. In any event, I hadn't returned to real life yet. It felt like I'd been debriefed and interviewed by every department of the United States government except the post office, and when I hadn't been talking to them, I'd been busy avoiding the media.

For a guy who never liked the media, it seemed like Novack had been doing round-the-clock interviews. I'd actually learned some things I didn't know by listening to him.

For instance, Novack said that an examination of Hennessey's financial records showed that he joined Emerson's group just before Charlie Harrison was killed. That was probably why he was hired in the first place, and why Laufer was the one that Karen had seen with her father.

Charlie must have gotten greedy and tried to extract

more money than Emerson was willing to pay, so it became necessary to hire extra muscle. Once Hennessey was aboard, he stayed, and probably was very useful when other problems came up that couldn't be solved by computer.

Emerson's creation of the Nolan Murray persona was brilliant. He must have killed the real Murray, maybe he had Hennessey do it, and then erased his life on computer. He appeared to make a mistake, leaving only the college transcript in Maine, but that was intentional. It gave him the chance to re-create Nolan Murray and then have Churchill take his place in death.

Emerson also was in a perfect position, as a local cop, to monitor police activity if it were closing in on "Murray." That was why most of the early murder-frauds were done locally.

Once he moved to the "big stage," the national attacks, he could have done it from anywhere. My guess was he insisted on only speaking to Janssen about the attack on the nuclear plant because Janssen was operating out of the police station, giving Emerson a vantage point to learn what was happening from both sides.

At the very end, Emerson had given Garrett the lead that sent him to interview Laufer's ex-girlfriend. She was lying, paid off by Emerson, and she would have been killed later on, had Emerson lived.

Gerard Timmerman called me three times, wanting me to come in and talk about my position within the firm. That fame I mentioned had apparently made me very employable, probably even "partner" material. Which would be good news, if I had any interest in it at all.

My uncle Reggie wanted me to join him and thereby double the size of his firm. Maybe I'd talk to him about it, after a while. I knew I'd eventually have to do something; I was just going to push it off for as long as possible.

Dr. Jenkins called me a couple of days after the surgery,

to apologize for being so cryptic before I went into the second room with Sheryl. All he had said was that I shouldn't let Sheryl take the pills, that it was "too late." He had promised Terry he would keep her secret, so he couldn't say more, yet he also couldn't allow Sheryl to take the pills.

Dr. Jenkins also confirmed most of my suspicions about how the Terry situation developed, without specifically saying so. It was obvious he was very helpful to her.

I spoke to Sheryl today; she called me for the second time this week. She told me that Karen is doing really well, that she was up and around and getting stronger every day. There was always the danger of rejection, but Dr. Jenkins was optimistic. Terry's heart was a perfect match, which increased the chance for long-term success.

Sheryl said that she wanted to see me, that she'd been thinking about me more and more. When she got to the point where she thought about me twenty-four hours a day, then that would make us even.

Karen was going to be out of the hospital within the week, though she'd need a lot of recuperation time at home. "Come over and I'll cook you dinner," Sheryl said. "Although it's been a while since I cooked, and I was never any good at it in the first place."

"I'll bring in pizza," I said.

"Much better idea," she agreed. Then, "Harvard, we didn't have the normal first couple of dates, and I don't know whether that will impact where we go. But right now, at this moment, I can't wait to see you."

"That's exactly how I feel," I said, because that was exactly how I felt. So we made tentative plans, depending on when Karen can go home.

I had wanted to tell her much more about how I felt, but I didn't. Which is okay, because it looks like we're going to have plenty of time.

Read on for an excerpt from David Rosenfelt's next book

AIRTIGHT

Coming soon in hardcover from Minotaur Books

The tabloids called it "The Judge-sicle Murder."

It was a ridiculous name for an event so horrific and tragic, but it sold newspapers, and generated web hits, so it stuck.

In the immediate aftermath, very little was known and reported in the media, so they compensated by detailing the same facts over and over. Judge Daniel Brennan had attended a charity dinner earlier that evening at the Woodcliff Lakes Hilton. Judge Brennan generally avoided those types of events whenever he could, but in this case felt an obligation.

The Guest of Honor was Judge Susan Dembeck, who was at that point a sitting judge on the bench of the Second Circuit Court of Appeals. Since Judge Brennan's nomination to that court was before the Senate, and he was replacing the retiring Judge Dembeck, he made the obvious and proper decision to support his future predecessor by attending the event.

Others at the dinner estimated that Judge Brennan left at ten thirty, and that was confirmed by closed-circuit cameras in the lobby. He stopped at a 7-Eleven, five minutes from his Alpine, New Jersey, home, to buy a few minor items. The proprietor of the establishment, one Harold Murphy, said that Judge Brennan was a frequent patron of the store. He said it on the *Today* show the following morning, in what the network breathlessly promoted as an exclusive interview, which aired seven minutes before *Good Morning America*'s breathlessly promoted exclusive interview with Mr. Murphy.

Among the items that Murphy described Judge Brennan as buying was a Fudgesicle. It was, he said, one of the judge's weaknesses, regardless of the season. As was the judge's apparent custom, Murphy said, that he started opening the Fudgesicle wrapper while walking to the door, such was his desire to eat it. Murphy seemed to cite this as evidence that the judge was a "regular guy."

Murphy didn't mention, and wasn't asked, the time that Judge Brennan arrived at the store. It was eleven forty five, meaning the ten-minute drive from hotel to store had apparently taken an hour and fifteen minutes.

It was ten minutes after midnight when Thomas Phillips, who lived four doors down from Judge Brennan, walked by the judge's house with his black lab, Duchess. In that affluent neighborhood, four doors down meant there was almost a quarter mile of separation between the two homes.

The judge's garage door was open, and his car was sitting inside, with its lights on. This was certainly an unusual occurrence, and Phillips called out the judge's name a few times. Getting no response, he walked towards the garage.

In the reflected light off the garage wall, he could see the judge's body, covered in blood that was slowly making its way towards where Phillips was standing. The Fudgesicle, melting but with the wrapper around the stick, was just a few inches from the victim's mouth, a fact that Phillips related when he gave his own round of exclusive interviews.

The murder of a judge would be a very significant story in its own right, especially when the victim was up for a Court of Appeals appointment. But the fact that this particular judge was "Danny" Brennan elevated it to a media firestorm.

Brennan was forty-two years old and a rising star in the legal system. It was a comfortable role for him to play, as he had considerable experience as a rising star.

He was a phenom as a basketball player at Englewood High School, moving on to Rutgers, where he earned First-Team All-America status. Rather than head to the NBA as a first round draft choice after one season, which he could certainly have done, he chose instead to stay all four years. He then pulled a "Bill Bradley," and went on to Oxford as a Rhodes Scholar.

When his studies had concluded, he finally moved on to the NBA, and within two years was the starting point guard for the Boston Celtics. It was during a playoff game against the Orlando Magic that on one play he cut right, while his knee cut left. He tore an ACL and MCL, which pretty much covers all the "CLs" a knee contains, and despite intensive rehab for a year and a half, he was never the same.

Confronted with physical limitations but no mental ones, Daniel Brennan went to Harvard Law, and began a rapid rise up the legal ladder.

A rise which ended in a garage, in a pool of blood and melted Fudgesicle.